A Rhapsody of Dreams

Whilst some of the names used are those of real people, the story, the context in which those names are used, the characterisations, and the incidents portrayed in this production are all fictitious. No identification with actual persons (living or deceased), places, buildings, and products is intended or should be inferred.

Print ISBN 978-1-0686686-1-6
E-Book ISBN 978-1-0686686-0-9

Book Cover and illustrations by the author

First Edition 2024

A Rhapsody of Dreams

By

Themighti Estpen

The glass guitar hovered, motionless in the void. Beyond space. Beyond time. Or was that before space and time. The glass sparkled from within; there were no other sources of light, just black velvet in all directions. The velvet crushed, waved, rippled; perhaps there was a breeze. With nothing to measure against, the scale of the guitar could not be guessed: it might be massive, it might be minute; the scale of the neck marked only by the frets.

From somewhere: a cosmic plectrum, the hand that wielded it hidden, or the plectrum moving of its own accord. A strum. Resonance. Then a chord; not a binding chord, a free-flowing, open chord.

The music took shape, penetrated the void, ruffling its velvet. From some distant body, an echo, a reverberation: cosmic feedback. The guitar wailed; the guitar screamed. Then it shattered; shattered into a million shards, each one spinning freely, racing outward, away from the now vanished plectrum.

Spinning and glinting, glinting and spinning; some splintering further. On one the glint deepens, transforms to a twinkle, and then blazes: let there be light.

The forest fronds swayed in the warm sticky breeze; the ant army continued their route march up the tree trunk: in line, obedient. Somewhere overhead a blistering sun beats down, its fiery curves obscured by the leafy canopy. It was several days since he had drunk; the dehydration had stopped him sweating now. An orchestra of insects serenaded him: their clicks and chirps; their humming and buzzing; their screeches and sighs rising and falling in crescendos and calandos.

His sight was blurred, the stems and trunks a hazy grey, the mottled green solid overhead. He tried to remember if he was in a group or alone. He tried to remember where he was headed, and why. He tried to remember his name. Ahead of him he heard a shout; the sound was magnetic, like an iron filing he was drawn towards it.

The twelve stood in a tight circle, shoulder-to-shoulder, facing inward; equidistant between them stands the thirteenth. He turns slowly; his eyes hold theirs in turn; most return the look, but one casts his eyes down. Avoidance. Light, akin to candlelight, flickers; it comes from many sources, but those sources remain unseen. He speaks: “This might be our first meeting, or it might be our last, but we must reach our outcome. You all know your place, your time. I send you out to grow our flock; take no spare robe; no pack; no money. We must remain strong; we must remain focussed; nothing must drive us from our paths. And believe me, those distractions will be many; the enemy knows us, he knows our purpose; he will do all that he can to thwart us. We must, simply must, strive for accuracy; one, two, points adrift and all will fail. I know that each of you is the best, the best that you can be; the training has been hard – on some of you more than others – but you have all reached the end. You must travel alone for the most part, although on a time your paths will cross – as they will cross with mine too. But so too our enemies!” As one they answered, a chant: “We will remain focussed; we will remain strong; we will reach our conclusion”.

One by one they flicker and go out. Now only two remain.

But Perhaps I am getting ahead of myself. Perhaps it was wrong to put the first pages before the introduction. You (and thank you for reading thus far) might think that you have just read (and I hope enjoyed) the opening to a piece of narrative. And narrative it might just be, but can I claim it all for my own? Perhaps a word or two of explanation before you read on. The text that precedes, and follows, needs some form of description; whether I am the right person to give it is another matter: I am biased. But, to the best of my knowledge, there is no other that can comment: I guard my find jealously. So, perhaps, the best that you are going to get is an explanation of how the text that you are about to read came into my hands; I will seek to remain impartial throughout. The story itself is straightforward enough – very down to earth in comparison to what is to follow! In fact, quite literally down to earth!

I have always loved motorcycling; whether it is on a Cruiser down the King's Road, a Dirt Bike along green lanes, or a Race Rep at the track – and sometimes on the road! But on this particular day, I was trying a new angle: on a huge thudding Paris

Dakar type bike, and across proper sand dunes, down in Northeast Egypt. It was an ordinary enough day, the giant orange disc of the sun hung dead centre in the azure blue wall of sky. Dune after dune rose before me, and I swept up them, the rear wheel spewing sand behind me, it made a swirling tan cloak, which swept out behind like some hero of old.

Cresting a ridge, I came to a brief halt; there was a huge depression in front of me, beyond it the largest dune that I had seen that day stood proud. I gunned the bike down the steep incline, and then started to climb the opposite dune; here the sand seemed more compact, the tyres gripped well, and the bike started to pick up speed. As it reached the apex, I realised that I was going too fast. I knew enough to know that if I braked then, that the front wheel would plough into the sand, with the most likely result of catapulting me over the handlebars! There was nothing for it; I would have to take the jump.

The bike soared into the air, the other side of the dune dropped away before me; for a brief moment, I hung motionless in the air, and then the bike started to descend. The bike landed with a huge thud halfway down the slope; the suspension soaked up much of the impact and I relaxed slightly, thinking that I had made a safe landing.

But then the bike suddenly stopped dead, caught by rocks just below the surface of the sand; and now I did fly over the handlebars, somersaulting in the air. I landed feet first, and heard a sharp, clear, crack; I felt the bone in my ankle break, and a flame of pain shot up my leg. Looking behind me, I saw that the front forks of the bike had fared about as well as my leg: they lay twisted and buckled; the rear wheel still span for a few moments, until the engine stalled and cut out. Silence descended.

Slowly, I dragged myself back toward the twisted wreck of the motorcycle, suddenly thirsty for the water in one of the rear panniers. As my hands dug into the sand to drag me along, they suddenly caught on what felt like the rim of an old earthenware pot, which struck me as bizarre. But I moved on to the bike ignoring it. I drank sparingly, not knowing how long until rescue might come; I had left a route back at the camp, but how long until they missed me?

I sat for several hours in silent thought, I had bound my ankle as best I could, but the pain was still a deep insistent throb. To pass the time, and take my mind off my ankle, I decided to investigate the pot further. Slowly, gingerly, I edged back to where part of its top lip was poking through the sand; in part, I went that way as there was some slight shade from a Westerly leaning dune. Digging the sand away from around it, I discovered, lying on its side, a tall, slender pot. It was completely intact, a wide cork stopper sealing the inside off from the sand. With a little effort, I pulled the plug away, and looked in the pot for its content.

My hand came away with one of several bundles of papers, all neatly tied with some kind of vine, it was still pliable, as though it had only recently been cut, but the papers that they bound seemed ancient.

Although the papers were undoubtedly ancient [at least so I assert, others have disagreed on this point] I was surprised to find that I could read them quite clearly. In the coming months that surprise was to be compounded, as others looked at the pages: some could not read them at all, others saw words other than those that I did.

I sat back to read, unable to stop once I had started. How long I read for, before rescue came, I cannot say; but what I can say is that I was gripped and taken away to another place as I read; a place with no pain, no beating sun, a place of contentment.

What I read I reproduce on the pages that precede, and follow, this introduction. I reproduce them exactly as I found them, in the same order. There is strong evidence to suggest that the pages had become muddled, and you, as reader, may wish to reorganise them in your mind, as I, and others, have sought to do.

One other change that I have made is to the language. The writing was not in any language that I know, or recognise; nor has it been recognised by others. And yet, strangely, I could understand every word; it is that understanding that has been reproduced here. Others that have seen the original have reached a similar understanding, although there was one of note that derived a completely different translation.

Whilst, initially, I thought that the collection was the work of several people, I now believe it to be the work of but one person. Albeit that it is written in different styles, in first and third person, and indeed the handwriting itself is remarkably different in style, shape and flow. Again, you must decide that for yourself.

Within the text, I found many hidden messages, some obvious, some cunningly hidden; there are probably some that I have not even spotted. Nothing would please me more than to hear about any that you, the reader, should discover.

I also leave you to decide if what unfolds is a work of fiction; or diaries; or histories, recorded as accurately as the scribe was able. In my opinion, they stand up as both; you, the reader, may decide: a work of fiction, or of fact? For my part, I believe them to be true, whatever the truth is that they tell. But from comments made by my publishers, I suspect that they believe it to be entire fiction throughout.

Slowly, now, I edged back to my bike; I had water, food too. I took a small sip of water; I still had plenty, but how long until rescue came - from my route, they had a start point, but how far might I have drifted from my course? I didn't eat. I had no hunger, except for the words, which I consumed voraciously.

I felt myself getting drowsy; through the heat, or through the pain, maybe both. I took those precious pages and placed them inside my jacket, pressed them against my heart, and then - despite the heat - zipped up my jacket to protect them.

The next thing I knew, I was catching the final rays of the sun as it dipped below the western dunes. The temperature dropped as though a switch had been flicked. Thinking they might still be searching for me, I flicked on the bike's light. Sure enough, some two hours later I heard the rhythmic thrum of rotor blades.

I remember little of the journey to the hospital, drifting in and out of consciousness - more so when they gave me something to relieve the pain. They tell me I slept for over twenty-four hours; it might have been more. When I awoke it was late afternoon, I was in a cool room. My hands flew to my chest; bizarrely, they had not removed my jacket. I felt the comforting press of the pages beneath it. They had cut off the trouser leg to get to my injured leg/foot/ankle, but made no attempt to remove them. Staff cuts, I guess? Or they had run out of hospital gowns? I was only another injured motorcyclist to them; I'd brought it all on myself!

Some months later, I returned to the spot of the discovery, and found other urns, containing other papers; but those are for another time, and another place, as I can see no connection between them, and what you are about to read.

If any of you that have chosen to read what follows feel moved to, then I would welcome your interpretation of what you read. I have made my own notes, but suspect, strongly, that others will have read a very different message into the text.

Themighti Estpen

Hovering before you is the huge silver globe; the sphere undulates; it is solid, but malleable. The lights flash: on-off, on-off. The sphere is jostled by others in the spatium-cingulus; they are many coloured. Silver. Spurious. Silken. Svelte. Stimulating. Scheming. Sardonic. Soft. Schematic. Suede. Soulful. Syllabic. Spatial. Smoky. Saffron. Sublime. Staccato. Stray. Surd. Sad. Semi-sarcomatic. Strobotic. Subcutaneous. Schmaltzy. Skinny. Sophismatic.

You are moving; the sphere is moving: apart, yet following each other. The colours change, but the silver remains: larger now, so large that you can hold it in the palm of your hand as it slips between your fingers to block everything else from view. The time stream flows. You move within it, by staying still; the stillness creates *G*, and that force subsumes you; your skin ripples; the liquid lens through which you look blinks. The current eddies, fast-eddies; it takes you too: cranberries and cream. Another shift, at first you think it is to deep purple, but the rainbow is ascendant; there is a genesis, and your knees are open to the sun; you wake up. Climbing your personal Solsbury Hill, a flick of the tail sends you spiralling down again; the silver sphere remains, but now you are inside it. There are tears; there are fears: a temporal jam, but no scone. Will the cranberries and cream suffice? Your life changes gear every day; each day takes an hour; each hour a minute; each minute a nanosecond, which lasts forever.

Interdum identidem. Interdum identidem. Interdum identidem. Interdum identidem. Interdum identidem. Interdum identidem. Interdum identidem. Interdum identidem. Interdum identidem. Interdum identidem. Interdum identidem. Interdum identidem. Interdum identidem. Interdum identidem.

Now you break the surface, ripples, stone, age, chaos, heat, light, so bright you cannot see. You watch your watch; you time your time; but all is at a standstill. The silver sphere splits without moving; it splits again, and again, and again. You think you see cells, but are they really molecules? Life takes shape before you; there are atoms: small, so small, that when you look again you see only the sphere, solid (semi-solid) once more.

You reach out to touch it and there is a spark: silver turns yellow, turns gold. The residents leave, they are Faith, and Hope; Charity remains at home, not yet called to the stage. Faith and Hope stride out, their work is just beginning. The golden sphere spins faster and faster, growing larger and larger; it fills the sky, and then retreats. It passes two other rocks, slightly smaller than the one on which you now stand, and then comes to rest. The rocks circle their prey, there are nine of them; the circles become elliptical, the dance a dervish. The prey smiles back, and blinks, benign; the hostility ends, but the dance continues.

Welcome to your future; you are quite alone.

A livid red disc scales an unblemished sky; a slow, ponderous process. Its course, serene, belies the trauma at its heart; millions of degrees of anger broil, swirl. The anger radiates down to the much smaller blue/green disc below.

Reflecting that anger, Judas pushed aside yet another damp vine; how long had he been lost in the jungle, he wondered. It had been around a week ago that he had met the others; plane crash victims, they had said; the memory of how he had come to be there was fast fading.

Two days ago, the group had pounced hungrily on a pair of lizards, tearing them apart, and eating the raw flesh; that was the last time that they had eaten. Drinking was much easier; everything was damp and dripping in this forsaken environment.

Almost before they realised it, the group stumbled out into a large clearing, about a mile across, but it wasn't this that held everyone's attention, however, for in the centre of the clearing was a growth of plants, the like of which Judas had never seen. The plants swayed somewhat as though in a breeze, although the air was still where Judas stood; the rustling of the leaves formed a beautiful music, subtle, barely heard, and yet compelling; the words Messina Straights entered his mind for a fleeting moment, and then were gone. There was a feminine curve about their growth, a mysterious pattern in the way they twined about each other; it was perhaps the most beautiful vision of his life.

Judas idly swatted at a blood-bloated mosquito on his sweat-stained neck, turning to his neighbour, to ask if he could see the same: he half expected to find this some heat-induced mirage. But no, his companion saw the same, albeit that he described the plants in a slightly different way.

As one, the group began to move forward, at first walking, then finally running until we came to a halt at the edge of the gently swaying fronds. My nose was assailed by their perfume; surely, if that aroma could be bottled it would outsell all other perfumes! But this was not something I wanted to share; I wanted it all for myself. The gentle sway of the broad olive-green leaves, which glistened in the sunlight, showing paler lines somewhat reminiscent of veins, created a cooling draft making it pleasant for me to stand there.

My neighbour was now some distance from me; the whole group seemed to have spread out. The rustling leaves seemed to call out my name: Judas, come closer. Tentatively, I reached forward, touching one of the petals, its colour a vibrant mix of peach, with splashes of purple, and red; much as lovers would touch on their first meeting, there was hesitancy, and gentleness in my touch. The petal was smooth, and soft, like silken skin, and at the same time both cool, and warm. The flower moved, seeming to press itself against my palm; there was a deep sigh, whether it was mine, or emanated from the flower I could not tell; I stepped further forward to be at once surrounded by gently swaying stems.

Without realising it, I reached up and plucked a petal; a tear trickled down my cheek at the thought of bringing any destruction to such a beautiful thing; but the tear dried on Judas's cheek as almost immediately the petal was replaced by a new one, if anything more radiant than the first.

Judas looked down at the petal, which was as large as his hand; other colours now became apparent, although Judas knew no name for them, they shifted constantly in the sunlight. Slowly, Judas lifted the petal to his lips, biting off the tip and chewing it. The taste was entirely new to him, although there was something in its taste and consistency that reminded him of meat, at the same time fruit, but also cakes, and pastries suggested themselves.

Inside the petal was a golden liquid, which on drinking was at once cool, and refreshing. Hungrily, Judas ate many petals, and washed them down with their own nectar.

His hunger sated, and thirst quenched, Judas looked around at his companions, they all wore smiles, and a faraway dreamy look in their eyes; Judas knew beyond doubt that he also looked as they.

One of the flowers twined forward, seeming to kiss Judas upon his cheek, as though the cue had been given, others snaked forward kissing Judas on every part of his body; thicker stems curved around his neck, and waist pulling him closer. Judas looked down, and saw that his clothes were gone, although he could not remember removing them; he gave himself up into their heavenly embrace, joining their song; they bit him, and drank his blood, but he felt no pain.

Many times, the sun set on the scene, and with its rising, nothing had changed, still the group stood entwined with the vegetation. After a time, and Judas could not say if that time was days, or weeks, or months – even years – he became aware that at the far edge of the clearing a ring of dark-skinned warriors had surrounded this Garden of Eden. Each had a vine tied about his waist, which disappeared into the forest behind them; at full stretch it stopped them 20 yards from where Judas and his companions were. They stood impassively in the clearing; each was dressed in animal skins, and carried an ebony and silver spear; their eyes were covered, and their ears were blocked.

Looking at them, though he could not see their eyes, Judas sensed pity; a frown creased his brow, why pity, surely not for him; pity for themselves perhaps for being unable to reach this harmonious garden.

Judas returned to his feast, even after all this time, each mouthful was still tastier than the last. How many more days or weeks he stayed there, Judas could not say, but all the time the warriors stood impassively, their spears planted on the ground before them, masked eyes seeming to look straight ahead.

Slowly the truth dawned on Judas. He wasn't ready for Paradise. He would have to leave at some point, but he knew that he could not; his body would refuse him, as his mind might too. Other realisations came to Judas too. He fell to his knees, and slowly, centimetres at a time, he started to edge away. The fronds became agitated, calling him back in their language, one that he had come to understand. Judas half turned to return, but in an agony of mind, and spirit he managed to continue his slow painful journey away; dimly he became aware of others, too, crawling away; that gave him some little strength.

Finally, he fell forward, prostrated at the feet of the nearest warrior; from under the edge of the mask, Judas sensed, rather than saw, two brown eyes looking down at him. At that moment, though no words passed between them, each knew the other, their desires, and why they were there; Judas knew why he had sensed pity; the warrior knew what Judas wanted from him. As one, the warriors' spears descended, I screamed in agony, and release. As one, the warriors turned and, with measured pace, walked back across the clearing, to become lost again in the main forest. The bodies lay in a ring around paradise; from paradise itself, came one last sigh. Judas was not yet ready for paradise. He had much to achieve.

Judas picked up the fine white feather of the quill and started to jab at the keys on the keypad; on the screen before him, the words were really beginning to flow.

It was one of the earliest lessons: there will be distractions. You have but one path to follow; many will try to drive you from it. These distractions will hold many forms, some base, obvious; some subtle hard to perceive. But you must hold true. To deviate from the path is to destroy our entire purpose. Your path will take many turns, appear in many alternates; sometimes it will be obvious, at others hard to find. But it will always be there for you. Each of you will walk a separate path; sometimes those paths will cross, or even run together for a while. Only once all those roads have been explored – without deviation – can we reach the final solution. Your training will show you how to avoid distraction; if you hold true, avoidance will not be hard; only the weak will fail.

The waves lapped softly against the sides of the longboat, pierced by the dragon-carved prow; their rhythm gentle now that they had left the Channel and entered the river.

Each of them was positioned at one of the vertices of the dodecagon that had been chalked upon the floor; the lines were precise, even, carefully drawn. Each had adopted the ready stance, Yoi Dachi, not because it had been commanded, but simply because it had become habit. At the centre, the Arch-Mage stood, a black silk bag, styled with silver thread in a pattern that was hard to determine, in his hand.

He had passed once around them already; as he had stood on front of them, he had dipped into the bag, drawn out a ball, and given this to them. Each held the ball in their right hand; except Judas, who held it tightly in his left. The markings on it were smooth, they could not be felt, but he could feel them imprinting themselves upon his brain: ***20***th. Now each was being given a second ball as he passed once more around them. Judas received his second ball with due reverence; its legend read ***9***th.

The Arch-Mage spoke now, "You each have your two targets, from the 1st to the 24th; you must visit only them; do not stray into another's target time zone. Visit yours, take careful notes, make observations, only interact with caution – above all else, change nothing! No close mingling with the subjects," he looked directly at Judas as he said this last, "many will not be as they seem, you must treat them all with caution!"

Thomas made to speak, anticipating him the Arch-Mage said, "No, Thomas, you may not swap with another! They have been selected with all due randomness; we must abide."

Simon-Peter asked, "Does it matter in which order we visit?"

"Not at all," came the reply, "you will probably wish to jump several times between the two, to allow for comparisons and analysis. You know how long you have to complete your tasks; ensure that you meet your deadlines! We must regroup at the given time and place, the moment upon which all hinges; it would be disastrous if you have not completed, thoroughly, your studies by then. Go now."

The Arch-Mage held each in his gaze in turn; each bowed – still keeping eye contact – and then blinked out. When Judas made his bow, and entered the maelstrom, only three others remained. The journey had begun. Or had it begun some while back? He wasn't sure. Already his memories were slipping; he tried to focus and failed; the time-fragments stung him like slivers of glass as they whistled around him. He reached out to steady himself against something, found something solid, maybe it was a tall standing stone, and then his feet were on solid ground. Was he in the right place? Was he in the right time? What were his numbers again? The balls had vanished.

Judas scrubbed hard at the stain, but soap and water seemed insufficient to remove it. He reached for the scrubbing brush, scraped it along the surface of the bar of soap, leaving freshly ploughed, but miniature, furrows along its surface; Judas renewed his efforts, scrubbing at the stain, the black, black stain; this stain must run deep, he thought to himself. The scrubbing brush too seemed to have little effect; in a rage Judas threw the brush into the basin of soapy water and started to scratch at the stain with his nails; rubbing harder and harder, faster and faster.

Red welts started to appear on his skin where the nails scored, growing deeper and broader, but still the stain remained; the deep, deep, stain. And now Judas's skin split under the constant rubbing and blood started to seep out, staining the feverishly moving nails. But if anything, this made Judas scratch the harder, the faster. With the increased effort whole strips of skin started to pull away as he scratched furiously at his forearm.

When Judas's insane frenzy reached the pinkie white bone, not only did he faint, but also, he knew that the stain had beaten him, that it must run all the way to his heart. Picking himself up from the bathroom floor, he left the room, and re-joined the party; followed by a trail of red.

The partygoers backed away from him, would not meet his eye, as he stumbled from the landing and down the stairs. Brain fuzzy and incoherent, Judas decided that he needed a drink; guests parted like

Moses' Red Sea as he stumbled for the kitchen. Judas's friend Peter stepped out in front of him, "For Christ's sake Judas," he shouted, "what have you done now?" "For exactly that," he mumbled, "exactly that".

WHO?

💣♋■⍓ □♐ ⍓□◆ ⬥♓●● ♑□ ⧫□ ♑
❒♏♋⧫ ●♏■♑⧫♒⬧ ⧫□ ⧫❒♋■⬧●♋⧫♏
⧫♒♓⬧ ◻♋⬧⬧♋♑♏📪 ♌♏●♓♏❖♓■♑ ♓⧫
⧫□ ♒♋❖♏ ♒♓♎♎♏■ ❍♏♋■♓■♑📪
⬧♏♍❒♏⧫ ❍♏⬧⬧♋♑♏⬧📬 ⧫♒♏ ⬧♏♍❒
♏⧫ □♐ ●♓♐♏ ♏❖♏■✍ 👌◆⧫ ✋ ❒
♏♑❒♏⧫ ⧫♒♋⧫ ⍓□◆❒ ⧫♓❍♏ ⬥♓●●
♌♏ ⬥♋⬧⧫♏♎🖳 ⧫♒♏ ❒♏♋● ⧫❒◆⧫
♒ ♓⬧ ♏●⬧♏⬥♒♏❒♏📪 ♓■ ♋ ⬧♏◻♋
❒♋⧫♏ ◻♋⬧⬧♋♑♏📬 ⧫♒♏❒♏ ⍓□◆
❒♏♋●●⍓ ❍◆⬧⧫ ❒♏♋♎ ♌♏⧫⬥♏♏■
⧫♒♏ ●♓■♏⬧🖉

Judas carefully transcribed the Men-I-Mem [mentally imparted memorandum], fully aware that it was a sackable offence; he knew full well the dangers of such information falling into the wrong hands, but the way his memory had been lately he feared that not to might cause even worse issues.

Men-I-Mem

From: The big cheese

To: The Boys

Subject: Souls on Fire

It has come to my attention that there is an increasing tendency to burn corpses, rather than returning them to the soil. As you know, it takes many weeks for the soul to properly leave the body. Burning bodies causes damage to the soul; in some cases, this can damage the soul irreparably; perhaps worse, the damage can go undetected before the soul is reissued.

There is nothing wrong in burning, if a suitable period has lapsed between death, and the torch; but you do not need me to remind you how long that has to be; it was clearly stated in one of your earliest classes.

You will each take urgent steps to bring this practice to an end.

Report back to me with the actions that you have undertaken, and their results, by □□/□□/□□.

What I did yesterday

Yesterday was a good day. It was fun. I saw my friends Peter and John. We went to the park. Then we had ice cream. Then we did kill lots and lots of unbelievers. Then we went home for tea. We had fish fingers. Yum, yum! I want to watch TV, but my mum said go to bed. So, I did. It was a good day.

Well, I have never really given it much thought!

The end came quickly; none had foreseen the speed and rapidity of the decline. He walked now along dusty and cracked ground; it might once have been a road. The burning wind caught at the tatters of his clothing; the chemical motes were visible within it. To either side of the path that he trod were mounds: of earth; of bricks; of bodies, of vehicles; of other things undeterminable. They made the road he travelled singular: there was neither turn to left nor right. The mounds were not particularly high; with a little effort he could probably have mounted them. But to what purpose? What lay beyond? Whilst there was a path before him, he might as well follow it. He had not seen another living soul for many weeks. He had not eaten for .... he could not remember the last time he had eaten, or drank. Even his name was lost, was it Jake? Jude? John? Joan? Looking down he could not tell. The rumbling noise was still behind him, he barely heard it anymore, only on the odd occasion when he stopped and focussed. It was like the rolling of rocks; an avalanche of scree; but it matched his pace, or was slower: whatever it was never gained on him. His skin was red and blistered; it might have been the sun or the chemicals that caused it. The sun had not set since his journey to nowhere had begun; the world hung still in space waiting for ....

Weren't cockroaches supposed to be the last things to die? A fleeting thought. Even they would have been company. Thoughts of roaches brought thoughts of how it had all begun. Or ended? It had started as a computer virus; its source had never been discovered; there was not time. The virus had taken shape and broken free, destroying, destroying, destroying. Behind it, millions of smashed monitors the only mark of its escape. The worm was free. The worm had turned. Many histories had told of the Worm of the World's End. None had pictured this particular worm, its shape and form. A silent infiltrator, it entered everything, and left behind nothing but wreckage.

The eleven were getting restless. Judas was late again. That in itself was not unusual; Judas was often late, having got side-tracked, diverted or lost. But this was late even for him. “Shall we just start?” queried Peter, “we have waited over a decade!”

“You know that we cannot, that would cause imbalance,” replied the Arch-Mage, their fulcrum. “Where was he last seen?”

“‘76,” offered John, “at least so he said.”

The Arch-Mage signalled to James and John, “Go and get him!” The impatience was beginning to show. They flickered, but returned: “The gates are closed!”

They looked at the rows upon rows of single-use orange travel suits. Next to them, the single 1976 suit, in pale green, the helmet’s visor wider. And then the 1977-onward suits, they were dark green, the helmets glass bubbles; dark green far outnumbered orange.

Judas let the pale green uniform slip to the floor, revealing the crumpled robes beneath. Looking around the room, he saw the expectant, but frustrated, faces looking to him for some kind of explanation. Hesitantly, he began, “I managed to find a way in, going to December ‘75 and just slipping over the threshold. But once there, no exit could I find! Something, or someone, had obscured them all. I will not tell you now of my adventures there, that can wait for another time, they are of no relevance here.

Judas was in the hallway drinking a glass of tea; at the other end of the hallway a pulse was generating. The pulse merged perfectly with Judas's mood: anger. Perhaps not anger, more self-loathing; frustration. His free hand clenched, the knuckles whitened. Judas looked in the mirror, but he did not see himself looking back; the image looked at Judas; Judas wanted to run, but the story kept moving as planned. The beat of the pulse grew louder; Judas looked along the corridor and saw the giant heart beating. Was this the centre, or was the centre 53 floors higher: the Pentium enabled brain. With a rueful smile Judas decided that it was actually 47 floors lower, in the sperm banks. Judas stood up, put on his leather jacket, revelling in his new image; he knew his image, he owned it; it was time for action.

Taking the express elevator, he descended to ground level; opening the door he stepped out into the grassy lane. Whistling a jaunty tune, he set off, heading roughly south; in the trees about him the birds also whistled a happy carefree tune. Behind him, the monster stirred, deprived of its soul it grew uneasy, restless; with lumbering steps it came in pursuit, but even at walking pace Judas soon widened the gap; he could see the vast shadow, stretched out before him, but soon that too was gone.

There was a below of frustration, frightening the birds who took to squawking flight. Smiling, Judas patted the future, which was taped to his chest. He was the Pied Piper. Reaching into his satchel, he took out his flute and started to play; soon the children came thronging around; dancing; spinning; laughing. They followed, their tiny feet beating a rhythm to accompany the trilling of the flute; they clapped, but that rhythm was different, 4:8. The sun started to set.

They camped that night on a hillside; it was still warm; the sky clear and black; the stars shone down, painfully bright. “Let me tell you now of your future,” said Judas, “this is what you must do.” Enthralled, the children sat quietly around him; their eyes shone like the stars. Judas knew that the future was safe; he would return to the building: they would have their god; but he would be a good god: benign; wise; irrefragable in his guidance. There would be only innocence.

Wildly, he threw himself down on top of the rumpled bedspread; bitter tears of humiliation stung his cheeks. How could he have been so wrong! For so long he had admired that perfect face: the soft downy beard, the angular cheekbones, the strong nose. But mostly the eyes. Eyes of such a deep, vibrant, blue that he often thought they were painted by a master artist. An artist who had captured the very twinkle of the stars and reproduced it to perfection.

He had seen the way that he looked at him; the signs had all been there; it was beyond lust; a deeper purer emotion. The occasional firm touch to his arm; the light pressure of leg against leg if they sat closely in a bar or restaurant; the whispers and confidences. They had all pointed to the same conclusion: a mutual attraction.

Even the time had been right; at this juncture society had ceased to judge; there was no shame, no stigma.

But he had been wrong, so wrong. It was just the two of them; the other three had left earlier. He could still feel the soft satin of his trousers on his fingertips as he moved forward with a kiss. A kiss that was not returned. A kiss that was spurned. A kiss that had drawn forth cruel laughter.

The tears were dried now on his face and slowly his heart hardened. Well, if I am not able to have him, then no other will, he thought. He spurned my kiss; there will come a time and a place when I will kiss him again – but that kiss will cast him down. A time when society declares the ultimate penalty as outcome for such an act.

He finally realised that he was trapped in a time maze. Now he was standing on a deserted Neolithic beach; a hot red sun blazed down thumping against his forehead. Step. He was balanced precariously on a speeding comet; all around him spacecraft of myriad designs waltzed: apparently silently, the sound of their engines swallowed in the vacuum. Step. And he was in a ballroom; now it was couples that waltzed. Round and round they span, gripped by a fever that came from the music from the string septet. Step. He was in a world of smoke and ash. Step. Cold winds buffeted him; icy fingers of frost, sharp shrapnel, stung at his skin and eyes: he was naked, still. Step. He stood on a floor of rapidly cooling lava – hot, but not burning. The world about him was newly formed, fresh, waking. Or was it a dying world? He wasn't sure. He took a step forward to examine his surroundings and they changed again. The air smelt of salt; wooden timbers creaked; canvas sails cracked in the wind. From the top mast a black flag fluttered; white, on the black, a skull above two crossed bones.

Would he ever find his way... ... home? Did he have a home? He remembered the soft feminine push that had set him off in the time maze; the whispered word in his ear: find the centre and you'll find my heart. He knew now that it had been a lie; she had no heart to give. Step. Still, there was a creak of wood, but now it was a sign that proclaimed: saloon. There were creaks of leather, too, and the jingle of spurs. A card table was overturned; six guns were drawn. He dived to avoid the bullets and found he was on the side of a hill, sweet wildflowers all around him. Two white clouds, alone in the sky, danced on an unfelt breeze. Dance. Was that the answer? His mind went back to the ballroom. Were the formal steps of the dance his way out of here? But Judas had never learned to dance; a soft shuffle was all that he had ever managed. He regretted it now. Could he learn by watching others, he wondered? He had to find the ballroom again. A goal now in his mind he stepped again; and again, and again, and again. The scenes changed, flickering like those in the old 'what the butler saw' machines. He nearly missed it. For a thousand years he had stepped; left foot, right foot. Scene after scene. Time after time he had wandered. But now here they were again; he watched, rapt.

He listened to the music for a couple of moments; he got the 1-2-3 of the beat in his mind. Now he watched the feet: on the first beat, he saw the men take a step forward, with their left feet. As though it was in a mirror, the women stepped back on their right foot. On the next beat, they stepped forward and to the right with their right feet (the feet made a kind of an upside-down "L" shape). Again, the women mirrored the step. Now there was a subtle shift of weight to the right; the third beat sounded, they slid their left feet over to the right and were standing with their feet nearly together. Mirror. Beat four, and the men's right feet moved backwards; their actions were mirrored. Five and they were stepping back and to the left with their left feet; again, that subtle shift of weight. On the sixth (and what appeared the final beat of the dance step) they slid their right feet forward until their two feet were together again. The steps were repeated, but with a slight circular turn. He watched, rapt and for the moment invisible. Then he began to move, matching the men.

There was something missing. Then he noticed the rise and fall; it was three-dimensional: the body moved forwards, backwards, side-to-side, but also up and down! He moved to the rhythm and the scene didn't change. He became visible. He saw a beautiful girl at the side of the floor; she stood shyly, her hands entwined and clasped before her. A stray ringlet had come loose from her hair; it curled down onto her left cheek, partly covering one of the richest brown eyes that he had ever seen. Those eyes were on him now. Without asking, he took her into his arms in the waltz stance; she came against him, close and warm. He moved his left leg forward; she mirrored, moving her right leg back. He could feel the warmth of her breath, within it a hint of cinnamon. From a small silver chain around her neck a single letter was hung: R. They danced and now the scene did change, but it changed to his will; he led the way. Her eyes did not leave his for a moment,

And then the dance was ending. "Will we dance again?" he asked her. "No doubt," she replied, her voice barely a whisper, "but maybe not until the final dance." With that, she was gone.

Brooding, ominous thunderheads filled the sky, reflecting his mood. Or perhaps causing it. His war axe in his right hand, the crude wooden shield on his left arm, and a smile of pure killing joy upon his lips he strode forward. Invincible, he hacked left and right; blood and gore covered him, darkening to black. Judas sported his new hairstyle, shaved sides, daubed with blue tattoos; the top, grown long, bound back with leather strands.

For the moment, he was unsure who his enemies were, just that he needed to kill them. To assassinate them all. The hillside on which he strode was now lumpen with the bodies of the fallen; the gore and the mud made them hard to separate from the rocks and boulders. Only their soft yielding as he advanced revealed their nature.

Lights flashed. Not strobotically fast, just above pulse rate. Perhaps it was a party? He pushed through the jelly of the time wall; the nourishment tube pulled free from his belly. It wasn't a party; it was a concert. For now, Judas was unsure who the band was; but then, right now, he was having trouble stringing a sentence toge... ... ...

He waded through the sea of people, who parted left and right. The venue floor was gloriously sticky beneath his feet; it felt like home. Behind him, and around him, the crowd closed in; he bobbed along with them, surging forward and back. They seemed to be keeping time with the lights, which were not synching with the music; Judas began to twitch.

What
is the
exact
nature
of tears?

He sat hunched, nestled, in the soft leather of the armchair; when he had seated himself it had been daylight, but that light was now gone, and the room had descended into darkness. It matched his mood. He stared intently at the device in his hand; it was supposed to tell him what was going on in the world, but its screen was blank. So too, it should provide him with lists of who his friends are; still, the screen was blank. "What should I do?" he asked it, but no reply was forthcoming. His eyes were as blank as the screen. How could this one small device have robbed him of everything? Will. Energy. Motivation. Direction. Purpose. All gone.

Outside, the thin crescent of a silvery moon rose; serenely it glided up into the night sky. It passed overhead and descended. Now the sun rose, chasing the trajectory of the moon. It set, and the moon took to the stage once more. MoonSunMoonSunMoonSunMoonSunMoonSunMoonSunMoonSunMoonSunMoonSunMoonSunMoonSunMoonSunMoonSunMoonSunMoonSun.

Judas saw none of this.

"Help!"

But no help came.

"Help me!"

Nothing.

"I am lost without you!"

A flicker.

"Save, me!"

Further flickers. And then, praises, the small white apple appeared on the screen. It held him; he could not look away.

The dated task list appeared. He did not remember writing it, but who else could have done so? Today's task was a killing. Briefly, Judas puzzled over the target; surely that could not be right? But of course it was right, the device said so. The location was clearly detailed, the method defined; there were minute-by-minute timings. No time to lose. He had momentum again. Purpose. And besides, he had seen tomorrow's task; now, that, he really was looking forward to!

He remembered the first time that he had received the gift. He had not asked for it, had not expected it. It just came upon him. He had been talking of a sorrow and the flood gates had opened. The tears had flooded his cheeks, although there had been no sobbing. Neither did he feel sad. He felt... ... ... peace? He felt a connection. He was joined to something much larger.

This page is intentionally blank.

He could remember, vividly, the first time. Like so many, he had started with the occasional joint. And then as he had learnt more, and seen through the propaganda, the occasional pill or two. But this was different; this was top-level.

It was a warm and balmy summer's evening; everything bathed in the golden light of that short period of time before dusk; the time so beloved by photographers. Perhaps a dozen of them sat on the stretch of grass in front of the pub; slightly more boys than girls made up their number. They had been there for three or four hours now, quietly chatting, laughing (the boys much louder than the girls); they were all drinking the beer that was brewed in the back room of the pub; it might have been called Hurricane. The group were dressed in a motley of colours: purples and greens, reds and yellows, golds and silvers, although one or two wore only black, harking back to an earlier time. With the careless abandon that only the combination of alcohol and dusk can bring, one or two were now rolling joints and passing them around the circle; briefly each face would be illuminated by a dark orange glow before the one next to it was similarly illumed.

Judas was sat next to Alan, who nudged him and passed on the joint; Judas took his turn and passed it to the girl next to him; she was one of the silver sisters. Judas admired Alan, although he was never quite sure why; he had that inexplicable charisma that some people had, and although he often tended to be obnoxious, especially when he had been drinking, he was a leader rather than a follower within the group. Recently, he had taken to wearing a loose brown woollen hat in the manner of the Rastafarians; occasionally, he would show off the dreadlocks he was growing underneath – Judas had never seen these on a white boy before. And Alan was very white of complexion; this was highlighted by the black of his hair and the blackheads that formed miniature patterns on his slightly bulbous nose.

A light breeze rustled the long grass by the trees as the last traces of twilight fled the sky. One or two of the group now lay entwined on the grass, gently caressing, making light rustling sounds of their own. Alan leaned closer to Judas, "follow me over to the trees," he said, nodding over to their right. The trees only formed a thin border between the grass and the road, but it was quiet within them. Alan held up a small white packet, "wanna try some smack?" he asked. Judas knew that Alan had occasionally used it in the past; he had always avoided it, but tonight, for reasons he could never identify, he nodded "yeah, why not!"

Alan led him across to a car, he had no idea whose it was, certainly not Alan's, he didn't drive; he may not have even known whose car it was. Alan pulled off the rear-view mirror; now Judas knew that Alan didn't know the owner of the car; their illicit presence sent a thrill through Judas. This was closely followed by a second thrill – anticipation and fear – as Alan unwrapped the small white packet to reveal some beige powder within.

He tipped the powder, showing great care, onto the mirror; they both giggled. Producing a razor blade, Alan chopped and cut the powder into two lines; one line was longer than the other. "You aren't used to it," explained Alan, pointing to the shorter line, "that will be more than enough for you." Other mixed emotions entwined with the anticipation: anger, why should he get the shorter line; fear, what if they were caught now by the police whilst in the act; relief, the longer line really might have been too much, Judas had no benchmark.

Judas had seen it done before, so when Alan asked him to, he was deftly able to role a £10 note into a narrow tube and pass it to Alan. Whilst Judas held the mirror for him, Alan sealed off one nostril with his forefinger and put the tube to the other; he ran the note along the line inhaling deeply through his one open nostril as he did. And then the roles were reversed, and it was Judas's turn; Judas was delighted to manage the line in a single sweep, without sneezing, coughing or spluttering.

He reared from the car, a proud and mighty stallion. He felt taller; he felt stronger; he felt... ... ... alive! Wow! This was the best! They strode back to join the group; two gunslingers marching into an unfamiliar bar: full of swagger and bravado. Judas felt the centre of attention; several of the group leant toward him their body language screamed: we love you; you are the master; you are the best of us all. One of the silver sisters was next to him again, and very close. He snaked his arm around her neck. She didn't throw it off as she often had before. Buoyed, Judas let his hand trail lower to caress her breast, naked below the thin cheesecloth shirt that she wore; "Judas! Don't do that!" she exclaimed, but she did nothing to remove his hand and even seemed to move closer.

Later, the group moved off, scrambling over the high wall of a nearby park; they would take their party there now that the pub was closing. They built a small fire, not really for its heat, more for the atmosphere. The other silver sister had joined him now; one sat either side of him; his heart and soul trumpeted loudly in pleasure as each hand stoked a stiffened nipple. Their hands moved across his chest, stroking, seeking to bring pleasure to their new master. This was it, the ultimate, he was the master of the universe, the lord of all he surveyed, the mighty would fall at his feet and he would trample them all!

Many times, he would seek to recreate that night. And many times, he would fail. Now, he couldn't remember much at all. Purpose, will, motivation, all had deserted him; only the dull ache of hunger remained, an itch he could never fully scratch.

He ran and ran as fast as he could, his breath coming it great steaming clouds as it hit the chill night air. Sweat ran down his forehead; his white shirt plastered to his sweat-sheened skin. Briefly, he glanced over his shoulder, but already it was too late: in a cloud of dust and stung by the shrapnel of flying gravel Life passed him by.

They had rented the entire thirty-seventh floor of the office block. It remained unfurnished, apart from a small coffee machine in one corner. The floor was covered in squares of coarse grey/blue carpet; with no partitions, there was a clear view to the glass on all four sides. The windows were partially shuttered; the setting sun, sliced and dissected by the slats, streamed through those on the western side of the building invigorating a million dust motes; beckoning them to dance for its pleasure.

The nine figures in the room were rendered tiny by the vastness of the space; they sat at the eight key points of the compass, backs close to the glass, with the ninth prone on the floor in the centre; his arms and legs were spread, his head pointing east. All nine were naked; the eight sat cross legged, arms spread, a lotus unfurling. Their eyes were shut, their foreheads furrowed in concentration; a sheen of sweat covered their bodies, although the room was cool.

Before them was spread a tapestry that could not be seen; its threads invisible to normal sight. Ten days ago, they had started to weave, the invisible threads at first carving a neat spider's web, anchored at eight points, its host in the centre. Slowly a richer pattern emerged, a thousand invisible colours; their combinations creating a million more shades of nothing. Each thread represented a thought, an idea, a person, or a possibility.

They were applying finishing touches now. The threads of possibility bound their enemies; they would not be able to interfere. The myriad circumstances depicted within the tapestry all led to one golden conclusion, one shining possibility, one clear moment in time. One birth.

The threads were strong; the weave made them so; a vast hem strengthened them further. The nine worked as one, a slow smile spreading on their lips as they surveyed their handiwork. They looked with swelling pride at some of the key moments depicted: the background and upbringing that shaped some of the principal characters (each represented by a single thread), forging their personalities; the subtle indoctrination; the flight on which the three would meet, strangers brought together on a row of slightly cramped seats; the spark that would unite them, join them; the future when the three became four – the birth that would change it all.

Now they were testing their work, eliminating doubt, ensnaring shadow. It was finished. All that remained was the speaking of the three words that would bring the colour, make it real, cast the events into motion.

And that was when it happened; the one possibility that they could never have imagined. This was not the work of an enemy, but one that they thought was one of them! His thread suddenly appeared within the scheme; he was on a small island in the north of the Atlantic. In one hand he held a wedge, and in the other a flame. The flame he played over a fissure beneath a huge sheet of ice-crusted snow; the wedge he drove into a small split in the rock floor before him. When both started to shift, his work was done, and he blinked out to another place. Slowly the sheet crept toward the growing fissure in the floor and the red glow that emanated from it.

The heat radiating from the fissure grew, speeding the approach of the ice sheet. And then a chunk of the ice had broken free and tumbled into the fissure. When frost met fire, the effect was cataclysmic. The fissure tore wider, a huge gaping maw; sheet upon sheet of compressed snow tumbled into its gap turning to instant steam. Explosions shook the mountainside and then the earth's exuberance poured forth; red rivers of molten rock meandered slowly from summit to valley floor; huge plumes of ash and steam clawed their way up into the atmosphere, seeking to escape the conflagration below.

Slowly the ashen smog spread its net, clearing the skies as one by one countries grounded their airlines amid safety fears (had He sown a seed of doubt here too?). Their plane would not take to the skies!

The thread that had represented that flight frayed and snapped, the threads that represented each of the other passengers twisted and snagged. To their horror, a small hole appeared in the fabric. With growing speed their tapestry unravelled; thread upon invisible thread withdrew. And then it was unmade, nothing remained but broken fragments of possibilities destroyed; short, disjointed, threads of nothing. Their dream lay before them, in tatters.

With some incredulity, he realised how frequently thirteen appeared between the numbers twelve and fourteen.

A warm breeze meandered down the street, plucking idly at the discarded newspaper; but without the strength to lift it. The sun had started to dip, obscured by the buildings now, but its warmth remained. Only a few folks occupied the street, some stood chatting, others making their way to destinations unknown; but their stride was relaxed, unhurried; lazy as the breeze.

Only one was moving quickly, her hips swaying slightly from side to side. Wearing a summer dress a shade or two off emerald-green, which finished a few inches above the knee; two thin shoulder straps held the dress in place; the wearer glad of the breeze on naked flesh. Judas smoothed down the material which had begun to ride slightly from the hip; for no reason that she could place her mood was one of distinct happiness; she felt joy with the world.

She passed two men standing idly chatting by the front of a coffee shop. The man facing her, without moving his head, let his eyes run up and down her figure coming to rest at a point just above the top of her dress; a ghost of a smile played across his lips. Judas's mood changed almost instantly: did he think that his admiring glances were welcomed, appreciated, did her a favour; or did he think that because he had not moved his head she could not tell where he was looking. She had heard all the arguments before: "if it's on show, it's there to be looked at"; "it's not rude to stare at a work of art"; "it's natural to respond to such provocation"! The weather was dictating what Judas wore, not her desire to be ogled at every opportunity. Why did they do it, especially the married ones; those that would probably hate the idea of someone ogling their wives.

Her heels clacking angrily now, Judas moved on. Another man was walking towards her, tall, clean cut and wearing shades. Judas almost laughed out loud, here was one who thought that because he was wearing shades, he could move his head to look directly at her and she would not know where he was looking!

In her mind's eye, Judas could feel the rough touch of hands upon her breasts, disinterested, almost perfunctory; so many minutes here for good measure before moving down her body – if she was 'lucky' often they would go straight for the treasure below. The hands were just as rough and unfeeling; a means to an end. She could feel the hard press of the hand's owner's mouth, the forceful exploring of the tongue, whipping her own tongue into submission; the press of a body on hers hot breath on her neck; but the press never there long enough for her to start to feel any pleasure – although occasionally she felt obliged to let him think otherwise if he had tried particularly hard.

Judas passed two more 'viewers', before reaching the door of her destination. She slipped into the cool interior; the club was crowded and noisy with dance music, but still more comfortable than outside. There were no men in the club at all. Now when eyes were turned to Judas, they were appreciative, complimentary; she was not an object of lust, but of beauty. Moving through the crowd, Judas saw a group of girls that she knew and made her way towards them.

They welcomed her to their group; their kisses were warm, tender, the tongues sweet tasting, gentle, exciting. Judas felt a soft hand on her breast; she tingled with pleasure; gentle fingers teased the swelling nipple beneath the material of her dress. She and her friends paired off to dance to the music, each exploring the other's body with their hands, the kisses deeper, longer, more passionate. The light show began, rainbow colours filled the room, swirling in and out of the pulsing music, around the throng of bodies; there were few gaps on the dance floor, the throng danced as one; felt as one; moaned softly as one. Dawn was still a long way off.

Men-I-Mem

From: Judas

To: The Big Cheese

Subject Soul Shortage

The population of the world is expanding too fast. There are now not enough souls to go round.

In some cases, we have been able to issue a communal soul shared by a group – should we call them a mob? – but in many cases no souls are available at birth. I do not need to remind you of the potential devastation of a fully-grown Homo Sap with no soul.

Fear most the enemy that you do not fear, for when he stings you the greater will be that sting.

The tiny boat bobbed on the vast sea. The sea was calm: nature's work done, the weather reverted, now the waves were tiny; little more than ripples on the glassy surface. Looking out, that was all that could be seen: water in all directions. That was indeed all there was: water. Or so Judas believed. The end had come quickly; the warming unabated; the politicians unable to agree. Slowly at first, but then more rapidly, the icecaps had melted. By the time the evidence was irrefutable it was too late. Tidal waves had swept the planet; except they did not recede; they flooded over land, and remained.

Judas had not seen another boat for at least a fortnight. He had given up rowing; there was no point, nowhere to head. Early rumour had spoken of a single landmass, still jutting above the ocean; on other occasions there were rumours of a vast boat, skippered by the visionary Kno'ar. This had amused Judas for days: overtaken by the past!

Eating was easy: the fish were plentiful, and, through some adaptation of nature, provided sufficient moisture for survival; thirst was ever present, but never life threatening. Judas wondered if there would be a rebirth, but it seemed unlikely, at least not in his lifetime.

Slipping over the side of the boat, he entered the water, as he had done every day for hours on end. But today something was different. Judas looked down at his feet lightly flapping in the water; they were longer, wider, and thinner than the last time he had noticed; toes now the longest part of the foot, and linked by a thin, but tough, membrane. His hands were not dissimilar. Judas ducked under the surface; water entered his mouth, but he felt no panic; he felt his lungs inflate, something was dispelled behind his ears; more water entered.

Looking down, Judas saw it, the landmass of which they had spoken; but it was not above the waves, it was below them. Others such as he swam there; their skin sleek, naked. He dived down toward them, and they darted toward him, circling him in playful greeting. Some he saw now had scales; their legs joined. A female swam close; he felt the slight warmth as her scaly legs (leg?) brushed against him. Her long hair flowed in the water, he could not determine its colour, but it was fair. Sleekly, she twined around him; he felt her breasts brush against his chest, the nipples hard. She twined round him once more; their mouths met in wet kiss; her tongue hot against his. Their hips met, and he entered her, the heat here twice that of her mouth. Their limbs wrapped around each other; they swam as one. Each time their hips slightly parted, Judas felt the slight chill of the water, and then as they closed together the heat seemed even more intense than before. She kissed him again; longer, slower, deeper; he felt her quivering in release, and he too released. As she guided him toward a cave in the undersea mass, Judas wondered what their offspring might look like.

HOW!

Chapter 43

The Nine Motivators of Man

There are nine true motivators of man. This truth was nearly stumbled upon once, by Sigmund Freud, but his own Prime-Motivator blinded him to the others; Freud later added the second motivator of the death drive. However, he had come too close to the truth, given time he might have arrived at the others, and he had to be replaced: there is great danger in man knowing the strength and power of his own psyche; it has the power to make all of this real, or unreal with a single brain wave.

You must therefore guard the knowledge that you are about to be given jealously, it should be discussed with no one but your tutor; this textbook must under no circumstances be removed from the classroom, nor should it be copied in either part or full.

These are the nine motivators:

MOTIVATOR:	REPRESENTED BY:
Love/Emotion	The Heart
Lust	The Genitals
Wealth	The Left [Open] Hand
Power/Leadership (also desire for Fame)	The Feet
Compassion	The Eyes
Hunger	The Stomach
Strength [Physical]	The Right [Clenched] Hand
Rationale/Logic	The Brain
Tribe/Community	The Torso

Not one of these motivators is more powerful than the others. There are some that are more base; for example, in the starving man, the hunger drive will almost always be the Prime-Motivator; this is rarely – but not always – the case when a regular source of food is available. Motivators too can work in reverse: in the anorexic, reverse hunger is the Prime Motivator; as in the zealot, reverse lust might be.

There is always only one Prime-Motivator, although often it can be difficult to split from some of its closer sub-motivators. Very few men can know their own prime-motivator, as they are often blind to it, or deny it: it is one of life's more amusing paradoxes that most might consider their prime-motivator as a weakness, and seek to mask it.

This too makes it difficult for others to identify, although they might believe they can, but add to that the complication that many use Sub-Motivators, to achieve their Prime-Motivator [as, for example, someone might use the Sub-Motivators of Wealth or Power to achieve their own personal Prime-Motivator of Lust], and the true Prime might be well masked, deeply buried. Prime and Sub Motivators can also change: a man, driven by Love can find himself consumed by Lust [for example], if his Love is unrequited.

There is a powerful school of thought, although it is not shared by this author, that there is a hierarchy of these motivators, with Hunger at its base. The implication being that once the Hunger drive has been satisfied man moves on to the next level; striving always to reach the top level. I will neither dignify, nor endorse this school of thought by telling you the motivator that is always depicted at the summit of what they refer to as Matlow's Hierarchy of Motives; I will simply say that in placing it there Matlow reveals much of himself, and his own Prime-Motivator. Students should, if they wish, study Matlow's work for themselves, and form their own conclusions. If they do choose to investigate Matlow's work, then I urge them to read also the works of Sayer, whilst they are very heavy going, and not at all easy reading, they represent an excellent counter point to Matlow's.

Matlow also goes on to argue the existence of a tenth motivator, outside and above his hierarchy, the motivator of Spirituality. In this, the author has some sympathy; but would argue that this state is simply the Prime and all the Sub Motivators aligned, and balanced in harmony. One must not, in the drive to achieve one's Prime-Motivator allow the others to go unfulfilled. Just as externally a healthy community is achieved when those with Power/Leadership [cf: Power/Leadership – The Feet] motivators have complementary aspirations, so it must be internally: for example, an unhealthy mix might be achieved if one's Prime-Motivator was Compassion, but Lust was in ascendancy over Love, or Hunger was overlooked. Internal and external balance is essential to achieve self, and group, harmony. Few truly understand this concept, seeing only conflict.

For a tribe, or community, to be successful, they need to have members with each discipline as their Prime-Motivators; these need to be in balance: naturally a community can happily hold larger numbers of one group than it can another; indeed, it is an unhealthy community if there is only a single Prime-Motivator; many sects, or cults, have this - although not necessarily the cult leader.

Eh bien, je n'y ai jamais vraiment réfléchi !

WHY!

His cheeks and neck were blotched with the hot, bright, red of rage, veins strained against the skin looking for release. His voice rose in pitch as he screamed at them; they had never seen him this angry! Small flecks of spittle flew from his lips; his face was so close to theirs that they all felt the hot saliva as it spattered them. "What the hell were you thinking! What on earth possessed you! Watch. Listen. Observe. Record. Watch. Listen. Observe. Record." With each word he smacked his right fist into the palm of his left hand for emphasis. "Who gave it to you to create possibilities! That is not for us to do; you know your mission; you know your directives; you know the rules; why! Why, why, why! Whose idea was it?"

The nine stood before him, despite several of them being much taller than Him, they stood shuffling their feet, heads bowed, like so many schoolboys caught smoking behind the pavilion. None of them wanted to speak, to risk that wrath being directed purely in their direction – it was hot enough when spread across the nine.

He prodded Bartholomew with a finger rigid as a stick, "Well?" Bartholomew swallowed, answering very, very, quietly: "But, er, you, I mean we… … … didn't you see the end result, the conclusion?"

"That is hardly the point!" came the retort, "You broke a fundamental rule of our creed!"

Thomas spoke, although the withering glare he received caused him to wish he had remained silent: "But surely the birth of that possibility made it all worthwhile? Why did you have to undo it, even if it was wrong; why perish that thread, unravel the scheme?"

When he answered, his voice increased even further in volume, "You know not what you do! Nothing is given to us to see clearly! We cannot see all ends! In your pride, you thought you could see them all; but you could not! It is not given for us to interfere!" Slowly he drew breath, the apoplectic rage cooled to a simmering wrath. "Go now, separately, from this place. Return to your given mission. Do only that that you have been told. Speak not one to another until I say that you might. You will not weave again! Punishment may come to you; on that I will ponder."

Slowly they departed, going out singly to demonstrate that they had heeded his words. Judas was last to leave, behind him he heard Him speak once more, although it was little more than a whisper: "This was not the first time that you betrayed me; it will not be the last." Judas did not risk responding, unsure whether he was being addressed or whether the comment was directed at another.

What is the True Nature of Jealousy?

In the mind's eye: movement: outside none; the kaleidoscope continued to turn. The four images (bodies?) met, joined, sprang apart again. At times they were one, centric, outward looking; at others four (eight?), the gaze inward, introspective. Intro or outro, occasionally retro: the style was all-important. The answer was here, in the pattern and he/you/I/we knew it; the design coalesced, the truth revealed; but too soon it had turned on again, and the pattern was lost, although another, perhaps better suggested itself. Desperately he/you/I/we tried to reverse the movement, but it seemed beyond control.

The image changed, and now the colours changed too, reds and yellows transmogrified to blacks and purples; four the only constant. Four is in itself strange, not a straight division of ten, yet every whole multiple of four ends in one of only five numbers: four itself, eight, two, six, or zero. And yet, zero, by definition, is the lack of a number; with that thought the colours fade, the images begin to blur: grey; one; slowing; stop.

Hurriedly he/you/I/we dismiss such heresy, and think instead of: four, and how it had infiltrated our language, disguising itself as: for: to show belonging, the possessive; also,: fore, too: coming first; in the beginning!

With this truth, the colours return, brighter, more vibrant; the speed of change increases: a vortex. He/You/I/We are drawn in once more, dimension travel opens again: the spatium-cingulus accessible again.

He/You/I/We, the four, become one; our place in time is identified, with gathering speed it approaches we are disgorged and our feet once more tread the new, familiar, virgin, path; it is 19_ _.

Capricious Extravagance

The spectre of הסחות דעת haunts my dreams;

Sleeping, awake, both. Night and day collide.

A wilful left turn, when the directions said right;

The many-eyed temptress: pursuit: no respite!

The chamber of doors beyond count,

Numb'red at random, foul hands at play.

The fault, never mine! 'Tis others, I cry:

They mask'd me, full-face, their ethereal cry:

Come join us, come join us, it matters no more.

Be free, take flight, from duty and task;

Your raiment cast off, bare-footed take flight;

To others, your burdens, a gift let them be.

But harsh, my addictions; a vice un-ask'd.

The leash, full-physical, imagined? Or both?

And now, sands of time, trickle to glass bulb below;

The last speck descends; the curtains draw closed.

Tempus fugit. הזמן חולף. El tiempo se detiene. Rewind.

All dials read zero, springs tight-wound coil free.

The page before me, blank, unfilled, full-bare;

No book as the other eleven; my worms fat, bloated, replete.

Words' end in my sights; to babble no more,

The towering challenge: assassination of the twenty-six.

Yon wordless night; on all sides, black drapes descend;

A, before I, before C. Then E? Or after C? Silver bullet, fly!

Yaw violently left, yaw myopically right; the cleats ripped free!

The world, mystery steep'd; the tannins break free.

No lime juice, no scurvy, no crew; the captain alone.

Don helm, take helm, aim for haim; haim precious Chaya!

Then, suddenly, becalmed; na'er e'en a gossamer whisper;

Heart slows too; breathing's last gasp! Set sextant to hope?

Day/night, day/night: strobotic, intense.

The end, it draws nigh; the end, endeth.

A new, new, beginning. I knew it was new,

Though knowledge comes not cheaply; it is hard-won!

And with that data imparted, binary, I became O.

Judas checked the front page of the newspaper, scanning date, and headline; it was then that he realised how far off course he must be.

Ten thousand pairs of eyes turned towards Judas: eyes of pale blue, mid blue, deep blue; eyes of hazel, light brown, dark brown; eyes of green; eyes of grey; even one pair of pink eyes belonging to a lugubrious albino.

Those eyes studied, worshiped, drank in his every movement, every nuance of his character. He was their master; they were his slaves; he had but to command it and they would leap to do it. They had all undergone rituals to bring them to this state, each one subtly different, and yet the same. Sleep was Judas's to give, or take; happiness, sorrow his to share out at his will.

Ten thousand pairs of eyes stared, transfixed as Judas plugged in his guitar; he swaggered, pounding out a riff, up to the microphone and started to sing.

Judas lay with his head resting on his knapsack, the midsummer sun beat down upon his body; the grass was soft beneath him, springy and fragrant; there was a gentle hum as insects went about their business. Below, a brook babbled, its music underscoring the scene; wild poppies swayed to the gentlest of breezes. A half-finished picnic lay before him. He could not remember being so happy before; he wondered if he would ever be as happy again. Lazily he watched as the dragons performed the intricate flight of their mating dance: male and female at times joined as one, at others far distant from each other. They must be the friendliest creatures in the world, thought Judas, his eyes following one of shimmering cerulean. It seemed that the entire population of the world lay back on the hillside to watch, so rare was this dance. A collective sigh rose up from the hillside; as though summoned by it the dragons drew closer.

The dragons swooped low, opening wide their proud mouths; flame billowed forth, scorching the earth, and the bodies that lay supine upon it. The peace of the scene was rent by screams; the dragons wheeled again, and Judas felt searing heat; his screams joined the chorus. Soon it seemed the whole world was ablaze, the flames leapt higher, fanned by the dragons' wings, caressing their bellies. The screaming had stopped; no human mouths remained to articulate their pain.

The dragons dropped logs into the centre of the blaze: building a mammoth nest; several now settled into the structure, and when they rose again gleaming eggs nestled where they had sat; soon the nest was filled with eggs; the blaze kept up, unabated.

Black White Black White Black White Black White Black White Black White Black White Black
White Black White Black White Black White Black White Black White Black White Black White
Black White Black White Black White Black White Black White Black White Black White Black
White Black White Black White Black White Black White Black White Black White Black White
Black White Black White Black White Black White Black White Black White Black White Black
White Black White Black White Black White Black White Black White Black White Black White
Black White Black White Black White Black White Black White Black White Black White Black
White Black White Black White Black White Black White Black White Black White Black White
Black White Black White Black White Black White Black White Black White Black White Black
White Black White Black White Black White Black White Black White Read White Black White
Black White Black White Black White Black White Black White Black White Black White Black
White Black White Black White Black White Black White Black White Black White Black White
Black White Black White Black White Black White Black White Black White Black White Black
White Black White Black White Black White Black White Black White Black White Black White
Black White Black White Black White Black White Black White Black White Black White Black
White Black White Black White Black White Black White Black White Black White Black White
Black White Black White Black White Black White Black White Black White Black White Black
White Black White Black White Black White Black White Black White Black White Black White
Black White Black White Black White Black White Black White Black White Black White Black
White Black White Black White Black White Black White Red White Black White Black White
Black White Black White Black White Black White Black White Black White Black White Black
White Black White Black White Black White Black White Black White Black White Black White
Black White Black White Black White Black White Black White Black White Black White Black
White Black White Black White Black White Black Read Black White Black White Black White
Black White Black White Black White Black White Black White Black White Black White Black
White Black White Black White Black White Black White Black White Black White Black White
Black White Black White Black White Black White Black White Black White Black White Black
White Black White Black White Black White Black White Black White Black White Black White
Black White Black White Black White Black White Black White Black White Black White Black
White Black White Black White Reed White Black White Black White Black White Black White
Black White Black White Black White Black White Black White Black White Black White Black
White Black White Black White Black White Black White Black White Black White Black White
Black White Black White Black White Black White Black White Black White Black White Black
White Black White Black White Black White Black White Black White Black White Black White
Black White Black White Black White Black White Black White Black White Black White Black
White Black White Black White Wred White Black White Black White Black White Black White
Black White Black White Black White Black White Black White Black White Black White Black
White Black White Black White Black White Black White Black White Black White Black White
Black White Black White Black White Black White Black White Black White Black White Black
White Black White Black White Black White Black White Black White Black White Black White
Black White Black White Black White Black White Black White Black White Black White Black
White Black White Black White Black White Black White Black White Black White Black White
Black White Black White Black White Black White Black White Black White Black White Black

The shelves were covered in a thick coating of dust; the spines of the books too were crusted with grime, although their titles could still easily be read. The room was only dimly lit, the flickering shadows revealing its source as candles. A robed figure moved around the room; on every wall there were shelves of books, scrolls, parchments, even the occasional blue ray tablet. There were no windows – or if there were, they were covered and shelved across. Judas ran his finger along the nearest bookshelf; it was his third circuit of the room and still he could not find the book he required. A pile of scrolls on the floor revealed his latest search.

His eyes ran along the spines taking in the titles: Aristotle and the acausal cosmic being, Genetic sleuths follow clues to elusive ancestral 'Adam', Against the Theory of Autodynamics, Ancient Indian aircraft technology, Another Space-Time perspective?, The collapse of the Antarctic ice sheet, Ueber Antimaterie, Binary perception: The tiger of consciousness, Diskussion ber Bioresonanz, Ueber die Entstehung von Blitze, How the brain works/How to understand reality, A case of professional hysteria on the Velikowski Manuscript, The Covariant Theory. (Time), What is DHA? (Docosahexaenioc acid), Eclipse/Alignment Update, The orgone accumulator, On the scientific concept of entropy, Evolutionists disproven, Full moon peak portends stock crash, world crisis? Astroharmonic & technical analysis, Fundamentals of quantum mechanics and relativity, About the future of Physics: The sustaining myth, Was ist Gentechnologie?, The holographic universe;

Physics Mysticism, How to construct a Time Machine, Get Laid Newsletter, issue 11: with Speed Seduction editorial, Levitation: It is very simple, 'The Merlin Project': Time pattern research, The Neurophone: Electronic Telepathy, The Exact Nature of the Catastrophe, Proving morphic fields, An introduction to a new geometrical physics, Particles & Waves : Wholes & Aspects, Gravity theory: The physics of the parallel world, Photonic mass a definitive exposition, PSI in der Sovjetunion, The once and future king, Pyramid energy: The Answer, Why there must be antiparticles. (Quantum-Mechanics), Do Quanta have mass?, Scientists reconsider life on Mars, The slide rule explained, Scientific dissertation on Shadows, Snowflake symmetry explained, Why?, Social toxicity showing effects in children, Science discovers the Soul, The Speed of Light, Synopsis: The Tarn of Eternity, Nikola Tesla's wireless power transmitter, Why does the universe exist?, Vector Particle Physics, Velikovski: The mythological evidence: comets and poem of Erra, The Voynich Manuscript. The Most Mysterious Manuscript in the World, The Enigma of the atomic tornadoes, Yin Yang and particles. Magic or mechanics?, Fragments of Behaviour: the Extensional Stance, Our distant future Leviathan,

He re-scanned the shelf, there was no doubt: someone had been here, the order of the books had changed. There were three titles missing; one of them was The AT1s Explained; this deeply troubled Judas. More troubling still, he could not remember the titles of the other two. Judas heard a creak of floorboards and whirled around; the candlelight guttered, and he saw the shining arc coming at his left side; it was slightly extended

Byron had claimed the words, but Judas felt certain that they had spilled from his pen; the fit, after all, was perfect!

I had a dream, which was not all a dream.
The bright sun was extinguish'd, and the stars
Did wander darkling in the eternal space,
Rayless, and pathless, and the icy earth
Swung blind and blackening in the moonless air;
Morn came and went—and came, and brought no day,
And men forgot their passions in the dread
Of this their desolation; and all hearts
Were chill'd into a selfish prayer for light:
And they did live by watchfires—and the thrones,
The palaces of crowned kings—the huts,
The habitations of all things which dwell,
Were burnt for beacons; cities were consum'd,
And men were gather'd round their blazing homes
To look once more into each other's face;
Happy were those who dwelt within the eye
Of the volcanos, and their mountain-torch:
A fearful hope was all the world contain'd;
Forests were set on fire—but hour by hour
They fell and faded—and the crackling trunks
Extinguish'd with a crash—and all was black.

Judas had been staying at the bed and breakfast for three weeks now; the last guests had gone home the previous day: the season was now over. That left just him and the landlady; she was forty something, carrying more fat than she might have liked, but to Judas, she was fine, curvaceous, the object of his lust. Each evening, he had sat by the bar, casting covert glances as she reached drinks down from the shelf, revealing more of her upper leg; stretching her t-shirt tighter over her breasts.

Tonight, she was wearing a shorter skirt than usual, and as Judas stole a glance at the front of her t-shirt, no bra. Judas ordered a calvados, not a drink that he was particularly keen on; it was simply its location on the top shelf behind the bar. "I did wonder whether to open up tonight," said Sandy, pouring out a generous, unmeasured glass, "Seeing as it is only you that is left, I thought it might be too quiet for you?"

"Not at all," replied Judas. "But why don't you join me for a drink?" In answer, Sandy reached back up to the top shelf and retrieved the Calvados, stretching up even more than earlier. She poured herself an equally generous measure, returned the bottle, and walked round to the front of the bar, saying: "I might as well join you this side, if you don't mind?" "Not at all!" Judas returned, feeling a stirring in his lower abdomen.

As she passed the end of the bar, Sandy dimmed the lights even further. The bar, which was in the basement area of the bed and breakfast, was already quite dark, with the comforting smell of stale, spilt, beer. Sandy pulled up a bar stool, close to Judas's, and slid onto it, her knees touching lightly against his.

They chatted lightly of nothing in particular into the evening, Sandy returning several times for the bottle, and each time pulling her stool that little bit nearer to Judas's; her knees now overlapped his own by same way, and touched with a firm, unyielding pressure.

"Now, don't forget," Sandy was saying, "tomorrow is cleaning day, so everything in your room will get a thorough going over; so, you need to be out by nine thirty." "And what if I am not, do I get hovered?" laughed Judas. "Definitely, and dusted" was the reply.

Sandy took another swig of the apple brandy, and shivered, "Brr, its cold down here!" she said. Judas who had been staring at Sandy's nipples, which seemed to be straining to breach through the thin cotton of the t-shirt replied: "Yes, I see you're cold." Then realising what he had said, stammered, "I mean I can see the gooseflesh on your arms." Sandy smiled and leaned forward, touching his cheek with the back of her hand, "Are you cold?" she asked. She was very close now, although it was only their legs that were actually touching, Judas fancied that he could feel her warmth against his own chest. "We both need another drink then!" he replied, his words a little slurred. Sandy slid down off the stool, supporting herself with a hand on his upper leg, her own thighs revealed somewhat as her skirt rode up with the friction of sliding from the stool.

They had two more drinks before Judas said that he ought to turn in; to his great disappointment, Sandy simply wished him a goodnight, Judas staggering slightly climbed the stairs to his room; there were, despite his hopes, no sounds of Sandy following. Judas sat in his room, but, realising that he must have misread the signs when there was no knock at his door, stripped, leaving his clothes scattered on the floor and slumped into bed.

He was awoken the following morning by Sandy entering his room singing quietly to herself, a feather duster in one hand, a small trug of cleaning chemicals in the other. She was dressed in a low-cut crop top, and a denim skirt even shorter than the night before, its hem frayed, the left side seam split a little. She started to move around the room, the duster darting here and there; there seemed to be an awful lot of dust in high to reach awkward places, requiring Sandy's close attention. Judas's eyes followed her around the room, watching the hem of her skirt every time she stretched up.

Sandy moved nearer to the bed, she leaned over Judas to dust along the headboard; he watched her breasts jiggling inside her t-shirt, as un-fettered as they had been the night before. "Come on," she said, "you should have been up and out by now! I told you I had the room to clean. Judas lay back, with his hands clasped behind his head, swallowed, and did his best to raise an eyebrow, in what he fancied was a quizzical fashion, "I'm waiting to be cleaned too!" he laughed.

Before he had a chance to react, or cover up the evidence of what he had been watching she had twitched the top sheet and blanket to the floor, "These bed clothes will need washing," she said, adding, "and you had better have a cold shower, from the look of it!" Although she was staring at him almost as much as he had been staring at her; she playfully dusted his chest with her duster. Red-faced, Judas hurried rather too quickly into the bathroom, turned on the shower and stepped into the cubicle. He closed his eyes, but all he could see was her breasts dancing before his eyes. Judas started to wash, in an attempt to divert his attention.

Judas felt a brief cold draft on his back, as the cubicle door opened and closed again, and then a warm pair of hands was soaping his back, " I told you that *I* do the cleaning!" she chided. The hands snaked up and over his shoulders, and now started to soap his pectorals; he could feel her breasts pressing into his back. Judas turned around to face her, she still had her top and skirt on, although both were now thoroughly soaked. "I don't mind doing my bit to help," he said, pulling up her top his soapy hands reaching for her rhythmically dancing boobs. Her hands had dropped lower, and she was lathering his abdomen, they now slid round his waist and pulled him closer; they were not dissimilar in height; now their lips pressed together, and then hers parted to accept his urgent, questing tongue.

Judas tore her top down the centre, and let it fall to the floor, kissing her cleavage before moving left and right to kiss, nibble, and suck the hardest nipples he had ever felt. Sandy's hands came up behind his head, and pushed him lower; his tongue probed her belly button, as his fingers undid the buttons of her skirt; completely sodden with water it fell heavily to the shower floor; beneath the skirt she had no further layers to remove! Judas moved lower, and Sandy screamed out in delight; presently, Judas felt her body quiver and shake with orgasm. Now it was Sandy's turn, and she sank before him, taking him into her mouth; her tongue was expert, and experienced, and Judas felt the pressure mount. Before his lust exploded, though, Sandy had climbed back up, her tongue sliding up his body and into his still hungry mouth. Her hands reached up and behind him, grabbing the top of the cubicle wall. In a quick movement, and much to Judas's surprise, she pulled herself up slightly, and then dropped back down, and he was inside her. He returned his attention to her breasts, as they bobbed up and down before his face, his hips joining with the rhythm of hers. He held off his moment of release for as long as possible, wishing that this moment would never end, but when she released her second orgasm her screams triggered his own release.

Wet, they lay on the bed, in each other's arms, stroking, gently caressing, until his ardour restored

Judas entered her again. When she asked, later, if he would stay with her throughout the winter closure, he nodded that he would. She had ensnared him, his power was gone, he was now no more than a mere plaything; there for her amusement, to be discarded once his usefulness, or appeal was gone. But Judas cared not, he was in love again.

The darkness was absolute. In its midst a figure squatted; knees tightly clasped scant inches from the chin. He sensed – nothing could be seen in this environment – the stalagmites and stalagmites that surrounded him. In his mind's eye they were close to him, the bars of a cage; but he knew this was not the case. There was a slow drip of water from all sides; trickling down the stalactites, lengthening them over the millennia. They splashed towards the floor slowly forming the stalagmites that rose towards the roof of the cave in slow, rocky, greeting. The figure rocked back and forth in time with the dripping. He had had a name once: Je…., Ju……, Jo……, but it would not come. He could not remember if he was hiding or searching. He had not eaten for several ……… he had no measure of time. His name had been J……, his name had been ……, his…….. h…….; the rhythm of the rocking increased. The figure's tongue extended and caught a few drops of water. Perhaps soon he too would become a slowly rising pillar of limestone, a gorged god. The rocking slowed; he hoped that if he stayed a while longer, he would forget the way out too.

WHERE?

The numbers are everything. It had been one of his first lessons. The numbers tell the true story; for some, they are all that mattered.

For reasons he didn't grasp, two numbers came to him: 144,000 and 666.

He divided 144,000 by 666 and was amazed to get 216.216216216216...

6 x 6 x 6 also gave him 216.

He remembered a name, was it Harshad, or was it Niven?

2 + 1 + 6 = 9. 216 ÷ 9 = 24. 24 x 6 = 144.

What did this tell him? Were his days numbered?

He thought back to the dividing. To him was given the 9^{th}C and 20^{th}C; the others, too, were given two. A span of 24 centuries. The crucial period. At the end Revelation would come.

His training was only just beginning. He lay still upon the rusty bedframe, the mattress coarse, even through the grey sheets; he was unsure if the grey of the sheets had come from centuries without being washed or if it was their natural colour, and they were fresh from the packet. He suspected the latter. As far as he could tell, he wasn't bound to the bed or restricted in anyway, but he was unable to move. A metallic grinding came from the frame, although he knew the bed had not moved in any way; perhaps it was adjusting itself to his weight. The bed was positioned in the middle of a broadly square room, equidistant from all points. The walls were painted a deep orange, bordering on brown; in the centre of each was a window, but the windows resided too high for him to see anything from them except the washed-out blue of the sky.

The two Shades approached the bed, one from each side – probably east and west, although it might equally have been north and south. He knew only that it was a prime direction.

"First he must learn to breathe," they said. The one to the east reached out and covered his mouth, forcing him to inhale through his nose; as he did so, she pressed firmly upward from the base of his chest. She withdrew her hand, and it was replaced by one dipping in from the west; this one clamped his nose, forcing him to exhale through his mouth; as he did so, she pressed down on his lower abdomen. The western hand withdrew. The one to the east reached out and covered his mouth, forcing him to inhale through his nose; as he did so, she pressed firmly upward from the base of his chest. She withdrew her hand, and it was replaced by one dipping in from the west; this one clamped his nose, forcing him to exhale through his mouth; as he did so, she pressed down on his lower abdomen. The western hand withdrew. The one to the east reached out and covered his mouth, forcing him to inhale through his nose; as he did so, she pressed firmly upward from the base of his chest. She withdrew her hand, and it was replaced by one dipping in from the west; this one clamped his nose, forcing him to exhale through his mouth; as he did so, she pressed down on his lower abdomen. The western hand withdrew. The one to the east reached out and covered his mouth, forcing him to inhale through his nose; as he did so, she pressed firmly upward from the base of his chest. She withdrew her hand, and it was replaced by one dipping in from the west; this one clamped his nose, forcing him to exhale through his mouth; as he did so, she pressed down on his lower abdomen. The western hand withdrew. The one to the east reached out and covered his mouth, forcing him to inhale through his nose; as he did so, she pressed firmly upward from the base of his chest. She withdrew her hand, and it was replaced by one dipping in from the west; this one clamped his nose, forcing him to exhale through his mouth; as he did so, she pressed down on his lower abdomen. The western hand withdrew. The one to the east reached out and covered his mouth, forcing him to inhale through his nose; as he did so, she pressed firmly upward from the base of his chest. She withdrew her hand, and it was replaced by one dipping in from the west; this one clamped his nose, forcing him to exhale through his mouth; as he did so, she pressed down on his lower abdomen. The western hand withdrew. The one to the east reached out and covered his mouth, forcing him to inhale through his nose; as he did so, she pressed firmly upward from the base of his chest. She withdrew her hand, and it was replaced by one dipping in from the west; this one clamped his nose, forcing him to exhale through his mouth; as he did so, she pressed down on his lower abdomen. The western hand withdrew. The one to the east reached out and covered his mouth, forcing him to inhale through his nose; as he did so, she pressed firmly upward from the base of his chest. She withdrew her hand, and it was replaced by one dipping in from the west; this one clamped his nose, forcing him to exhale through his mouth; as he did so, she pressed down on his lower abdomen. The western hand withdrew. The one to the east reached out and covered his mouth, forcing him to inhale through his nose; as he did so, she pressed firmly upward from the base of his chest. She withdrew her hand, and it was replaced by one dipping in from the west; this one clamped his nose, forcing him to exhale through his mouth; as he did so, she pressed down on his lower abdomen. The western hand withdrew. The one to the east reached out and covered his mouth, forcing him to inhale through his nose; as he did so, she pressed firmly upward from the base of his chest. She withdrew her hand, and it was replaced by one dipping in from the west; this one clamped his nose, forcing him to exhale through his mouth; as he did so, she pressed down on his lower abdomen. The western hand withdrew. The one to the east reached out and covered his mouth, forcing him to inhale through his nose; as he did so, she pressed firmly upward from the base of his chest. She withdrew her hand, and it was replaced by one dipping in from the west; this one clamped his nose, forcing him to exhale through his mouth; as he did so, she pressed down on his lower abdomen. The western hand withdrew. The one to the east reached out and covered his mouth, forcing him to inhale through his nose; as he did so, she pressed firmly upward from the base of his chest. She withdrew her hand, and it was replaced by one dipping in from the west; this one clamped his nose, forcing him to exhale through his mouth; as he did so, she pressed down on his lower abdomen. The western hand withdrew. The one to the east reached out and covered his mouth, forcing him to inhale through his nose; as he did so, she pressed firmly upward from the base of his chest. She withdrew her hand, and it was replaced by one dipping in from the west; this one clamped his nose, forcing him to exhale through his mouth; as he did so, she pressed down on his lower abdomen. The western hand withdrew. The one to the east reached out and covered his mouth, forcing him to inhale through his nose; as he did so, she pressed firmly upward from the base of his chest. She withdrew her hand, and it was replaced by one dipping in from the west; this one clamped his nose, forcing him to exhale through his mouth; as he did so, she pressed down on his lower abdomen. The western hand withdrew. The one to the east reached out and covered his mouth, forcing him to inhale through his nose; as he did so, she pressed firmly upward from the base of his chest. She withdrew her hand, and it was replaced by one dipping in from the west; this one clamped his nose, forcing him to exhale through his mouth; as he did so, she pressed down on his lower abdomen. The western hand withdrew. The one to the east reached out and covered his mouth, forcing him to inhale through his nose; as he did so, she pressed firmly upward from the base of his chest. She withdrew her hand, and it was replaced by one dipping in from the west; this one clamped his nose, forcing him to exhale through his mouth; as he did so, she pressed down on his lower abdomen. The western hand withdrew. The one to the east reached out and covered his mouth, forcing him to inhale through his nose; as he did so, she pressed firmly upward from the base of his chest. She withdrew her hand, and it was replaced by one dipping in from the west; this one clamped his nose, forcing him to exhale through his mouth; as he did so, she pressed down on his lower abdomen. The western hand withdrew. The one to the east reached out and covered his mouth, forcing him to inhale through his nose; as he did so, she pressed firmly upward from the base of his chest. She withdrew her hand, and it was replaced by one dipping in from the west; this one clamped his nose, forcing him to exhale through his mouth; as he did so, she pressed down on his lower abdomen. The western hand withdrew. The one to the east reached out and covered his mouth, forcing him to inhale through his nose; as he did so, she pressed firmly upward from the base of his chest.

She withdrew her hand, and it was replaced by one dipping in from the west; this one clamped his nose, forcing him to exhale through his mouth; as he did so, she pressed down on his lower abdomen. The western hand withdrew... ... If you wish to understand, you must read every word. There is no skipping to the end.

For what was probably a whole year, that four step dance marked his entire existence; it might have been much longer. At what may have been the six-month point, the hands ceased the dance; without thought or effort Judas breathed in, passively, through his nose, raising his ribcage; then he exhaled, taut, through his slightly parted lips; tightening the muscles across his abdomen. A dozen breaths later and the hands resumed their dance. The Shades seemed pleased with the progress made, but there were no further pauses as the months rolled by.

How to Turn a Black Mood White.

A Beginner's Guide

Outside the rain battered the thin, barely adequate, roof tiles; like so many impatient fingers drumming upon a table the windows too rattled within their frames as the rain battered them. It was the perfect day for staying in and trying to make further progress with his thesis.

Picking up his fake Mont Blanc fountain pen and a sheet of cream-toned paper, Judas began to write:

Time travel is of course impossible. One can only live in the now; yesterday is gone, vanished; tomorrow hasn't happened yet and therefore you cannot visit something that does not exist. If you could somehow travel back a day, it would no longer be yesterday, it would become the now.

Thus, it follows that every moment is the now and therefore time travel is infinitely possible as the only time that exists is the now. Everything happens in the now. And, therefore, if you exist (that's a whole other thesis), then you too exist in the now. There is but one moment, and within it everything happens, so we all live in the past, the present and the future, simultaneously.

Capture an insect in a jar. Inspect that jar an hour later. Is the insect still there? You've just invented the time machine; that jar transported the fly from the then to the now (of course to the insect, they were both the nows). But can that experiment be reversed? With certainty! Open the jar and remove the insect, is the jar now empty? As empty as it was before capturing the insect? ... ...

Judas paused before completing the reverse-experiment text and re-read his words. Nope that would never do. Far too many 'therefores and nowhere near enough words, this was supposed to be a thesis, not a précis of one!

The entrance to the club was dingy, it might once have been a deep and lustrous black, now it was a dusty grey. At least the bits that could be seen were grey, nearly all of the walls, and much of the glass, had been over-sprayed with graffiti: testimonies to music icons, loved ones, hated political movements; a myriad of names preceding 'woz ere'. Two bouncers stood nonchalantly on either side of the door; both chewed casually, one on gum, the other on a cocktail stick. Both had come from the typical bouncer mould: huge barrel chests, close cropped hair, goatees; this was not a salubrious club, so they wore leather, not dinner, jackets. Judas mooched past, trying to portray an aura of toughness that he neither felt nor knew how to show. He stopped at the ticket window; there she was, the vision of loveliness: thick hair, black and spiked; black eye liner and lipstick, applied thick and broad; black fishnet covered one arm; her dress was black leather (Judas knew that below the counter it would be very short and that there would be more fishnet); her nails were the only concession to colour, a purple so dark to seem almost black, the nails themselves sharpened to pointed talons.

She was slouched over the counter; before her a forgotten cigarette burning in an ashtray. Barely looking up, she acknowledged Judas only with a "Yeah?"

"Awright," said Judas, in his best drawl, "gis a ticket."

"Oo for?"

Judas was stumped, he was only here to see her, the only reason that he had been coming here, every day, for the past three weeks; ever since he had found out that his Rachel (at least, that is how he thought of her, he had never told her this, or anyone else except his pillow) worked there. But then he realised that there would only be one gig that night, as there was every night. Was she teasing him? Or did she think he wanted a ticket for another night?

"Oh, yeah, fer t'nites show," he said. Silently, she slid a ticket towards him; Judas pushed £4.35, all in loose change, through the gap in exchange. He scanned the name of the main group on the ticket, saying: "Yeah, I fink The Lost Sheep and Teenage M F Death Squad are brilliant, really quite special." He realised he was losing the accent, so quickly added: "d'you reckon 'em?" No one iterated the words that the M and the F stood for, not for prudish reasons, it was just colloquial.

"They're a'right."

"You com'in in'a d'gig?"

She moved her shoulders slightly, a half-hearted shrug: "Maybe, dunno."

"I'll look out for you." He felt the stare of one or both of the bouncers and decided it was time to move on, abruptly, and far too quickly, he left the window. He called back, too late, and too quietly, "I'll buy you a drink." There was nothing to indicate that she had heard.

Inside everything reflected the same shades of black; Judas felt more comfortable in the dark, he too was in black, hardly noticeable. The support acts: Kill My Mother and Wooarghhhh, had whipped the crowd into a seething frenzy of half shambling, half pogoing, ecstasy. It was at the end of TMFDS's first number that Judas spotted Rachel. It took three more numbers for Judas to manoeuvre his way through the crowd to her side. She did not hear his first offer of a drink, so he was overjoyed to be able to put a hand on her arm (the fishnet felt so good) and put his mouth close to her ear (she smelt divine) to re-shout his offer. She did not answer, but turned toward the bar; Judas followed her, managing to retain the contact of his hand on her arm.

Showing off, he ordered two Blood Suckers (Vodka, Tequila, Tomato Juice and Beetroot Juice). She took the drink, without a word of thanks, and started to head back to the mosh pit. Judas followed her through the press: a faithful puppy. The crush pressed them together; Judas's arm was around her waist, the hand pressed firmly to the soft flesh just below her hip bone; whilst most of his hand grasped leather, his ring and pinkie fingers trailed just below the hem of her skirt. Judas was in a personal heaven. He was here, with his Rachel, touching her, she was pressed against him; tonight, he would walk her home, and they would kiss. Maybe she would invite him in for coffee. Maybe he should kiss her now. Dare he? Why not, surely, she would not be this close if she did not like him.

Rachel raised the glass to her lips, tipping it steeply; such was the etiquette of the young with this drink that she deliberately let the drink overspill her lips and run down her chin – striking the pose of the bohemian vampire. Avidly, Judas watched the liquid bead and roll down that perfect chin. He willed it to continue, in rapt hope of the next part of the ritual. Driven by his thoughts – or gravity – the small stream on the left of her lips dropped from her chin to splash redly onto the pale white of the flesh above her breastbone. He knew the ritual, now he, as the perfect vampire-gentleman, should lean forward and lick it off, smearing his own lips with red. But for the briefest of moments, he hesitated; supposing she had not noticed, did not want him to; his mind raced forward, and he imagined the sting of a slapped cheek. And then the moment was over; before he could decide, or move, she had swallowed down the rest of her drink in one and was gone, slipping off through the crowd wiping the red away with the back of her hand. He tried to follow, but where she seemed to find a path and gaps, he found none. Perhaps she just wanted the toilet, and would be back, he thought. Maybe she had gone to buy drinks, this was the modern world. Or to get a better spot to watch The Lost Sheep. But she did not return. Twice more he saw her in the club that night, each time with a different drink, and a different man. He was to see her one last time that night: as the club disgorged its noisy sweating contents onto the street, there she was, locked in a passionate embrace with one of the bouncers. Both his hands grasped her buttocks as she writhed against him. Then they were walking off down the street, her hand around his waist, his around her shoulders, the hand idly caressing her breast. Judas turned up a side street, to vomit against the wall; he sank to the ground in floods of tears, sitting in his own filth he rocked back and forth. He needed a new religion.

Bene, ego numquam multum cogita-verat!

Judas sat back in his chair, put down his pencil and let out a long steady stream of breath; he interlinked his fingers, and pushed the palms away from him hearing the joints crack, the sound magnified in the quiet of his room.

He had done it. He had finally done it! He had recorded every joke, every pun, every double-entendre, every anagram, every acronym, every cross-linked name, and every reference point in the Illuminatus Trilogy.

Inspecting his work, he was not surprised to discover that he had written 23 chapters, filling 1,776 pages. He picked pages at random, chuckling over their content; surely this was one of the ******** books that had ever been written?

The dark figure on horseback was silhouetted against the horizon; briefly, the moonlight caught the tip of a scythe. Hesitantly the man approached, looking up at the mounted figure; "Is it my time?" he asked. The pale skeletal face rolled upward gleaming near bright as the moon itself; mocking laughter spilled from thin translucent lips: "That time might never come!"

The answer troubled him deeply, though he knew not why. "But surely in the end, you must come for us all?" he asked; "you have taken so many already!" The horse snorted, voicing his Master's disgust, the mounted figure glared: "And how dare you make that accusation! You who have taken more than I!" "That's not true; it's a lie!" he replied. "I would hurt nothing, neither man nor beast."

The translucent lips pulled back from tombstone teeth in an approximation of a grin: "Oh, but you will! If you haven't already, you will – many of great import too; perhaps even the greatest one of all." The horse reared; below it the man screamed, not in fear of the flailing hooves, but of what had just been said; a scream of pure denial. With that rider and horse turned and started to trot away; the hooves muffled by the turf. He looked back once, to offer a parting word: "For you see, I am you, and you are me!" The screams rose in pitch and then descended into barely audible sobbing.

They were all gathered together in the training room; it's walls crudely plastered, painted a dull brown. Overhead the dusty rafters held the gloom and the sweat of a thousand sessions. The instructor, big as a bear, but fast as a striking snake, stood behind them. "Fighting stance!" he commanded. As one they took the pose; their kiai shook dust from the rafters. "Jab." They struck at a shadow in response. "Jab." "Jab." Their forward arms snapped outward at each command. "Counter!" This time the other arm whipped forward, accompanied by a twist of the hip.

"Jab. Jab-jab. Counter".

"Jab. Jab-jab. Counter".

"Oi tsuki. Oi tsuki-oi tsuki. Gyaku tsuki"

The commands came without pause. This was the one hundredth day; these were the only two attacks that they had learned. Those, one stance and two blocks. That was all they had learned.

"Oi tsuki. Oi tsuki-oi tsuki. Gyaku tsuki"

"Oi tsuki. Oi tsuki-oi tsuki. Gyaku tsuki"

"Oi tsuki. Oi tsuki-oi tsuki. Gyaku tsuki"

But today there was one change: punch bags descended from the ceiling, one in front of each of them. Now instead of striking shadows, they struck bags. For another one hundred and fifty days they struck bags, with the same two punches. And then in what seemed a veritable flurry they learnt three kicks: mai geri, mawashi geri, soto geri. Instead of bags, they faced each other, now the front row moved: step/punch, step/punch, step/kick, step/kick, step/kick. The second row stepped backward, mirroring their steps, but instead of attacking they blocked: step/block, step/block, step/block, step/block, step/block. Without pause the roles, and the direction of movement, reversed.

For days beyond count they continued this dance. There was no pause, there was no sleeping, there was no eating or drinking. There was nothing else. Just the dance. At some point new techniques, new blocks, new stances were introduced. The dance became more complex, spinning and whirling, leaping. After years beyond count, they were finally permitted to dance freestyle, to face each other in combat. Bodies littered the floor now. Three emerged from the room, leaving the other, unmoving, bodies behind. The first batch had completed their physical training. But this was just the beginning, not the end: the mental, the spiritual, the magickal all these and more were to follow.

"Only three! But we need twelve!" he roared.

Judas urged his steed to an even faster pace, as he entered the woods; the moon cast flickering shadows to either side; damp branches lashed at his face. Suddenly, Judas was thrown violently over the horse's neck: the animal had run into a low, but sturdy, branch; the impact had broken its neck. Without hesitation, Judas leapt up and blindly ran on: he had long ago forgotten if he was chasing after something, or fleeing.

The sun was just beginning to set. Or was it rise? He always got east and west muddled up! The path that he was following led through a wood; the trees were not packed particularly closely together, but they were heavy with moss. Their leaves, too, were sparse. Did that mean spring? Or autumn? None of his pointers seemed to be working effectively. Soon, it would be time to stop for a break, a small snack and some water; but he felt fit and fresh, so determined to do a little bit more walking.

Presently, he came to a point where another path crossed his. "Do I carry straight on, turn left, or turn right?" Judas said to himself; his voice seemed unnaturally loud in the hushed woods. There was no one to answer, of course. But it also made him conscious that he had not heard the sounds of any wildlife for a long time: no rustling in the undergrowth; no chirrups from birds. He was pretty sure that he should carry straight on, which should soon bring him out of the woods, but he wanted to be certain, so rummaged through his bag for the map. Opening it, he ran his finger along the path that he was fairly sure he was on, to the place where he thought he was probably now standing. The map was very clear: a turn to the right. Judas's brow furrowed, that did not feel right; surely that would lead him deeper into the woods? He looked at the map again; it would be fatal to make a mistake now: he was already well behind schedule. But no, he was either reading the map incorrectly, or it was a right turn. He stood for a while longer. What to do: to follow his instinct; or, follow the map. "Well," he voiced out loud again, "my instinct has certainly been known to let me down on occasion, but surely a map cannot make a mistake, can it? I'll do what the map is telling me to do."

And with that, he plunged into the woods. The trees grew denser all around him; the path narrowed, in places it disappeared altogether. But Judas forged on. Several hours passed, and it ought to have been getting dark, but the intensity of the light did not seem to have changed at all. Judas paused to check his map; he was still following the path that it had declared. Later, and still in that same half-light, he reached an impassable point; the trees stood bough to bough; there was no forcing through them, neither was there a circuitous path to left or right. He would have to turn back and look for an alternative route.

Judas turned, but the path behind him was gone. There was nothing but the trees. Trees on every side. Had there been any gaps, they might have felt like prison bars; but there were no gaps to be seen. He turned again through 360 degrees; as he finished his circle, the trees had pressed in closer. He could hardly move. Now he could not move at all. They pressed in, constricting his chest. He could hardly draw in air, and still they pressed in. He heard the leaves rustling: they sounded like cruel laughter.

There was a desperate need to fill in the blanks.

Judas sat on top of the high garden wall, looking out across the village square, it was still, partially, in the grey-brown light of dawn, it was deserted. The only sound came from the clock at the west-end of the square: it had just started to strike six o'clock.

Judas rolled himself a mean cigarette, using almost as much paper as he did tobacco; his legs swung from side to side, a counterpoint pendulum to the clock. Judas had just finished the cigarette, when a lone figure entered the square. He was pushing a cart, from which he took a broom, and started to sweep the area, pausing occasionally to light his pipe.

Another figure crossed the square, they called casual, but indistinct greetings to each other.

As the sweeper was scraping the last of the dirt up into his cart, a tractor entered the square; behind, it pulled a trailer, laden with trellises and tabletops. Two men jumped from the tractor and started to pull the trellis poles off, dropping them to the floor in a seemingly random fashion. Both men paused for wheezing laughter, their breath clouding in the air, as a high pile of trellises toppled from the trolley, narrowly missing them.

The sweeper sidled over, and little work was done, as they exchanged gossip, and cigarettes, for the next half an hour.

Eventually, the stalls began to take shape, until all were assembled in four zigzagging rows. These early performers drove off, to return, presently, with candy-striped awnings, roofing every stall in turn.

Next came the stallholders, each in a large car, towing a trailer full of wares. Hurriedly they spread their profusion of goods on their individual stalls; signs were erected, advertising their content. All the while they called friendly greetings to each other:

"Morning!"

"New line in nylons!"

"Still cold!"

"See you in The Bull lunchtime?"

"Morning!"

"Morning!"

"Morning!"

"Morning!"

It seemed to Judas only a short time before all the commodities were laid out on display. He jumped down off the wall, and went to look closer. Passing by fruit stalls, flower stalls, book stalls, bric-a-brac stalls, fish stalls, meat stalls, pie stalls, sweet stalls, card stalls, clothes stalls, kitchen stalls, and others selling a mixture of many things.

Two schoolboys rushed through the market, books clutched in their hands; one bumped into Judas and looked up, he seemed troubled that he had never seen me before; they both ran off, calling greetings to a few of the stall owners.

As the market began to get busier, I left, taking a side road down to the nearby stream. Sentencing was about to begin.

Their eyes have seen all that had happened in Egypt to Pharaoh, to all his officials and to all his land; the history books had recorded it. With their own eyes they saw those great trials, those signs and great wonders.

But to this day, still, they did not possess a mind that understood, or eyes that saw or ears that heard.

He would give them ten times twelve score years of free will. And if they failed, he would wipe the slate one last time.

Freedom, life itself, is that strangest of things;

Wings spread wide.

Enclosed within bars no more; and yet

Something remained in that empty cage;

Never to be released!

He is known as Judas Iscariot (e.g., Mark 3:19). Some have explained this as being derived from an Aramaic version of a Latin word meaning assassin. But the most (un)likely explanation is that he came from a village called Kerioth.

Thus didst the mighty ones gather;
He, clothed in white at their head.
Brows' furrowed; perplexed;
Worry, heavy 'pon their shoulders.
"How has it come to this?" asked He,
"That the fourth who rose up,
"The world, he did not take for his own?"
A silence pervaded the room.
Of speech, none thought to make bold!

"Herr Wolf rose, but was not victorious;
"His armies defeated; routed; slain; captured.
"His slow march across the globe, about-faced;
"Like dominoes, like Jericho, they crumbled and fell!"

All knew the plans that were drawn:
The fourth, more evil than all before;
The world would he trample underfoot!

Leviathan, serpent, beast: moulded in one!

Then, cometh the sword-tongued one,

To sweep him away; to cast him to the depths!

But what now? The Evil One o'er thrown;

But fragmented, not gone.

'Though not o'erthrown by the one destined

Beliefs, spread wide, amongst many;

no longer in one! Evil seed!

Is the whole world turned evil?

Repentance lost?

The end? A new end?

The beginning?

A new beginning?

Pre-planned history undone?

Rewritten!

Ten thousand pairs of eyes turned towards Judas: eyes of pale blue, mid blue, deep blue; eyes of hazel, light brown, dark brown; eyes of green; eyes of grey; even one pair of pink eyes belonging to a lugubrious albino.

Those eyes studied, worshiped, drank in his every movement, every nuance of his character. He was their master; they were his slaves; he had but to command it and they would leap to do it. They had all undergone rituals to bring them to this state, each one subtly different, and yet the same. Sleep was Judas's to give, or take; happiness, sorrow his to share out at his will.

Ten thousand pairs of eyes stared, transfixed as Judas drew his sword, pointed it at the sun and cried out in a voice of command:

A gentle breeze now filled the sail; it stretched, convex, from the mast; pulled taught, pulling them on. They shipped oars and the drumbeat ceased. The gentle lapping of the water, the soft creak of wood, were calming; they belied the appearance of the men: leather and mail clad; axes and knives at hand; shields mounted port and starboard.

He had taken enough of Rakel's scorn. It had been that, that had pushed him to the front of the volunteers to join the raiding party, heading for a new destination. It would be his first taste of real battle; the practice fights had been real enough in their own way; he had often emerged bruised and bloody. But it was only rarely that these had proved fatal to the unlucky few. Not so in that which was to come; death would be real to many. Like Judas, most sat in brooding silence; they knew that battle was near. The day before, they had left the Channel, mooring at the mouth of the River Seine. At first light, they set off, rowing at first; now they started to see wisps of smoke curling up into the sky: the home fires of Rouen.

They saw, now, the moorings ahead; the warlords signalled for readiness, fierce grins on their faces. As they neared, they saw someone jump up from the decking and run deeper into the town. A solemn bell sounded out; its peel told them their arrival would not be a complete surprise, but their foe would have little time to prepare. With a soft bump, the longboats butted the moorings; some would remain behind to secure them, but Judas and his fellows raced behind their warlords towards the town centre.

Rounding a corner, they saw a hastily prepared defence force heading towards them, rapiers drawn. A rictus grin spread across Judas's face; his axe was already in his hands. He and his fellows were tall, burly, muscled; the defence seemed slight in comparison; his grin grew. And then the two factions met; the defenders were controlled in their approach; the raiders far less so, fighting with reckless abandon. Their momentum alone scattered some of the defence, who fell to the ground, initially uninjured, but moments later bloodied and axe-marked. Judas's first kill was one of these; he saw him stumble before him; as he tried to rise, Judas's axe bit into his neck. A howl escaped from between his lips as he swung his axe now left, now right; he was not taking careful aim; he slashed with careless abandon. Judas did not even really try to defend himself; he felt no sense of threat. Soon his face, his arms, his leather jerkin (Judas had no money for mail) were stained with blood.

Several braziers had been kicked over; the wooden frames of the buildings quickly caught; and now gusts of smoke thronged between the warring factions too. The soot and grime mingled with the blood and the sweat until the invaders took on the look of dark-skinned warriors. Many French lay dead, but Judas could see no Vikings lying amongst them. A young enemy stood before him now; barely out of his teens, somewhat foppish in look. The adversary took up a traditional, tutored, fighting stance; Judas laughed, cruelly, pushed the sword to one side and slashed obliquely. The axe smashed through cheek and jaw; the Frenchman fell to his knees. Judas did not wait to see if the blow had been fatal, he was onto the next of his foes.

The massacre did not take long. Soon all the defenders lay dead or dying (or had fled). The invaders fragmented somewhat, moving out into the town's streets; they were now searching for houses to raid, plunder to steal, and perhaps a wandering male or two to kill. And women. Women to rape.

Judas found himself alone in one of the streets; the noise, the screams told him where his fellow raiders were, and what they were doing. He was not concerned to be alone; the bloodlust was still fully upon him; the enemy had proved to be of little concern. His mind turned to which house he should raid first; at random he picked one, kicking open its door. In the room before him he saw a cooking fire, a table and chairs, and on the table bread and roasted fowl. Beside the table stood a woman; her dark hair had been tied back, but much of it had escaped the confines of the string and tumbled over her shoulder. She wore white: a button-up blouse, although the buttons from the neck to halfway down were not fastened; her skirt too was white. She looked at him steadily; Judas did not see fear, he could not quite interpret the look. He strode into the room and across to the table; he ripped flesh from the bird and crammed his mouth, the juices running down his chin and into his beard.

To his surprise, she came towards him; she spoke, but he did not know her language. With a napkin, she dabbed some of the juices from his chin; she stepped back a little; here and there blood and soot now stained her clothes. Her fingers traced his bicep, "Si forte!" she said. He did not know what it meant; she tapped her breastbone, "Je Suis Rachelle." On hearing that name he forgot all about the bread and meat, he tore open the remaining buttons of her blouse; her breasts were soon streaked with black and red from his fingers. He pushed up her skirt and took her there on the table; her screams were loud, but they were screams of pleasure, not fear or pain. Or so it seemed to him.

Judas did not take long to finish. As he returned his attention to the chicken and the bread, she rose from the table, naked and stained all over from Judas's grime. She went to the door, pushed it closed and slid a bolt. "Maintenant tu es à moi," she said. Now it was Judas who she pushed down on the table; within moments he was ready and inside her again.

It would be a long while before he continued with his journey from Rouen to Paris.

He remembered the first time that he had received the gift. He had not asked for it, had not expected it. It just came upon him. He had been talking of a joy and the flood gates had opened. The tears had flooded his cheeks, although there had been no sobbing. The tears did not seem to match his mood, in one way, although in another they matched perfectly. He felt... ... ... peace? He felt a connection. He was joined to something much larger.

For the twenty-fourth time, he dropped the needle onto the record: Stiff Live Stiffs. The was no mistaking it, he must have been there: plain as day, he heard Ian Dury declare: “it’s Judas, Judas is on stage.”

The crowd pressed Judas forward; he could not remember ever being in such a large crowd before.

“Lost Sheep, Lost Sheep” the crowd chanted. They were the hottest property that year.

Judas was pressed up against the barrier at the edge of the road: the Lost Sheep were on a walk about. Judas gasped as they came closer, surely that was the Arch-Mage leading them! As they drew level, Judas called out, “Arch-Mage!” He whirled, and walked towards Judas. “Arch-Mage,” Judas repeated. The reply was, “No, I am his brother, the black sheep of the family, he probably hasn’t mentioned me!”

His mind raced, was this truth, or schizophrenia: the bad to balance the good? He let the crowd draw him away; they were surging towards the vast stadium, where the concert was to be held. For a while he tried to fight his way out of the crowd, but soon gave up: you can’t fight destiny; he was swept into the specially built stadium.

Judas sat unhappily on the grass, all the groups that had appeared so far had been mediocre, and received only polite applause. The crowd had been intent on drinking, and ingesting a plethora of narcotics; the smoke could not be avoided, it hung over the crowd, sweet and heady. The Lost Sheep were next to come on; the final act of the day.

Without warning, the lights went out; the crowd leapt to their feet; the excitement rose to fever pitch. For

fully five minutes the crowd shouted and screamed, until suddenly, at deafening volume lone guitar chords sliced through the darkness. It was an old Rolling Stones number: Honky Tonk Women. The guitarist sustained the opening for at least ten minutes, until, in a heartbeat, the lights all flared on, and the rest of the band joined in.

It was indeed the Arch-Mage who played the guitar, Judas was convinced, he could see him now; a black aura surrounded him, where usually it was white. The crowd were mesmerised, and under his control; they failed to notice the subtle way in which he changed the words, the commands that he was now imparting, which the music would cement in their subconscious, until activated.

It was all too much for Judas, he retched, turning to race for the exit, clutching stomach, and mouth. Behind him the crowd bayed in glee.

A fragment of lyric.

And now, now, now, now, I've lost everything,

I give to you my... ...

What did he have to give? He knew it must be important. He had to give... ...

Was it a message that he had to give? Or, were the lyrics themselves the message?

He tapped, tapped, tapped at his forehead. Come on, Judas, think. Think!

The swirling mists balled the orange flare of the torches; he fancied that the fingers of the mist rolled the flames, shaping them, moulding them, a living moving work of art. Dozens of the glowing balls bobbed along the path behind him; he could not see the carriers, or the brands from which the flames arose. Their pace was even, slightly slower than his; he did not know if they pursued him or some other quarry; their purpose might even be entirely innocent. The disembodied flares passed under what he guessed must be a tree – it was something that had held millions of tiny droplets of mist, which it now sprinkled lightly across the torches. They hissed and spluttered, but their flames did not dim.

Suddenly, before him, the path came to an abrupt end. A sheer drop was before his toes; he did not know how far the drop might be, it might be a few feet; it might be hundreds – he had been ascending all day. Tendrils of mist swirled before him; maidens' skirts promising a glimpse of what lay below, but only teasing, never revealing.

Cold fingers of mist crept over the edge of the precipice grasping for his feet but without the strength to pull him downward. He had passed many such breaks in the path during the day, before the mists had come; none of the fissures had been more than two or three feet in width, an easy jump to the other side. But now the mist refused him the knowledge of the width of this crack; indeed, it would not reveal if it was simply a fissure or the very edge of the mountain with a sheer drop to the valley below.

The torches drew nearer. Did they seek him? Would they attack him? Push him to the floor – or over the edge? He sensed animosity in their midst; he heard something hiss; was it the mist venturing too near to the flames, or was it the sound of hounds straining on their leashes, straining to be on him, to sink their fangs into his flesh. Perhaps they were not torches that flared, but the eyes of ferocious, slavering, hounds their height comparable with proud stallions. In his mind's eye the lights paired, proving his theory.

Judas turned back to the fissure. He would jump. He would make a leap of faith. Better to jump, rather than to be pushed. He had been jumping such gaps all day; others had gone before him, they must have leapt here too, and survived. Or had they fallen to their deaths hundreds of feet below, their bodies tattered and torn, food for the carrion beasts? Of course, that could not be the case; reports of such a dangerous gap would have reached the village by now, wouldn't they?

Would it help if he knew the nature of those who pursued him; knew their intentions toward him? Why risk the leap if it was not necessary for his own preservation? But he offered his own answer, if he waited to see it would be too late; if they wished him harm, they would have him.

Judas glanced back. The torches were much nearer. He turned again to the gap; the mists teased him still. Should he leap upward and across – the ledge the other side might be higher than this one. Or should he just go for length. He had decided. Inside he screwed up his resolve, using its forces to propel him as far as he could; he took a few paces back and then sprinted for the edge. He felt the toes of his leading foot arrive at the edge; he leapt. His arms windmilled, his legs still sprinting over thin air; the mist was all around him now; he could see nothing, even the glow of the torches was gone. And then suddenly he knew what lay before him, with a rush he

There is no Hope

The street ahead was dark; the orange glow of the streetlights seemed powerless to infiltrate the black of night. A chill wind blew, enough to whip leaves along the street before its wake; to prise questing fingers through any gaps in clothing: its quest for flesh overriding all. Several small groups of people populated the street, most headed in a singular direction: summoned by a fizzing neon that proclaimed “Dance”. A hushed expectancy filled the night air, the only other sound was the rustle of dried leaves as they sought to gather together in doorways, and against walls, seeking protection in numbers.

Amongst the thronging groups one character stands out as unusual, although this is simply as he walks alone, in a group of one. But there are other differences too, hidden ones. For starters, his whole energy is focused on aligning his blue chakra: massaging it, tuning it, preparing it for its task. Some might say that the use for which he was intending it was to waste its fantastic potential; but for Judas there was no higher purpose: ahead of him strode the vision that was Rachel.

His pace matched hers, as he rehearsed his lines. When ready, he would catch her up, and open with an expression of surprise at seeing her here, followed by an enquiry on her destination, then the request that they might head there together.

Ahead one of the girls in Rachel’s group laughed, he heard the word “lapdog”, but no more, the rest lost in a sudden flurry of passing leaves. Suddenly, the girls stopped; instinctively, Judas stopped too. And that is how they caught him as they turned, stationary, ten paces behind them. Judas's mind froze; he could think of no plausible reason why he should be standing there in the middle of the street, although, after the event, dozens of reasons would present themselves.

One of the girls spoke, "Going somewhere? Or just pretending to be a lamppost?" Judas thought her name might be 'Becca, she was the shortest of the group, slightly dumpy, wearing a hideous floral print dress; but there was only one girl that could hold his interest, and that bordered on obsession. The rest of the girls in the group giggled loudly, flushing with amusement; Rachel's laugh was not quite as boisterous as the others, but it was enough to send any comforting blue images fleeing from Judas's mind, to be replaced by unhelpful, melancholy, brown. He tried to speak, but no words came. Sudden inspiration came from the flashing neon that cast a small halo around Rachel's hair, but he could not get beyond the first phonetic, each time it caught in his throat. "Dawdling?" suggested 'Becca, helpfully, to increasing giggles all round. "Dangling?" added one of the others, tall and thin, slightly pinched looking, as though the victim of being stretched on a rack. "Dribbling?" scored the biggest laugh yet.

Judas tried a different opening word, "Rachel, I was hoping that ...." But before he could finish Rachel had cut him short, "Just leave me alone, Judas." Her voice was soft, Judas heard another emotion in it, was it kindness, or perhaps caring? But then Rachel saw the looks from her fellow revellers, and added, with vitriol, "You're pathetic. A right wimp. Now buzz off!" They turned, and carried on toward the dancehall, leaving Judas rooted to the spot, neither able to follow, nor flee.

In truth, he had long outgrown the desk. The twelve of them sat with their knees scrunched up against the worn wood; the chair, too, was several sizes too small. Why couldn't he see that they had grown? As though he had read that very thought, the mortar-boarded figure at the front of the room changed direction: "Can you people not see, if every good act had its reward, then everyone would indeed do good things, act well, give generously. But they would not be doing good for the sake of good, they would be doing it for themselves. The compassion would not be there for many. Just greed. I will help this person – but only because I will get more for myself in return. I will give to this person, because I will receive tenfold in return.

"Just as I cannot reward every good act, neither can I punish every bad one. Not yet, at least. Sure, if there was retribution for every misdemeanour, pain for every crime. Then evil would stop, but not because the perpetrators no longer wished to act in an evil way, only because every crime would be met with punishment. But that would not remove the evil from their hearts. It might even strengthen it.

"There is a wisdom in living within the laws that He has provided. But, too, there is a higher wisdom. The wisdom that creates balance. Order and Chaos must be balanced. His world can be neither pure Chaos, nor pure Order."

When you move onto combat classes, you will find that if you can identify the Prime-Motivator of your opponent, then you will beat him every time.

Let us now move on, and examine each of these motivators in turn.

Power/Leadership (also desire for Fame) – The Feet

Students must first understand that with each of the motivators, there can be degrees of aspiration. It might initially surprise students to know that a tribe can run very successfully even though a number of its members are principally motivated by their Feet; as long as their aspirations differ. One might be content in leading a small group, such as a hunting party; another might be content with running a farm. It is only when there are a number of men [please be aware that the author uses "men" in its oldest and most traditional sense of the word), vying for the post of Chieftain, or King, or to some extent General or Captain, that conflict will undoubtedly occur.

Let us consider why the feet represent this motivator; to truly feel this, it might help you to be standing now. Place your feet roughly a shoulder's width apart and parallel with each other (in combat you will learn more of Heiko Dachi), hold your tome in both hands before you; feel its weight. Now, transfer it to your left hand and hold it out to the left. Can you feel how the

The mist came down, a shutter on the sun; premature night.

And I, lost on the moors, ne'er a sole in sight!

The fog, damp, eerie, grey motes dancing around;

The sound, both muffled, and amplified: the screech of an owl!

Forward I stumbled unsure of my route, but unable to stand still.

For long I plodded, unsure where I trod, until, with a shock:

Off there, to the left, those upstanding stones,

Jaw-less, misaligned, teeth, set firm in a grin;

Had I not passed them a scant hour past? Their moss all too familiar!

In despair, to the ground I fell; from my jaws: a howl of frustration flew.

Grey mist swallowed that scream, closed in tight all around: a vice.

An echo? No, the tone deeper, from a rumbling throat!

And now a steady rhythm: pad-pad, pad-pad;

In mind's eye, an image – unbidden, formed, all too clear:

Coat shaggy, jaws flecked: saliva and blood: a wolf, most large!

Pad-pad, pad-pad; the sounds grew louder, came in from the left.

So off right I sped, heart thumping, straining to be free.

The soft, clear, steps followed on, now somewhat off right;

Veering left, on I ran; the atavistic beast still close, just behind;

His angle of approach oft changed, and I its reverse in swift flight.

The howl of the hunter pealed out through deep fog; a bell tolling for me;

Its potency: muscle freezing; I stopped, all movement gone.

By my toes: a ravine, quite deep, but, not too hard to leap;

The gully's jaws, at an angle, the unwary ankle to snap; clean break!

Muscles suddenly freed, o'er the ravine I leapt, my flight continued anon.

My zigzag route changed as often as his; beyond count of time in length;

But now: a silence, the padding had stopped, all told!

I slowed in my flight, and there, up ahead,

My heart filled with joy, my eyes tears o'relief:

A light, cutting through haze of mist and tears, a soft orange glow!

Its source was revealed: an inn, with a blazing fire in the grate;

A welcome of cheer, a smiling host, and a pint.

Sitting down by the hearth, I warmed up chilled bones;

My eyes drawn into the flames, captivated by their hypnotic flicker;

My ears catching clear snatches of conversations that floated all around.

But one, in particular, I heard above all others; its message quite clear:

The words that were spoken echoing on in my mind:

"They say that it is, on nights such as this,

"That the ghost of old Shep wanders o'er the moors;

"Most loved was he by his master, Bill of The Grange."

"They both died together, out there on those moors most fell;

"Bill by the ravine, his nemesis, his doom;

"And Shep, by his side, ever faithful laid down to die.

"And that's how they found them, together at the end;

"Shep's paws on his chest – big as a wolf's so they say!"

From the flames before me, or so I fancied, as I looked, stared deep;

Two eyes stared back out, canine in look;

A log suddenly split, the crack a deep-throated bark.

Was that how it was, I wondered in awe, on that dark fateful day:

Had the ghost-spirit of Shep herded me here; death-cheater at last?

Bueno, ¡realmente nunca lo he pensado mucho!

The walls of the room were white, possibly plastic. The floor and ceiling were also covered in the white material; no joins could be detected at any juncture. The only variation to the white was the thin grey line that marked the outline of the door and the two barred windows high up in the wall opposite the door. In the centre of the room there was a desk, also in white; the desk was bare, with the exception of a small laptop computer. This was not white it was a bright crimson red that might once have been fluid. The room was brightly lit, although the source of the lighting was hidden.

A man was hunched over the computer – although it was impossible to tell the figure's gender from look, clothed as it was from head to foot in black cloth. There was a thin gap in the material aligned to the figure's eyes, although no eyes could be seen.

The figure stared intently at the computer screen, on it a spreadsheet stood open. The spreadsheet's title was: Voices_To_Be_Silenced.xlsx. In the first column of the sheet a long list of initials could be seen:

Z Đ
Y R
T R
R V Z
R S
R H

R G
P S
P McC
N P
M ZuH
M X
M T
M L K
M J & K R
M H T
M G
M D C
M C
M F A
L H O
J W B
J M H
J M
J L
J J
J I
J H
J F K
J D M
J C
I G
G W B
G I M
G H
F S S
E P

C H
B M
B B
B A J M
A L
A II
A H
A A

In the three columns adjacent to this first were one of three markings, against some there was a ✓; against others an ✗; the third symbol was P. There were two further columns with entries, against each set of initials; the first column contained the entry method and the second scapegoat; both linked to other tabs on the spreadsheet. The figure's fists clenched and unclenched in frustration.

That was it, Judas decided. He was getting out of the assassination game. For every ✓ that appeared on the sheet it seemed that two or three more Ps appeared at the bottom; the ✗s also remained unresolved, a testament to the occasions when even his finely detailed Method could not foresee all outcomes. The ramifications were just getting too intense; what had started out as one simple eradication – albeit one agreed to rather hastily, over too much wine – was now spiralling out of control. It was easy for the others, they just passed judgement; eleven judges to his one executioner. When had they been given that right; hadn't the mantra been:

Observe, Record, Report; Don't Interfere? When had that changed? Had he missed (or forgotten) a Men-I-Mem?

Perhaps he should let the fates decide. Judas pressed keys at random, his eyes focussed away from the keypad and outward to the tiny wisps of white that drifted lazily across the bright azure of the Aegean sky.

Judas's attention returned to the room; he lifted the wooden goblet that rested on the table to his lips – it was a concession to a simpler time – and drank thirstily. He coughed and spluttered: the goblet did not contain what he was expecting; proof if any more was needed of how out of hand things were getting.

He looked with vindication at the screen when he saw the message that glowed upon it: Are you sure that you want to delete the file Voices_To_Be_Silenced.xls?

The dark olive of his eyes roamed to the eastern wall of the room, and the tools of his trade: rifles and handguns, swords and daggers, cords, umbrellas, liquid-filled phials, crossbows, car keys, pill bottles, gas canisters, throwing stars, even a number of caged animals. Whilst he could not say that he enjoyed his job, he thought, there was no doubt that he was very, very, good at it. Although there had been a few failed attempts (×s flashed before his eyes), not once had there been even a hint of suspicion of his involvement – how could there have been when you were able to slip from one moment to the next; time did not pass him by.

Judas accepted the computer's offer.

He closed the door behind him as he left the room, tapping a code into the number pad just below the handle. A message flashed up on the door: Are you sure that you want to delete Assn_Stor.rm? As his fingers touched the green button he was whisked away on a howl of venomous anger, jostled by angry chronos spheres, he was wrenched up only to be deposited moments earlier/later on the damp and yielding soil of a rain-soaked Irish potato field.

The walls of the room were cream; motivational phrases and graphics plastered the walls, their huge letters a mix of prime colours; the effect jarred the eyes. But Peter found them calming. He leaned back in his chair, his Church's brogues, polished to a gleam, were placed on the table. The table itself was a huge single slice of a giant redwood that had been slaughtered for the purpose; the bark was still visible around its rim, but the table was so lacquered and varnished that even that was smooth to the touch. Casually he fingered the cuff of his Budd shirt, smoothing away imaginary fluff; he let a slim stream of strawberry and mint vape escape from his pursed lips. It had been many years, maybe decades, since they had all sat together. As was his way, he would single one of them out for verbal destruction. He felt a frisson of excitement as he looked around the table to choose which one it would be: Andrew, James, John, Philip, Bartie, Thomas, Matthew, James, Jude, Simon, Judas, Levi, Matthias or Paul (who was late to the party). Briefly, it flitted through his mind, why do they always refer to us as twelve, but that hardly mattered: he was going to be the number one. Slowly he took each of them in, Andrew's benign beaming face; Bartie twirling his pen; John reading papers on the desk in front of him; Judas… … was that a love bite on Judas's neck, partially covered but the crumpled, badly ironed, collar of his white shirt; it was drawn together with a floral tie, the knot far too small. Yes, it was! Sweet simple Judas. With a girl! He almost laughed out loud; the thought was ridiculous: no one could possibly fancy Judas, he was far too blah. But that decided it for him. Judas was going down.

The Chief Executive Mage was beaming in by satellite for the conference, from wherever he'd planted himself in the world. He was forever jetting off around the world, Peter had no idea why, there was no need for him to do so. The screen flickered to life and there he was: bronzed, his dark hair curled to his collar, his beard freshly trimmed and oiled. "Reports!" he barked. Peter smiled inwardly again, so he was in one of those moods; this would be easy, he turned to Judas, "Why don't you go first J.I.?" and was delighted to see the blind panic flash behind his eyes.

"Yes, um, of course. Thank you. Very kind. An honour." Wildly Judas looked around the table, a cornered animal looking for escape. Oh, this was wonderful thought Peter; he hadn't even prepared anything, it would be almost too easy! He beamed at Judas, "Your comments are always so insightful, Judas, I am so looking forward to hearing you speak! Please, do go on."

"Yes, indeed, I will. But, er, before I do, I thought maybe, if you all agree, er, perhaps we might, I mean should, do a little bit of blue sky thinking, um..." Peter interrupted him with: "Blue Sky Thinking, how quaint!" But something was wrong, the CEM was speaking from the screen, "This sounds excellent, Judas, how does it work?" Peter felt his spirits drop, how could the CEM have forgotten such a base technique. But Judas was buoyed, he too had noticed the CEM's apparent forgetfulness, "Let me run this up the flagpole," he was saying, "I want to reach out to you all; together we are stronger; but let's step outside the box." The CEM was nodding. Peter was glowering, but he kept it in, he might recover it yet.

Judas continued: "Let's put ourselves in the shoes of the opposition, Peter, if you were them, what would you be doing?" Oh, very clever. A returned ball. How had he managed that; Peter fingered his collar, he was perspiring, he didn't want to spoil the silk. "I'd be going for our root, for our heart. There is no point going for our low-hanging fruit, that will only cure some short-term hunger; it will not shake our tree, that stands firm, we..." the voice from the sat-link was speaking: "Specifics please, Peter." His confidence was returning now, "Our brand is our heart, it is what we stand for. It is strong; it has stood for thousands of years. It is revered. If I were them, I would seek to damage it, to discredit it. I would somehow sabotage it, try to tear it down; I would..."

"Exactly my point!" Judas had stolen it from him, taken it for his own, "they will seek to fragment us, to set us bickering amongst ourselves, set brother against brother, we must stand shoulder to shoulder. We must love each other; we must be one, not twelve, or even fourteen."

The CEM was delighted, "Judas, I want you to lead this project for me; the rest will support you, take all the resources that you need." Peter was distraught; he'd lost his grab for the crown. And to Judas of all people; Judas that always bumbled along and winged it! How had that happened? Judas was usually a cert to make a mess of things with his lack of preparation, his penchant for winging it. It must be Judas's woman, whoever she was, she was somehow lending him strength. He would have to find her and seduce her. Or kill her.

He had never really been one for the phenomenon of social media; although he could see it had its place. Of course, he had profiles on all of them – even those that were yet to come. Once, he had even started to develop his own site; it was going to be called PeepsLinx, it would guarantee its members a minimum number of automatically generated friends based on the things they said and shared, and also on the places that they visited. He didn't see how it could fail, both at its surface purpose and its buried one: the ability to preach to, and influence, its members. He could do with the fans. They might even make his job easier.

Judas had spent the day drinking sour red wine, he was feeling moribund, and yet at the same time full of himself. He had spent the last hour writing a post under one of his many aliases (he was using PenPalPerson, today); he scanned through its contents again, it made him laugh. Ergo, it must be good, he thought, so with little further consideration of the ramifications (why had he worked on nine, all too revealing; he could have stopped at eight, or made up a tenth – but that was red wine for you!) he pressed Post. And there it was, for all to see:

After much research, investigation and analysis, it can be revealed that users of social media can be categorised into one of only nine groups:

A)#TheClassRoomJoker*.* *The guy who always thought it was cool to yell out in class. Rarely makes* *posts of his own but places oh-so-witty comments on others, no matter how serious the topic.*

B)#TheItsAConspiracy*. Issues dire warnings about how when you 'like' something it feeds straight into MI5, the CIA, the FBI, Interpol, and everywhere besides; immediately placing you on a most wanted list. And how if you send an e-mail with your name in it, the recipient can immediately access all your personal details, make withdrawals from your bank account; and substitute your name for theirs on all the MI5, the CIA, the FBI and Interpol lists. Believes in The Man.*

C)#ThePedant*. Sometimes known as #TheFactualist. Notes missing, or misplaced, apostrophes (so hates B and D). Quotes obscure literature. Peppers their post with historical facts and dates. Always has an answer for everything.*

D)#TheLookAtMeImWonderful *(cf, Bonzo Dog Doo Dah Band, Look At Me, I'm Wonderful). Believes themselves to be the centre of the universe. Truly thinks that the whole world will be interested that they are: brushing their teeth/going to the corner shop for a pint of milk/reorganising and colour coding their sock draw/washing their hair/&&&&. Invented the Selfie.*

E)#TheQuietOne*. Spends a lot of time looking at other people's pages. Never makes their own comments or posts – on their own page or anyone else's.*

F)#TheFiftySomethingGoingOnSeventeen*. Uses lts ov txt spk (usually incorrectly). LOL. Coz they thinks they iz dahn wiv d'kids. Innit. Smileyface.*

G)#TheCaresAboutEverything*. Posts and re-posts any cause, anything that might tug at the heartstrings. Sponsored by Kleenex. Doesn't matter how truthful, or very clearly made-up-for-something-to-do, they might be.*

H)#TheIveGotSomethingToSell. *Sometimes they are also known as #TheSelfPromoter. Has something that they want you to buy. Lots of hype. Lots of 'please like' and 'please re-post' requests. Churns out at least twenty-five posts each day. Understandably, often confused with the #TheLookAtMeImWonderful. Look out for my forthcoming book, DVD and t-shirt entitled How to Spot the Difference Between a Look at Me I'm Wonderful and an I've Got Something to Sell. Available from all good stores.*

I)#TheTotallyandUtterlyInebriatedByTheAllConsumingExuberanceofthePlethoraofTheirOwnVerbosityRarelyActuallyNeverUsesOneWordWhenTwentyWillDoASpadeIsNeverCalledASpadeNoSirItIsActuallyaManualImplementfortheLiftingandTurningofSoil*. Doesn't understand Twitter.*

Of course, it is unlikely that you will recognise which category you fall into – only your best friend will tell you. Unless you are like me, I don't seem to fit into any of the above .... Which one do you think you might be?

Judas pushed back his chair and waited for the flack to start.

The True Cost of Loyalty

He had listened to so many music discs, watched so many films, read so many books, attended so many concerts, that he knew he did not want to be a rock & roll star. He needed to be, *had to be*, a rock & roll star. Last week he had bought himself a glittering red flying-v guitar, now he stood before his bedroom mirror his left hip thrust forward, the guitar hanging casually (but reverentially) from his shoulder. He really did look the part. Now all he needed was to achieve instant overnight fame.

He had decided to abandon completely his roots and his artistic integrity; that way was too slow. His would be the fast route; once he had achieved worldwide success, then he might return to the music that he believed in and educate the world. But not now, not yet.

The cool breeze and light drizzle did nothing to dampen the enthusiasm of the queue of wannabes; they were buoyed by the roving cameras and plethora of fawning warm-up men. The ritual was firmly established now: inane questions would be followed by inane answers. The *expression du jour* was “I want it so badly” hotly followed by “It'd be a dream come true”.

He was surrounded by giggling and screaming girls, the occasional misplaced pensioner, and lads who felt their boyish charms would take them all the way. Cautiously, Judas adjusted his age, he needed to be old enough to have a story to tell (and what a story he had prepared!), but not so old that he was treated as one of the novelty acts gratuitously filmed in the hope that they would completely fuck up and constitute a moment's entertainment in the final cut. Slowly the file of hopelessly hopeless hopefuls snaked forward nearing the gaping maw of the temporary audition structure.

Inside, his humanity was stripped away and he became a number, badged 14732 by a sullen-faced, hopelessly bored, teenaged 'researcher'. And then he waited. And waited. And waited. For his moment to arrive. Finally, with all the ceremony of the next customer's number being called in the supermarket delicatessen queue, he was ushered into the presence of the Four Fates.

Their desk was slightly curved; at its left-hand end sat Steven Moirae, resplendent in his robes, comfortable on his gilded throne; preternaturally white teeth gleaming in the slight gloom. The chairs of the three other judges appeared (to their owners) to be unnaturally shortened so that the desk sat unnaturally high before them. Here sat Lachesis, who had achieved some genuine musical success during the last couple of years singing of memories and times gone by; Clotho, whose sibling was a genuine star, but who, herself, lived only for the moment; lastly on the shortest of the chairs, Atropos who claimed he could see the future of rock and roll (although he called it popular music in his idiosyncratic way) – he was fierce of opinion, but generally ignored by Steven.

Facing the judges, he announced himself: "I am not a number, I am The Betrayer and music is in my soul!" Lachesis opened the rote: "What is the dream?" The Betrayer took a moment, stoking the smoulder within his eyes, before replying; "I want to soar with the eagles; I want to touch hearts and souls; I want to save the world from musical strangulation; I want to *be*!" A flicker of recognition passed across Atropos's eyes, but was soon swallowed; "Who are you doing this for?" he asked. "I am doing it for me. I am doing it for the children of the world. But mostly," he looked up to the distant framework that supported the ceiling, "I am doing it for my beloved parents who were taken by foul pestilence this last year." He launched into his carefully prepared story of loss and horror. When he had finished, both Lachesis and Clotho had deep kohl tracts staining their otherwise perfect faces; Atropos was smiling wryly; surreptitiously, Stephen pressed keys on his ever-present calculator with the end of his pencil. Stephen took a long pull from his goblet before waving regally, "You may proceed."

The Betrayer took his place, angling his feet (as he had been told to) to trace the inverted V that formed the top of the letter Y pasted with gaffa tape to the floor before him. The spotlight burned into his eyes; he turned its fire into passion and expelled it in haunting, perfect, musical phrases. Cleverly he had chosen one of Lachesis's songs to perform; her vote would be his. Atropos too would support him; The Betrayer had shown him a version of the future. One more vote would do it and then it would be easy:

manipulation through television was a simple conjurer's mechanic that he had learnt many years ago. He just needed that one more vote.

As he was ushered from the room he slipped left, down a quiet passage, making his circuitous way through the labyrinthine corridors to the rear door from which The Fates would emerge at the end of the day. He had chosen his spot well, Clotho walked down the passage towards him, she was quite alone. The Betrayer stepped from the shadows; there may have been a moment's fear in her eyes, but so taut was her face that it was incapable of betraying expression. Then she smiled and told him how beautiful his performance had been. Breaking at least a dozen rules, and several more taboos, The Betrayer notched up his aura until he saw the pupils' of her eyes dilate; she was his. He pushed open the door to her dressing room; before it had closed behind them, she was pressing herself against him, her lips rising to meet his. They were softer than he had expected and her perfume more subtle. Her breasts, however, were exactly as he had expected: as he slid open the deep red silk of her blouse they stood before him solid as unripe fruit, the nipples growing unnaturally long as he caressed them. She ripped hungrily at his own clothing until it was all in a jumbled heap upon the floor. Both her hands grasped the cock that he had especially lengthened for the occasion. She kissed him once more, her lips wet with anticipation, before she sank down to her knees before him and took his entire length in her mouth.

In a move that she would never be able to describe the next day (was it a dance move?), he had reached down spun her round so that her legs now scrapped the low ceiling; he was still buried in her mouth but now her clothes, all red silk and black leather, were beside his on the floor (although neatly folded) and he had begun to explore her with his tongue. His hands clasped tightly to the cheeks of her arse, which was as firm as the tits which now pressed into his stomach. When he felt the flesh of her (smooth well-toned) thighs start to tremble he lifted his mouth away from her shaven pussy and bit into their milky softness. Her eyes flew open, and she shouted in pain; but now – in another shift that she was never able to explain – his face was before her eyes and the shout turned to a long groan as he entered her. Her purple-manicured talons sunk into the flesh of his back as she hungrily kissed him, tasting her own juices. Somehow, they were now on the long low couch; their two bellies, slick with sweat, squishing together.

As she came, she whispered in his ears, in her soft southern-hemisphere accent, the words he had so longed to hear: "I am so going to be voting for you tomorrow!"

It was completely dark in the room now; idly he traced the invisible scars of her surgeries and treatments whilst she slept beside him. Of course, she would want to wear him on her arm like a badge of merit now, but it was a price worth paying: he would not now have to seduce Steven. Victory, and international fame, was assured. He just had to try not to lose his humanity along the way again; yes 14732 was going to enjoy his rise to the top.

Ten thousand pairs of eyes turned towards Judas: eyes of pale blue, mid blue, deep blue; eyes of hazel, light brown, dark brown; eyes of green; eyes of grey; even one pair of pink eyes belonging to a lugubrious albino.

Those eyes studied, worshiped, drank in his every movement, every nuance of his character. He was their master; they were his slaves; he had but to command it and they would leap to do it. They had all undergone rituals to bring them to this state, each one subtly different, and yet the same. Sleep was Judas's to give, or take; happiness, sorrow his to share out at his will.

Ten thousand pairs of eyes stared, transfixed as Judas adjusted his cassock, gripped the edge of the pulpit, and started to quote, fervently, from the book before him.

There's Always Hope

Reflecting the dying embers of the fire, the music too fades; just the dull static hiss as the cassette winds to its end remains. Time to change the music. In affirmation, a burning coal shifts, rolling lower in the grate; momentarily, red sparks fly.

Judas touches the eject button; softly the mechanism pops open the door. He retrieves the cassette, returning it first to its case and then to its allocated spot on the shelf. The order was vital. He had tried many methods: alphabetical by artist; alphabetical by album title; by genre; in date order of release (that one had worked particularly well); in date order of purchase (that had not worked at all!); once, seeking to be obscure, by opening note; in order of favouritism, from least favourite, to most favourite; by colour; using the first word of each title to create a narrative. His current filing method, though, was by far the best; he did not dare to spoil it.

Selecting the next tape, he removed it from the case, which he placed on his mantlepiece, he was about to pop it into the still open door of the Marantz, when he realised that that would not do at all. He ran his finger up the bank of players, past Teac, Philips, Sony; past Binatone (what had possessed him to buy that!), Bush, Aiwa, Denon, JVC, Tascam, Siemens, Technics... ... ... He stopped at the Nakamichi; perfect! The cassette slid into place; Judas returned to his chair; the music started to flow.

Revitalised, the fire too sprang back to life; tongues of flame flickering against the soot-black back of the fireplace. Judas continued to study them, to hear their guidance; occasionally he would write a word or a phrase in the notebook on his lap.

It was Christmas. To Judas Christmas was always better in the early 1900's, however, all routes were blocked, and there was no way he could reach it.

Even the Arch-Mage does not have the power of creation. A statement.

It was then that he began the model. He was working in $^{1}/_{20}{}^{th}$ and intending to build a scale model of London in 1905, his favourite year. The houses were easy, a few well-chosen words and a perfect model would appear in his hand; he would set it down, populating the streets that he had marked out on the baseboard. Next came streetlights, gas-fuelled, of course; chestnut stalls followed; then an aroma of fresh baking, as he filled the shops.

Now Judas made carriages, but they needed horses to pull them; these were much harder, and took several attempts before he was able to set them down, and let them commence their work. Cats and dogs followed, then sparrows, and robins. Seeing the robins hopping around reminded Judas of another important detail: snow; he blew grey clouds into existence, and sent them scudding across the model. Soon everything was coated in a layer of crisp white.

Sound effects followed: children laughing, jovial parental shouts, tinkers and tradesmen: "Merry Christmas!" "Merry Christmas!" The faint tinkling of bells, and, overall, an atmosphere of quiet excitement, of expectancy.

Still Judas remained unsatisfied; there was a final detail; though he knew it was wrong, he could not stop himself. At first, his spells produced nothing, but finally the first appeared in his hand: a tiny man shuffling around, but with a withered arm, and a humped back. Judas set him down, and he scuttled off, like a mouse given reprieve from a cat, into one of the houses. Judas tried again, but every one that he produced, male or female, adult or child was deformed in some way. Soon the town was swarming, none of them seeming to notice the other's deformities; all were happy, as they sang and danced in the streets. "Merry Christmas!" The thud of a snowball. "Merry Christmas!" The stamping of feet. "Hot chestnuts, farthing a bag!" "Merry Christmas!"

Judas lay down in his scale Thames and started to cry.

The leader of the rag-tag bunch looked Judas up and down, "So, you want to become a Ghost Pilot, do you?"

Silently he entered the room full of shadows; he himself, black and faint too. They moved around him like gossamer smoke; their touch was cold as fog. He slipped amongst them, chilled (and yet also strangely warmed) by their embrace. He knew he was amongst friends; no harm could befall him here; soon he would be whole again. A light caress passed across his ill-defined thigh and moved on; cold nibbled his suggestion of an ear. A whisper: where have you been sweet young thing, do you love us no more? Never that, came the reply, I love you all. They drew close around him now; with each touch the black darkened, became more solid, started to take a more defined form. The shadows moved in and out in a strangely geometric dance; cold tendrils traced the now unmistakable form of a heavily muscled chest.

The shadows tumbled to the floor and as they rose ebony calves and thighs rose to meet the chest. The shadows converged between legs and chest and then drew back (as an artist might to admire his canvas) there stood a proud and erect jet-black cock. They converged on it once more; he felt their touch, more intense now, urgent, questing, exploring: shadow lips and shadow hips. The cock quivered; newly formed hands and arms drew the shadows in, pushed them closer. It grew hot, the only source of heat in the room. He felt himself build towards orgasm; the shadows tasted it too, willed it on. And then white spurted into the room, anointing the shadows. Everywhere it touched the shadows solidified; taking form: male and female. All black;

even teeth; even eyes. The shadows that remained danced around the new forms; that same geometric dance; until they too took form.

Silently, they swept from the room; the orgy over, the mission just beginning.

If your enemy is about to strike you: strike him first. But, you must not strike him unless you are sure that he is about to strike you.

To strike early is to destroy the rhythm.

Fear not to move forward with the slowness of the hour hand; fear only to stand still. But when you strike, strike with the swiftness of the second hand; see in your mind's eye, the movements and attacks of your opponent flowing at the speed of the minute hand; take time, and make it your own.

Judas shut and locked his front door with an air of finality; but, as he turned and headed down the drive the keys remained dangling in the lock, glinting burnished red in the setting sun.

Judas shouldered the pack, which contained all he had left in the world; how had it come to this, he wondered. He had had it all: wealth, property, fast cars, women, even a yacht; the lifestyle, the image, the career, and more. And now: nothing.

It had been so quick, so sudden, and then, like a house of cards, it had all fallen down.

He turned the corner and, head down, shuffling already, headed off. Judas was unsure as to where he was headed, how he would live, where; it simply felt right to walk, to move. He feared that if he stopped, stood still, that he would never move again. The itch of the sackcloth was already fading to a familiar warmth; for now, his face was clean, but he knew that soon it would be smeared with black. He coughed; throaty, coarse. He hawked phlegm. The look was complete.

With a startling suddenness, he and I became you. And with that moment came insight: with a fervour bordering on hysteria, you picked up the nearest writing implement and (truthfully more insightful than either of us had ever been) you wrote:

The first rays of spring sunshine touched the branch of my tree, scampering along the branch, I greeted the sun with a sigh; another day, I thought, time to dig up a few nuts for breakfast. Absently I began to groom and fluff up my tail, the grey of the fur curving up and over my head to form a slight shade from the brightening sun.

Turning, I descended to the ground, and, following the map that I had memorised, I began to trace the route to where I knew that breakfast was buried. After scraping the earth to one side, I uncovered a pair of ripe acorns; taking one of them between my paws, I raised it to my mouth. My sharp teeth made short work of the shell, to reveal the juicy flesh underneath.

There was plenty of food in store, and fresh food was beginning to grow anew; but suddenly my heart sank, when I remembered why there was so much food in store: last autumn, my mate and I had taken great stores of food, and buried them ready for the coming winter, and early spring, when we had planned to start our family. Already we had prepared names for them: Ril, Ryn, and Rak, for the boys that we would have; Krill, Kryn, and Krak for the girls. We had found a beautiful towering oak tree for our home.

But now it was gone, all gone. As the memory filled me, I discarded my half-eaten breakfast. The memory was clear, so dreadfully clear in my mind: we had been chasing each other up and down trees and around the field; stopping occasionally and panting for breath. I heard the sound of the approaching feet, “Run!” I cried, diving for the tree. But my wife did not seem to hear, or she thought that it was a part of the game; I was halfway up the tree when I turned to see that she had not followed. At that moment, the beast came crashing into the clearing, panting through bared fangs.

I knew the name of these creatures; I had heard it called many times. It was “Boy”; I had heard the strange two-legged creatures that always accompanied them calling after them; Here Boy, they would call, Come on Boy. Fetch the stick Boy.

It seemed that the two-legged creatures controlled the Boy; they would follow them sometimes, a piece of rope around their necks wherever they went.

And now here was one, a large specimen, with saliva dripping from yellow fangs, bearing down on my mate. “Kyryn,” I called out in horror, “run!” But it was too late, I froze in revulsion as I saw him catch her up in his fangs, shake her, and then toss her into the air; she turned several times in the air before falling to the ground. I heard the crunch of splintering bones. The beast pawed at Kyryn’s broken frame, sending a shrill squeak from her mouth.

At that moment, the two-legged beast entered the clearing, “What have you got there, boy?” it asked. “Come on, leave it alone, it’s time to go home.” Grabbing the beast by the band around its neck, he pulled him away, and out of sight.

Slowly, I descended from the tree and approached the still form; as I approached, her eyes flickered, and opened. “Skyrryl!” she whispered my name, and sighed, it was her last breath.

That was last autumn, and the grief was still heavy on me. I was lonely; so alone. All our dreams had been shattered in that one moment. Now I had nothing.

Behind me, I heard the soft pad of paws, instinctively I prepared to run; I knew the sound of those paws: it was a beast smaller than the Boy, but with sharper teeth, and sharp steely claws; they always hunted alone, and I did not know their name. But then I knew what I should do, rather than run, I turned to face the beast; I stood my ground as the beast bore down on me. I stood still as the beast pounced, claws gleaming in the sunlight. “Kyryn,” I cried, “I am coming to join you!” My heart felt a lightening of the sadness, and for the first time since autumn, I smiled.

Vel, jeg har egentlig aldri tenkt så mye på det!

Thus, it came to be that the great secret was revealed to Judas. W***h***ere he had once thought that none existed, suddenly was it revealed. Wh***e***n late one night he finally cracked the code, the answer became obvious; it had been there all along: hidden, but only just. Fou***r*** times he rechecked his work to ensure that there could be no mistake; but it was clear, the message undeniable; dare he record it, he wondered. I've s***e***en much that was before now hidden, mused Judas; what more might there be if I look with care? But th***i***s was perhaps a task for a new day, he thought, until a moment later a thrill of fear ran through him: what if by the morning the memory was gone, would another find it? Moving ***s***lowly along the corridor of the bed-sit, he entered the kitchen, the kettle, heavy with limescale took some while to boil, before he could make himself a black coffee. Idly, he l***i***nked the spiders' webs that covered the kitchenette walls, in his mind's eye; their tracery threatening to reveal yet more truths, in fear he shrank back: too much truth will kill you, he had once been told!

Finally, a***n*** intrusive whistle escaped from the boiling kettle, and Judas poured the boiling liquid onto the coffee granules; from the odour escaping the milk bottle on the table he was glad that it was a black coffee that he needed. Taking his ***d***irty mug back to his tiny room, he picked up the pencil once more. A chill shiv***e***r ran through him: the point of the pencil was broken; dark forces were at work: a warning: stop there, this should not be written. Defiantly, wh***e***n all about him swirled, he stood, and when he had stopped shaking, and the fear had subsided, he cast around his room, looking for a sharpener, or another pencil. None: they had i***d***entified them all, they were missing broken, or blunted; the one pen that he found spat venomous indigo across his face and shirt, before slithering off into a corner, and through a crack in the skirting. Now, without the ***h***ope of making a successful imprint of his memory, despair took him; he cast himself to the floor, wailing and gnashing his teeth. Now, finally, terr***i***ble thoughts receded, and a degree of sanity returned: Judas's thoughts spiralled out laterally, seeking a solution. He dredged his min***d***, what was it that he had been taught about memory; and then it came, associate the important words with an image; but what image he wondered. Galloping bison, od***d***ly, were the first image that came; but had the Native Americans not wiped them all out? A glass guitar came n***e***xt, but that was entirely wrong, something else, perhaps even a bigger secret: love really was the answer. Images came faster, so***n***ic vibration accompanying them, but still nothing that fitted. In frustration, Judas s***w***ept up a pile of books, selected one at random, and started to underline letters; his own blood the ink. Some of the letters stra***i***ned for release; they stood out, unmarked, but marked all the same. Holding scissors, a serra***t***ed blade; age old but sharp, Judas cut out the letters. Scattering the letters as ***H***eaven sent confetti, Judas turned to read the messages revelled. Here was a note from his new w***i***fe, though he did not know her, and one from his mother; but here was the true meaning! At last, the future foretold a***n*** epic epidemic, a future philosophy, a tactical text, a guide for guidance; and end. But then the cool breeze, reali***t***y check from the opened window; the secret lost, never to be regained. And now he became I a shift in it, t***h***e focus, I became myself again and felt the fierce joy of creation; how good it was to be alive, to be me. My pencil case was filled to an ov***e***rflowing; creativity to the fore; the pencil my sword, the protractor my shield. The everlasting light bulb would ***t***ake the place of my everlasting light, an everlasting beacon, to an everlasting love; it's going to be alright. Dark thoughts were forgotten, and d***e***ep joy broke free; bright light scoured the grime from the windows and flooded in; an epiphany. This sentence the true revealer, a ne***x***us that bound the truth; none could miss the misplaced x, its place in the pattern; its revelation. The needle sank towards the record, bu***t*** it skipped the first bars; the speakers crackled and hissed; the condition of the record was so bad that no one could tell what it was; only the beat was clear. It might have been from the seventies, s***o*** anarchistic, so agnostic, were those times; was it The Saints double single: One, Two, Three, Four?

The needle followed the spiral scratch ***n***earing the centre of the record and further revelations; at another time and in another place, it could have been The Revealing Science of God – although certainly not in this part of London and so close to Finsbury Circus. Judas remembered another time and anoth***e***r address: Dahlia Gardens, Mitcham, it had two very separate, yet two very distinct, memories; both of them good. Another memory stirred, and he lit up a Gaul***o***ises to ignite it further; he inhaled deeply on the pungent smoke (he would often claim that it was dried garlic mixed with the tobacco that gave them their distinct aroma) and let his mind drift back to the discotheque where he had always felt out of place, except this one time; the smoke of the Gauloises became the representation of dry ice; the base drone grew deeper.

Suddenly and unexpectedly all the clocks o***f*** note in the room began to chime, reminding him not only of his responsibilities but also how often an f was missed in text as the reader sounded it as a v; it was a warning and a clue – he really did have to give it more thought. Perhaps colour was an answer, he mused; but tha***t*** would reveal too much; what was the point of a hidden message that was visible to all! Judas had committed too many crimes and breac***h***ed security too many times to take further risks; he put his faith in the ability of the reader to read *between* the lines, to see what lay beyond the obvious; small clues pointing to the larger mystery. The stereo too joined the cacophony, or was that ***e***nergy just the disc it was playing; time and the popular music press would tell!

Deep within himself, he felt his arrogance take a***g***gressive hold and blossom – ever would that be his downfall, both now and into the future until that one climatic day. Diving and rolling as though under foe's fire, clea***r***ing the settee he leveled the remote control at the stereo and changed tracks; a rich and vibrant orange filled the room; calm was restored a different motivator achieved ascendancy. The truth was now so close that he felt almost able r***e***ach out to touch it; he saw its rich pattern transcribed within the weave of the carpet; only the threadbare patch held secrets as yet unrevealed.

The time had come to take his leave, this knowledge I h***a***ve to share, he thought; his thoughts turned to covering his tracks, to the code that he might use to keep the knowledge from untrained eyes. Nothing so deep that its meaning would mayhap get los***t*** forever; groups of four, perhaps, or the removal of every fifth word? Now he drew forth the anti-Enigma's device and primed it***s*** circuits; its tubes hummed and then grew bright, "Take a note AE" he started. For the next three hours he spoke into the machine's huge ***e***longated tulip shaped mouthpiece, watching the shredded ticker tape that flew from its output nozzle; each of which he tied off with raffia tape.

Each of the eleven bundles he carefully placed within ar***c***haic envelopes, carefully addressing each in green ink to designate the contents' meaning and the code used. The premises he would of course need to sterilize; the pile, ***r***oughly covered with muslin, that contained what remained of the bodies that he had been using to fuel the machines must be dispersed; the rune-encrusted furniture destroyed; maybe even a fresh coat of paint, Judas mused! Summoning the droid-servitors he gave his instructions; th***e*** tasks shared amongst the three.

Turning his back on that particular chapter of his life, a better Judas sallied forth; he chuckled quietly to himself over the image that he had chosen: tatters and rags, his few belongings tied in a large spotted handkerchief on the end of a stick. The sun had just slunk down beyond the horizon leaving purple skies resplendent in its stead; reaching the crossroads at the end of his street Judas consulted his map; he turned right his faithful cat, Tommy, by his side. Judas drew forth the watch from his weskit pocket as the four panting, glistening, black horses pulled to a halt beside him; the stagecoach was on schedule. And then they were spreading their wings soaring up to a far distant star, the coachman's maniacal laughter roaring in his ears.

The new chapters began with a flourish, the characters carefully matched, and positions set; the premise determined. The twelve stood facing each other, at their backs a recently erected standing stone; ley power fizzled at their centre, straight from Helvellyn by way of the Thurcaston Stones. Neolithicism turned Bronze and the leaves fell from the trees; its alert to them that it was time for them to begin their education – although none could remember if they were to be educated, or were the educators! And then he was caught once more in the eddies, engulfed within their dynamic and deposited quite alone. Time after time he knew that this might be the last time, but hope drove its need through him, spurring him on; hope and his Master's whip cracking at his heels.

The new basis was easily established; most of his notes, jottings and mac***h***inations remained intact (the musings too); Judas adopted a new filing system for them, their order was paramount. Soon, he was the same self-assured person that he had always been; even the p***a***ranoia had abated (although he was still fairly sure that he was being followed). Strapping the tools of his trades around his waist he turned to greet the s***t***ill new millennium; it would come to be known as the era of hope and despair. Judas knew that the part he played was that of the small cog, but a cog around o***t***hers, from which mighty wheels flew; without his solid support the machine would stall or, worse, crash and burn.

He entered the market square, just as the traders were clearing down for the t***h***eatre of night; quickly he selected his mark and sauntered over, his wide-brimmed fedora shading his eyes from the setting sun. "What news on tonight's happening," he inquired, "will all the usual suspects be th***e***re and will there be stimulants aplenty?" "Oh aye," came the reply, "number 42, usual time; I can – erm – help you with the necessary p***r***eparations now if you like?" He reached into his back pocket and pulled out a small white paper packet, "twenty ***e***ach" he said. Judas handed over two twenty pounds notes and was passed two of the tiny vellum wh***i***te paper squares, carefully folded, which he immediately slipped into the felt band of his fedora.

As the last remnants of the rusty sunset slipped below the horizon, Judas sidled pa***s***t the last lamp post and down a narrow alley between two rows of crumbling (but still occupied) houses; he needed a quiet spot. Crouching down on his haunches, Judas fumbled in his pockets for some matches; on locating them he next reached into the band of his hat and drew out the first of the papers. A brief gust of wind sent papers and dust scurrying down the alley; scanning one of the Guardian's headlines he was amused to see who had made the headlines that particular day! Returning to the matter in hand he glanced down at his hands, and the package therein; glowing tiny beads of excitement-induced perspiration stood out on his brow. He unfolded the paper, struck his match and started to read; he hadn't quite grasped who had instigated it, or why poetry had been outlawed.

Blest pair of Sirens, pledges of Heav'n's joy,

Sphere-born harmonious Sisters, Voice and Verse,

Wed your divine sounds, and mixt power employ

Dead things with inbreath'd sense able to pierce,

And to our high-rais'd fantasy present

That undisturbed Song of pure concent,

Ay sung before that saphire-colour'd throne

To Him that sits thereon

With Saintly shout and solemn Jubilee,

Where the bright Seraphim in burning row

Their loud up-lifted Angel trumpets blow,

And the Cherubic host in thousand choirs

Touch their immortal Harps of golden wires,

With those just Spirits that wear victorious Palms,

Hymns devout and holy Psalms

Singing everlastingly;

That we on Earth with undiscording voice

May rightly answer that melodious noise;

As once we did, till disproportion'd sin

Jarr'd against Nature's chime, and with harsh din

Broke the fair music that all creatures made

To their great Lord, whose love their motion sway'd

In first obedience, and their state of good.

And keep in tune with Heav'n, till God ere long

To His celestial consort us unite,

To live with Him, and sing in endless morn of light.

And then he was Milton no more.

Upon reading the second paper, Judas slapped his brow, how can he have been so blind!

With a wry smile on his face, he started to paint onto the piece of parchment. There's more than people when it comes to assassination, he mused, like Babel before it, this will kill language for millions! The start was slow, in the first few days he managed only a half dozen letters (шесть, he said, chuckling!).

But slowly he filled the page with 45 characters:

А	Б	В	Г	Д	Є	Ж
Ꙃ	Ꙁ	И	І	К	Л	М
Н	О	П	Р	С	Т	ȣ
ОУ	Ф					

Х	Ѡ	Ц	Ч	Ш	Щ	Ъ
ЪІ	Ь	Ѣ	Ꙗ	Ѥ	Ю	Ѫ
Ѭ	Ѧ	Ѩ	Ѯ	Ѱ	Ѳ	Ѵ
Ҁ						

That was the hard part. Creating the words was easy. And then he loosed them upon the world!

There are days, and there are days. Today was the day that I'd received the devastating news, "I'm sorry to say that... ...", no, it's too raw, too painful to finish the sentence right now.

Here I stood in the middle of the street like one of those living statues; humanity flowed past me: I was the rock in the middle of their fast-flowing stream; their faces, their clothes, blurred into vibrant colourful streaks. And me, frozen to the spot, my phone halfway between my ear and my pocket; my mouth was probably open, but I couldn't feel it. I couldn't feel anything. The tide of humanity receded, briefly, and I staggered as though they had been supporting me; I was at the kerbside, my toes over its edge. But it felt like a cliff to me, I was on a precipice, a fall of a thousand feet before me. I swayed, buffeted by an unseen wind; instinctively I reached out to steady myself. My hands met cold metal; that cold steadied me, grounded me; some semblance of normality returned.

The metal belonged to a car. My car. And yet I was sure that I hadn't parked it here. On the windshield there was a slightly crumpled piece of paper, on it: some scrawled text. For a while I stared blankly at it, my brow creased – although I wasn't really having any deep thoughts. My first mundane fear that it was to report damage to my car was dissipated as I read its brief contents: "Drive west for 100 miles." That was it. No further explanation, no author's name, nothing. How ridiculous. Who on earth would follow such a statement... order... request... which of these was it? Well on this particular day, I was that person!

I still preferred the physical reality of paper to the intangibility of the electronic device, so as I slid onto the soft leather of the driver's seat, I reached in the glove box for my map. Its ancient pages yellowed, the ink faded, the edges worn and frayed. My index finger traced a line across the page, right to left; one hundred miles would bring me to Burnham-on-Sea. Well, that wasn't quite true: ninety-nine and a half miles would bring me to Burnham-on-Sea; one hundred miles would see me in the sea! That would just be plumb-crazy! Reaching forward, my thumb hovered over the ignition sensor; I felt the faint tingle as its green light scanned my papillary ridges. The car rose on its cushion of air and then started to drift forward as I engaged the primary thrusters. "Where to?" the car's soft robo-feminine voice asked. "Burnham-on-Sea," I answered, "no hurry." Despite my last words, there was a lurch as the car sped forward. The neon signs on either side of the street blurred into vibrant streaks. There was an occasional jolt as the car avoided those with less sophisticated guidance/crash avoidance systems, but not enough to stop me sinking back into my reverie.

I thought at first about the caller, the imparter of the news. Then my thoughts were sliding down into the unfairness of life. Why me? What had I ever done wrong, lyrics of the ancient song slipped into my consciousness: I've never done good things; I've never done bad things; I never did anything out of the blue. The seat next to me was empty except for the map book. Empty as it had always been. Central had never succeeded in finding me a partner; it seemed that my mindset was too atavistic, anachronistic, and a dozen other istics besides. Not one person in the whole wide world. My heart was as empty as the car seat. I had never known my parents, but that was not unusual: all children went straight from the womb and into education. It was better that way. Central said so: gave everyone equal opportunities. The whole world was equal now; one equal happy mass; we were happy because Central told us that we were; they could prove it with graphs.

Outside the car, the neon-coated concrete was waning as we left the city behind. Out here, in the in-betweens, there was little to see, the occasional stunted, twisted, straggly bush, clinging stubbornly to the dry crumbling soil. We didn't need plants and trees anymore, Central gave us the air that we breathed; we didn't need livestock, Central gave us the wholesome (although bland) food that we ate. As far as I could remember, I had only left the city once before; there had been no need to; nowhere to travel to. Although I understood the concept of the sea, I had never actually seen it.

I must have dozed, as the next thing I knew we were passing through another city, awash with artificial colour. Two more cities came and went and then on the distant horizon I saw something blue and twinkling. But this was not a blue I had seen before, this seemed to be... ... a real blue: natural, not manufactured. It made my heart skip a beat.

As I sped towards the blue, I felt a warmth in my heart that I had never known before, a sense of peace, maybe even a sense of belonging. Now we were on the outskirts of Burnham; some of the buildings had painted advertisements applied to their surfaces! Of course, many had the normal neon signs, but my eyes were drawn to the painted ones, like ball bearings to a magnet. As my car slowed, I was shocked to discover what appeared to be communal eating houses! Surely no one would eat with others voluntarily! Eating was a thing of privacy, a function to be undertaken in the privacy of the home, like one's toilet or ablutions. But yes, as the car slowed more, I could see them: groups of people sitting together, eating, drinking, talking and laughing! Maybe I was more modern than I thought.

It was early evening as the car pulled into one of the designated Stopping & Charging bays. The door hissed open, and I was standing on the deserted pavement; in front of me a broad strip of yellow dirt, no, that wasn't the word! Soil? No. Dust? No. Sand? Yes, that was it, sand! The sand ran down until it met that voluptuous blue, which lapped up and down caressing its fringes. Giving in to an impulse that I don't understand, I removed my shoes and socks and stepped onto the sand. The sensation was almost electric: I felt its comforting warmth between my toes; it felt real; solid yet yielding: I was walking on the soft belly of Mother Earth. Slowly I walked along its breadth, until I reached the gentle lapping of the sea; now that was caressing my toes – a cold, but thrilling, chill. It receded and I was on warm sand again. For a long while I stood there warm|cold|warm|cold|warm|cold|warm|cold|warm|cold|.

So, this was my journey's end? Ninety-nine and a half miles. Ninety-nine and a half miles from "I'm sorry to say that I have to tell you… …". Was this it? I began to wonder why I had come. What mad impulse… …

But then I saw a stronger twinkling out on the blue; no, it was nine twinkles, bright against the darkening sea. Nine points of light, equidistant, fixed in their proximity with each other and yet gently bobbing. I walked out into the sea. It rose to my ankles, my calves, my knees. What strange impulse drove me towards those lights: a moth to flame. The water reached my waist and then I was swimming; I didn't even know that I could swim! I tasted the water's saltiness on my lips, felt its sting in my eyes, but still I strove on. I could make out a deeper blackness below the lights, which I saw held them some two demins or so above the surface of the water; it was a small boat, with nine candles secured around its perimeter.

Finally, I drew alongside it and pulled myself up to peer in. The boat was not long, and there she was laid in the bottom of it, almost filling its entire length.

She was clothed in shimmering white samite with gold brocade at the flared cuffs; a necklace of pearls and sapphires, like so much sea and foam. Long, curling, auburn hair was spread across each shoulder; a face of such beauty that even the finest artist could not better it (or so I believed). For one horrific moment I thought that she was dead, but then her eyes – eyes of the deepest green – fluttered open and she was smiling. “Judas, you came!” she said.

The next thing I knew, I was in the boat, lying to her right; she was propped on one elbow, slightly above me. Her lips brushed mine: soft, warm, sweet. The boat was moving, slowly. “Where are we going?” I asked. “We have many, many, hundreds of miles more to travel yet!” came her reply. It didn’t matter, I knew wherever it was that it would be home. And it had all started with a note. I knew I was going to be out of circulation again for a while.

Judas trudged the moors for several hours before he came on the lonely pub, seemingly in the middle of nowhere.

Pushing open the carved oaken door, he entered the well-lit pub. A huge fire burnt in the grate against the back wall; the landlord leant on the bar, chatting with three customers, one of whom seemed to be the local bobby. At a table, two other men sat playing dominoes; another two played darts; one man sat in the corner, reading Sporting Life.

No one looked up as Judas entered; he walked to the bar and waited patiently. The landlord was patently in the middle of a joke, though Judas could hear none of it. Eventually, he must have reached the end, for they all threw their heads back roaring with laughter; the bobby pushed back his helmet, and with a red and white handkerchief he dabbed at his sweating forehead, and blood-shot jowls, his moustaches bristled.

Still, no one paid any attention to Judas; becoming angry he reached for a tankard and poured himself a pint, expecting to be reprimanded by the landlord at any moment; still, no one acknowledged him. Judas went and sat at the remaining table.

“I wonder why we never get any visitors in here.” called one of the domino players. “Too far away from anywhere, I guess,” replied the landlord.

Was Judas really invisible to them, he wondered. He made his way across to the domino players, waving a hand in front of their faces, but this elicited no response: they carried on with a story, about a cow named Bessie. Judas banged the table, and all the dominoes fell down, but within a blink they had all resumed their original positions.

Judas helped himself to another pint, but left the pub soon after, too unsettled to relax. From his periphery, he thought he saw the Arch-Mage slipping out of a side door, but he was unable to will himself to return to check: Too nervous that it would indeed be him.

Lazing back in the armchair, Judas let the sound of Pink Floyd fill the room; the volume was cranked to full; the speakers, and the room itself, shook and pulsed to the music. He could almost see the chords falling out of the four speakers, the sounds taking on a colour of their own. He stubbed out the roll-up, pushing the chair back against the wall; the track was building to its climax.

The whispered voice of Roger Waters pleaded: "Be careful with that axe, Eugene." Judas's voice joined the following scream as, in the middle of the room, at a point equidistant from the four speakers, a shape began to form. It was a dim outline at first, gradually solidifying into the form of a dark-skinned native, dressed in a dirty loincloth, and bedecked with cheap Woolworth's jewellery; the cruelly barbed axe in the left hand, however, was what drew Judas's attention. Was this vision?

Judas clutched the arms of the chair as the warrior advanced, the axe raised high. The axe descended, with frightening speed, Judas felt it bite into his skull, there was no pain for a moment, but then the blood filled his eyes, the pain came, and he saw no more.

How was it even possible? The ground was covered in a thick blanket of Sakura blossom, and yet the trees themselves were still laden. It gave him a fix on the month, if not the year. The black, lacquered, wood of his leg greaves was now spotted with the blossom, as were the greaves of his fellows. The twinned daishō, rested comfortably on each hip; the katana on his left hip, the wakizashi on the right. Judas was not sure how long he had been here in Hokkaido, probably a lifetime. The Arch-Mage had taken to calling himself Sakanoue Tamuramaro.

Whether it was some strange filter effect of the blossom, or testimony to this being an off-kilter alternative, he was uncertain, but the sun hanged pink and bloated in the sky. They moved silently through the trees; the last village was not far. The trees now started to thin out, a sure sign that they were almost at the village; their pace slowed, until, at a sign from the front, they halted. Final orders were not required; Sakanoue had briefed them – drilled them – to perfection. Again, with no visible signal, one hundred pairs of swords were drawn, silently, simultaneously, rapidly. And then they were running. Silent, still.

It seemed that they would make the outskirts of the village without detection; but suddenly a shout went up: “Ware! Invasion! To arms, to arms!” with a speed which shocked them, almost brought them to a halt, the village’s defenders were running to meet them; their own swords were drawn. And they were not silent; they screamed cries of war; battle-cries;

primal screams of hate. The two sides met; battle was joined; swords whirled in arcs of destruction and death. Now both sides gave voice; the kiai to startle, to distract, to bring fear. Judas faced two; carving a cross as first the wakizashi descended, cutting one opponent from right shoulder to waist, then down came the katana, cutting the other from left shoulder to right hip. Judas felt a sting on his upper arm; in the gap twixt one piece of lacquered wood and another. That had been careless of him. In the battle lust he felt no pain, but could feel red fluids dribbling down the bicep; fully focused, he cut down the perpetrator. Then another opponent, and then another.

Almost as quickly as it had started, the battle was done. The village's defenders lay dead or dying; only three of Sakanoue's force lay with them.

They entered the village, fearing no ambush – that would have been dishonourable. The women of the village came forward to meet them, moving rapidly, but with short strides hampered by their clothing. They carried bowls of steaming rice; silently they fed the invaders, deftly moving the chopsticks between bowl and lips. Judas looked down at the one who fed him; she was young, shorter than most of the others; her hair was black, her skin creamy-white. A ghost of a smile passed across her lips. She knew that she was a spoil of war, but did not seem to mind; she held his gaze steadily. Other women moved amongst them with skins of sake; Judas drank deeply. Of course, Sakanoue was first to be served;

he had not proclaimed himself, but his aura gave away his status, his rank.

"Now, I am Shogun," he said, sheathing both swords, simultaneously, in a single flowing movement. Judas did not know the word. It was new to him.

Behind them, the support force began to enter the village: supply wagons, blacksmiths, cooks; the children, herded by matrons; the women – Judas had three war-wives now, he hoped that they would get on with each other.

The sound of shouting and laughter greeted me as I left the cave. There must have been several hundred of them, running and dancing about the floor of the valley; all of them between four and twelve years I guessed (although now I know better); slowly I descended the hill.

As I approached the children, they stopped their cavorting and turned inquisitive eyes towards me. A hush fell over the valley, and I came to a stop a few yards from them. They looked up at me, as though they had never seen anything like me; I checked my appearance: it seemed normal.

One of the children nearest me, a girl with rusty hair and a face full of freckles, started towards me; buoyed by her courage a few more moved forward. She stopped near my side and looked curiously up at me. Her hand moved out to touch my hip, but then she pulled it quickly back, as though fearing that she would be burnt. When she found that she was unhurt her hand reached steadily up and took my hand; I smiled down at her. She giggled, quietly at first, then louder. Swiftly the laughter spread amongst the children, more hands reached up and pulled me into their midst.

Too late did I see the knives glinting in the sun, rise, and fall; then rise again, dripping blood.

The crowd pressed Judas forward; he could not remember ever being in such a large crowd before.

"Lost Sheep, Lost Sheep" the crowd chanted. They were the hottest property that year.

Judas was pressed up against the barrier at the edge of the road: the Lost Sheep were on a walk about. Judas gasped as they came closer, surely that was the Arch-Mage leading them! As they drew level, Judas called out, "Arch-Mage!" He whirled, and walked towards Judas. "Arch-Mage," Judas repeated. The reply was, "No, I am his brother, the black sheep of the family, he probably hasn't mentioned me!"

His mind raced, was this truth, or schizophrenia: the bad to balance the good. He let the crowd draw him away; they were surging toward the vast stadium, where the concert was to be held. For a while he tried to fight his way out of the crowd, but soon gave up: you can't fight destiny; he was swept into the specially built stadium.

Judas sat unhappily on the grass, all the groups that had appeared so far had been mediocre, and received only polite applause. The crowd had been intent on drinking, and ingesting a plethora of narcotics; the smoke could not be avoided, it hung over the crowd, sweet and heady. The Lost Sheep were next on, the final act of the day.

Without warning, the lights went out; the crowd leapt to their feet; the excitement rose to fever pitch. For

fully five minutes the crowd shouted and screamed, until suddenly, at deafening volume lone guitar chords sliced through the darkness. It was an old Sex Pistols number: Holidays in the Sun. The guitarist sustained the opening for at least ten minutes, until, in a heartbeat, the lights all flared on, and the rest of the band joined in.

Ten thousand pairs of eyes turned towards Judas: eyes of pale blue, mid blue, deep blue; eyes of hazel, light brown, dark brown; eyes of green; eyes of grey; even one pair of pink eyes belonging to a lugubrious albino.

Those eyes studied, worshiped, drank in his every movement, every nuance of his character. He was their master; they were his slaves; he had but to command it and they would leap to do it. They had all undergone rituals to bring them to this state, each one subtly different, and yet the same. Sleep was Judas's to give, or take; happiness, sorrow his to share out at his will.

Ten thousand pairs of eyes stared, transfixed as Judas shuffled up to the microphone in the beat club and started to chant his latest poem "Is It All Black?"

WHEN!

It was indeed the Arch-Mage that played the guitar, Judas was convinced, he could see him now; a black aura surrounded him, where usually it was white. The crowd were mesmerised, and under his control; they failed to notice the subtle way in which he changed the words, the commands that he was now imparting, which the music would cement in their subconscious, until activated.

It was all too much for Judas, he retched, turning to race for the exit, clutching stomach, and mouth. Behind him the crowd bayed in glee.

He'd done it! Over his leather jacket, he now wore an excrement covered denim cut-off. Beneath the fast-drying crud, the fresh logo stood out: a chopper, with three wings, face on; an amalgam of bike and tri-plane; above it the words 'Ghost Pilots' on an arched rocker; below, a mirrored arch, with the single word, 'Spacetimecontinuum'. He stood outside the clubhouse, surrounded by his new brothers; they all wore the same cut-offs. Except for Rick. Rick's had the logo, but the only wording read 'Prospect'. He and Judas had joined at the same time, but he hadn't yet made the grade. Today was Judas's day: the party was in his honour, the new member of the brotherhood. The women moved amongst them, dressed also in denim and leather, but with much, much, less material (of course they wore no patches); they were handing out beers. One, Rose, all tumbling blonde curls and curves, handed a can to Judas, who downed half of it in one; the other half he poured over her t-shirt burying his face between her dancing breasts; from the brothers a roar of approval went up. She pulled the tight t-shirt up to let her huge breast flop out; Judas kissed a nipple, slapped her arse and shouted out, "Maybe later baby, there's drinking to be done now!" "You go for it!" she cried back, handing him another beer, "I'll be waiting!" She dropped to her knees in front of him, sucking loudly at his crotch. "Well, I guess I could do both!" he laughed. As though it was the treat she'd been waiting all her life for, she'd unzipped him and gorged herself, sucking wildly, loudly. The Master at Arms wandered past, "Don't choke her Jude!" he roared.

These were his brothers now. So much better than the eleven he had had before; there were thirty or more of these. Plus the women. The old brothers never seemed to be very interested in women; Jude just didn't get that: what wasn't to like!

He was rapping now with three of the other brothers: Col, Sam and Joe; Rose was still hungrily feasting below. Morticia wandered across to the group; she'd been named for her long, straight, jet black hair. She wore a black lacy top, already completely undone, and tiny cropped denim shorts, the top button open and part of the fly down. She yanked at Rose's hair, "My turn!" she purred, pushing Rose aside. Rose simply shuffled across to the next brother, Col, but it probably didn't matter to her which of them it was. Jude's eyes widened: Rose had been good, but Morticia was amazing! As a Prospect, he'd only been able to watch such antics from afar; now he was in their centre and loving every minute!

As the yellow sun faded to orange and dipped behind horizon several blazes sprang up from old oil drums that had had their lids removed; this wasn't so much for the need of heat, it was just that they enjoyed burning stuff. The flames seemed to swallow the sun's colours, stealing its orange and sending it flickering into the darkening sky. The orange also shone back from the chrome of the bikes as they too took on the hue; it caressed them like the gentlest polishing cloth.

Morticia had finished Jude off; his seed was now fast-drying on her blouse and across her tits. She stood draped at his side; one arm idly around his neck, the other caressing her own nipple. Occasionally she would reach up to kiss his neck between the fine blonde hair of his head, which hung across his shoulders, and the slightly coarser hair of his bushy beard. Later, when they rode out, she was behind him on his bike; her top still undone, her breasts crushed against the patch on his back.

Judas entered the reception of the plush offices of London's top legal firm; he was confident and jaunty as he strode toward the reception desk: he knew this was the job for him. He gave a slight, last-minute adjustment to his tie as he approached the desk. The interview would be a formality, and he knew it. Especially with his qualifications!

Judas strode self-assuredly up to the reception desk. "I am here for the interview for the marketing position." He announced. The receptionist looked at him strangely; Judas realised that she must have been tipped off already that he was shortly to join the firm, and was memorising his face. Judas made a mental note, a good first impression, he could see that he could nurture her to better things, perhaps she might even join his department: he would need a good strong PA.

But now the receptionist was looking flustered, and started to stutter, "Er, um, the, er, interview? Marketing?

Judas's opinion of her changed instantly: she would have to go. You simply could not have such a dizzy representative of the firm as the first person people might meet. He became short with her: "Yes woman! The interview. With Mr Powys-Maurice! In the paper!" he waived it at her to illustrate.

"Er, that was er, last er month I think er, I mean, just a minute." She picked up the telephone, turned her back on him, and started talking quietly but animatedly into it.

This really was too much for Judas; first thing Monday, she would be gone! She was rude, vague, inefficient, and mumbled!

Judas felt a hesitant arm on his shoulder, and a voice: "Come along, sir, this way." He turned. It was a security guard, the touch was slightly too over-familiar for Judas's liking, but at least he was getting somewhere. "At last! Which floor are we off to?"

He moved Judas off down the corridor, away from the reception desk, and the few other employees that were around the area, then his tone dropped, and his grip tightened, he hissed into Judas's ear: "Listen you fucking tramp, don't you ever come into these fucking offices again! Piss off back outside to your cider bottle and your cardboard boxes. If you ever come through those doors again, I'll break both your fucking legs!"

He took Judas to a back door and pushed him roughly down the steps. Judas looked at the paper: last night's bed sheets; and his tie, which was not around his neck, but holding up his filthy, torn trousers: retrieved from some dustbin or other. He was not going to be back on his feet just yet then. Judas began to cry: all those years spent studying at Cambridge, wasted.

Still, there was always the cider.

Nåväl, jag har aldrig tänkt så mycket på det!

Buri edhe rewi thin youw illf indt helo cati onof thek eywh ichi sits elfb urie dand thel ocat iono fthe trea sure that itun lock sfir stgo toth epla cewh eret hean cien tson ceme ttop rocl aimt olis tena ndon occa sion toju dget here youw illf indt heke yloo kfor thep lace wher e52. 5683 69cr osse swit h-0. 9451 89an dthe nwit hthe keyc lutc hedt ight toyo urbr east goyo ucar eful lyso utha ndun toca esar swel lfor here will theb egin ning befo unda ndth etru thre veal edbu ttel lnon eofy ourd isco very lest illf ortu nefo llow youf orth eres tofy ourd ayst ruly.

This page has been created using white ink.

He had forgotten about the scrap of paper that the slightly stooped man in the granny glasses had thrust into his hands all those weeks before. But now it lay on the desk before him, spread flat but still showing the myriad creases earned during its time languishing in his pocket. Upon it was The Answer. For decades great minds had struggled over the meaning of this particular text; its author had dismissed it as nonsense saying its purpose was simply to confuse and amuse.

But now that he had cracked the code, the truth lay naked before him. Like all the great puzzles, once their key is known, it is revealed as simplistic, even glaringly obvious (briefly his mind touched on the fun that he had had with the How Many Indians matchstick puzzle; it remained one of his favourites).

Amazingly, the key to the code had even been set out in the cryptic message itself!

I am U

And U = R me and

W = E

All together – A and L together = L

See (C) = How they run

Unable to resist the habit of a lifetime, he had included the joke that Walrus thus translated to Elvis. And that word was part of the key; in some cases, he had had to transpose whole words, in others only a single letter had needed changing for the truth to appear. He looked down at the page on which he had set out the code; it was a simple case of including the key word, then the rest of the alphabet to find the revised coding; real schoolboy stuff – once you knew! And the typical arrogant conceit of using your own name for the code key would not have been the first – were they truly one, he wondered?

A	B	C	D	E	F	G	H	I	J	K	L	M
E	L	V	I	S	A	B	C	D	F	G	H	J
N	O	P	Q	R	S	T	U	V	W	X	Y	Z
K	M	N	O	P	Q	R	T	U	W	X	Y	Z

It was the meaning of the rest which was so revealing of his insight to the times in which he lived, and the future that he foresaw. Some of it needed no translation, or only very little: If the sun don't come = If the Son don't come.

He looked at the translation again. Surely, he must have got verse three wrong; could that really be true! It shook the very foundations of his teachings. It did not take a great leap to realise what Mister City Policeman stood for as soon as you realised that he was far more likely to refer to officers of the law as Pigs (in a sty, see how they snide).

A warm breeze meandered down the street, plucking idly at the discarded newspaper; but without the strength to lift it. The sun had started to dip, obscured by the buildings now; but its warmth remained. Only a few folks occupied the street, some stood chatting, others making their way to destinations unknown; but their stride was relaxed, unhurried; lazy as the breeze.

Only one was moving quickly, her hips swaying slightly from side to side. Wearing a summer dress a shade or two off emerald green, which finished a few inches above the knee; two thin shoulder straps held the dress in place; the wearer glad of the breeze on naked flesh. Judas smoothed down the material which had begun to ride slightly from the hip; for no reason that she could place her mood was one of distinct happiness; she felt joy with the world.

She passed two men standing idly chatting by the front of a coffee shop. The man facing her, without moving his head, let his eyes run up and down her figure coming to rest at a point just above the top of her dress; a ghost of a smile played across his lips. Judas's mood changed almost instantly: did he think that his admiring glances were welcomed, appreciated, did her a favour; or did he think that because he had not moved his head she could not tell where he was looking. She had heard all the arguments before: "if it's on show, it's there to be looked at"; "it's not rude to stare at a work of art"; "it's natural to respond to such provocation"! The weather was dictating what Judas wore, not the desire to be ogled at every opportunity. Why did they do it, especially the married ones; those that would probably hate the idea of someone ogling their wives.

Her heels clacking angrily now, Judas moved on. Another man was walking towards her, tall, clean cut and wearing shades. Judas almost laughed out loud, here was one who thought that because he was wearing shades, he could move his head to look directly at her and she would not know where he was looking!

In her mind's eye, Judas could feel the rough touch of hands upon her breasts, disinterested, almost perfunctory; so many minutes here for good measure before moving down her body – if she was 'lucky' often they would go straight for the treasure below. The hands were just as rough and unfeeling; a means to an end. She could feel the hard press of the hand-owner's mouth, the forceful exploring of the tongue, whipping her own tongue into submission; the press of a body on hers, hot breath on her neck; but the press never there long enough for her to start to feel any pleasure – although occasionally she felt obliged to let him think otherwise if he had tried particularly hard.

Judas passed two more 'viewers', before reaching the door of her destination. Home at last! She was so lucky to have a man like Richard, so unlike the rest: gentle, caring and considerate. As always, he came rushing down the hall to meet her arms wide; a smile of pure pleasure on his handsome face. The strong square jaw was now inches from her face, the aquiline nose almost touching hers; softly, Richard pushed back Judas's hair and kissed her in greeting. Richard asked about her day: he was genuinely interested; it was not a cursory question. He listened closely as they walked down the hall arm in arm; Judas unburdened herself: all the worries of the day washed away as she told him about them. The notes that she had promised herself she would make were forgotten; everything could wait. This was her heaven; the world could fall apart around her, but as long as she still had Richard none of it would matter.

The dinner was ready and waiting on the table – Richard was a great cook! There was a soft pop as the cork left the wine bottle, and he was pouring her a glass of chilled rosé; perfect for the weather. They took their time over dinner; they always did. The food was light and full of flavour; although there were three courses at the end Judas was content but without feeling over-full. The starter was simple, scallops with just a sprinkling of crispy bacon snips; this was followed by tender pieces of lamb with an orangey pasta salad. Judas could not identify all the ingredients of the salad, they were so finely chopped, but their combination was stunning. For dessert there was a light lemon soufflé, tiny pieces of brittle caramel providing a crunch that somehow highlighted the softness of the dessert.

Now Richard gently took her hand and led her up the stairs to their room. She knew what was to follow: gentle, tender, unhurried lovemaking; it would last for hours, and then they would sleep, entwined, until morning. This was all that mattered.

The crowd pressed Judas forward; he could not remember ever being in such a large crowd before.

"Lost Sheep, Lost Sheep" the crowd chanted. They were the hottest property that year.

Judas was pressed up against the barrier at the edge of the road: the Lost Sheep were on a walk about. Judas gasped as they came closer, surely that was the Arch-Mage leading them! As they drew level, Judas called out, "Arch-Mage!" He whirled, and walked towards Judas. "Arch-Mage," Judas repeated. The reply was, "No, I am his brother, the black sheep of the family, he probably hasn't mentioned me!"

His mind raced, was this truth, or schizophrenia: the bad to balance the good. He let the crowd draw him away; they were surging toward the vast stadium, where the concert was to be held. For a while he tried to fight his way out of the crowd, but soon gave up: you can't fight destiny; he was swept into the specially built stadium.

Judas sat unhappily on the grass, all the groups that had appeared so far had been mediocre, and received only polite applause. The crowd had been intent on drinking, and ingesting a plethora of narcotics; the smoke could not be avoided, it hung over the crowd, sweet and heady. The Lost Sheep were next on, the final act of the day.

Without warning, the lights went out; the crowd leapt to their feet; the excitement rose to fever pitch. For

fully five minutes the crowd shouted and screamed, until suddenly, at deafening volume lone guitar chords sliced through the darkness. It was an old Slipknot number: Pulse of the Maggots. The guitarist sustained the opening for at least ten minutes, missing the usual opening chant, until, in a heartbeat, the lights all flared on, and the rest of the band joined in.

It was indeed the Arch-Mage that played the guitar, Judas was convinced, he could see him now; a black aura surrounded him, where usually it was white. The crowd were mesmerised, and under his control; they failed to notice the subtle way in which he changed the words, the commands that he was now imparting, which the music would cement in their subconscious, until activated.

It was all too much for Judas, he retched, turning to race for the exit, clutching stomach, and mouth. Behind him the crowd bayed in glee.

WHY?

Each of the motivators can have different branches, and roots. This is perhaps easiest to grasp, initially, if one thinks of The Heart. There are many types of Love; all of them – or none of them – can be thought of as *True Love*. There is love of parent, love of child, love of sibling, love of friend, love of relation, and love of life partner. The Greeks named most, but not all, of them: Eros, Philia, Erotoropia, Storge, Philautia, Pragma, Agápe. Many these days cease the hunt for life partner too swiftly, believing that through The Eyes they have identified that which they should have seen with The Heart; such a choice is rarely happy.

Ten thousand pairs of eyes turned towards Judas: eyes of pale blue, mid blue, deep blue; eyes of hazel, light brown, dark brown; eyes of green; eyes of grey; even one pair of pink eyes belonging to a lugubrious albino.

Those eyes studied, worshiped, drank in his every movement, every nuance of his character. He was their master; they were his slaves; he had but to command it and they would leap to do it. They had all undergone rituals to bring them to this state, each one subtly different, and yet the same. Sleep was Judas's to give, or take; happiness, sorrow his to share out at his will.

Ten thousand pairs of eyes stared, transfixed as an already sweating Judas threw off his towelling robe, strode to the centre of the ring to have his gloves inspected, and then returned, dancing lightly on tiptoe, to his corner to await the first bell.

The Nine temptations.

Colours flickered and changed; subtle hues of red, blue and green interspersed the cool white. LEDs. He had a time fix.

I am born black; my soul, though, is white; happy am I.

I am born yellow; my soul, though, is white; happy am I.

I am born white; my soul, though, is black; evil am I.

I feel the warm sun beat upon my back.

I smell the sweet nectar of the mango.

I smile at the day before me.

I feel the cool mud squidge between my toes.

I hear the creak of wicker; the creak of my back.

The tiny white grains are more precious than pearls.

My eyes glitter green, reflections of the lucre before me.

With my pencil I draw lines, deciding fates: the scrap heap for you.

My heart, cold, caged; the calculator rules.

And now I am home.

My toes trace the tracks of the fresh-brushed path.

The gentlest, warmest, of kisses, a welcome.

The pearls of rice now swollen, and tender, plated for supper.

The arched pillars that front my town-dwelling;

A cold welcome: gin and tonic awaits me.

Once before he had taken a rib and formed from it a daughter. And that daughter had become mother, grandmother, great grandmother of all. In the beginning, he had wandered together with them in the garden. Until their first sin, that is.

Later he had done the same, taken a rib, and formed from it a son. Except this time, it was his own rib that he took. A rib which he had put into the womb of a woman to gestate.

But still there had been many who disbelieved. Many who refused to grow up. To become adult.

Judas rolled himself another joint. He was aiming for a fat one, but ended up with something looking like an overripe runner bean; but it was late, and no one seemed to notice.

He waived the spliff airily, looking for the next topic of conversation: they had done space, God [and religion], best guitarist, scale, what they would do if they were invisible, most obscure CD they had found; interspersed, naturally, with an awful lot of giggling, and nonsense-speak.

"You know the trouble with this country?" he began.

"Too small?" offered Simon.

"Too cold?" opined Matt.

"So out of date?" quipped Luke, "Or is that us?"

"No, none of them. Well, actually all of them, but I mean no, that's not what I meant." started Judas. "Law," he carried on, "that's the problem!"

"What law?" asked Peter?

"Just all of them. They are all crazy, we would be better off without them!"

Simon threw another log on the fire, which for the first time that evening actually hit its target. Other than the fire, the only other source of light in the room was the few candles that they had lit, although several of these had now burnt out. The flat's owner (at the moment, no one could remember who that was) had pasted posters to the wall in lieu of wallpaper, the posters covered a period spanning over a hundred years, with examples of stage performances: plays, music hall, concerts, gigs, raves, happenings, festivals, and so on. Simon took the joint, saying: "Noo, noo, noo! We need laws; they help us. I wouldn't break the law." He took a deep drag. The room collapsed into laughter; what are you doing right now, Luke wanted to know. It took a moment or two for Simon to catch on: "Oh! This!" he held up the joint, like some venerable holy relic, "well that's just a silly law; there's no harm in this, it doesn't hurt anybody."

"So, why don't you take heroin?" quizzed Judas.

"Because that's a crazy drug to take."

"Not because it is against the law?"

"Well, yes, I mean no, both, or is it neither."

"So, if heroin wasn't illegal, you still wouldn't take it?"

"No, I'm not that crazy!"

Judas had him hooked, and reeled him in: "So, you don't take heroin, not because it is against the law, but because you are not crazy; and the man that does take it is crazy, so the law does not stop him, so the law is a waste!"

Judas pressed home his point: "Matt, if it was perfectly legal to kill people, would you go off on a killing spree?" He shook his head. Judas carried on, "Would any of you?" Heads shook like so many toy dogs in car rear windows. "And, Peter, if there were no property laws, would you start stealing?"

"No, of course not!"

"So, again, it is not the law that stops you doing it, and the law does not stop the thief doing it, so the law is a waste.

"No! You've got it all wrong!" I cried, before realising that I was not even supposed to be there. Fortunately, in their befuddled state, it did not register, although one or two did look around to see who had spoken; the moment passed, and I had not been revealed. I smiled wryly; the smoke must have been affecting me too!

"Look at it this way too." Judas carried on, "We have more laws now than ever, and more crime than ever: which truthfully breeds which? You know when we had the two biggest increases in crime. When the first courts of justice opened, and when the police force was invented! Law does not prevent crime. If all the laws went, overnight," he tried to click his fingers, but failed, "there might be a small upsurge of petty crime: looting shops, that sort of thing. But then that would soon die down, and I promise you there would be far less crime than there ever has been."

The room went quiet, as they digested Judas's point. It was hard to find a fault in it, at the moment: it filled them with hope, and enthusiasm for a bright new tomorrow. It was just such a shame that by the morning it would all be forgotten.

WHERE!

Judas had been growing his hair. Tight white curls now covered his head. He was very proud of his new look; he fancied that it made him look quite wolfish. He could feel the fingers of the warm noon-day sun softly massaging him along the spine; its warmth infused him, gave him energy. He could feel its rays even through the thick white curls of hair that covered his back; the curls ran down his sides. The ends, around his belly, were less white, stained with mud; slightly matted. He had not noticed this for a moment; he was intent upon eating: there was so much lush grass to enjoy.

The grass was stiff, juicy; he could feel its slight roughness against his tongue. Around him many others feasted too; this was the supper of the mighty ones!

Soon the daily ritual would begin; the one who was not a sheep would come; they would bunch together, not quite in fear. It was something else. Respect? Obedience? Worship? The other was fleeter of foot, with sleeker hair, both black and white. Judas and his friends never made it easy for him; they pretended not to understand the ritual. They feigned ignorance of their intended destination.

Belly full, body awash with contentment, Judas laid down on the lush green carpet, dozing, dreaming of when he used to be... ... ... or was it what he would be?

He was quite lost.

"You know what I think the next step of evolution is for humans." Luke broke the silence. "Our little fingers," he raised his, and waived it in illustration, "will fall off, and we will grow another thumb! Just think what fantastic grip we will have! Then we really will be catching up with the monkeys!"

Nine. The crucial number. So much revolves around it. This workshop considers the number nine, its implications on the order and structure of society. Throughout history, the enemy that I will not name has sought to obscure its importance. We will open with perhaps his most audacious move, the move away from the harmony of nine. When first men set in line their method of counting, the block was nine; in an act of pure evil he created the zero and threw it into the numbers mix; what previously had followed the sequence 1, 2 ,3 ,4 ,5 ,6 ,7 ,8 ,9, 11, 12, 13, 14, 15, 16, 17, 18, 19, 21, 22 and so forth suddenly became 1, 2, 3, 4, 6, 7, 8, 9, 10, 11, 12, 13, 14, 15, 16, 17, 18, 19, 20, 21, 22.

No longer were there nine days in the week; no longer were there 14months in a year (13 months as we would now count them, curse it!), with the additional week of devotions to our master in the middle of the year and the five days for harvest. Now the week became seven days, and the months of random length and they were reduced to only 12.

Firstmonth

1	2	3	4	5	6	7	8	9
11	12	13	14	15	16	17	18	19
21	22	23	24	25	26	27	28	29

Tuesmonth

1	2	3	4	5	6	7	8	9
11	12	13	14	15	16	17	18	19
21	22	23	24	25	26	27	28	29

Thirdsome

1	2	3	4	5	6	7	8	9
11	12	13	14	15	16	17	18	19
21	22	23	24	25	26	27	28	29

Budsmonth

1	2	3	4	5	6	7	8	9
11	12	13	14	15	16	17	18	19
21	22	23	24	25	26	27	28	29

Leafsmonth

1	2	3	4	5	6	7	8	9
11	12	13	14	15	16	17	18	19
21	22	23	24	25	26	27	28	29

Blossomtyme

1	2	3	4	5	6	7	8	9
11	12	13	14	15	16	17	18	19
21	22	23	24	25	26	27	28	29

Sunswarm

1	2	3	4	5	6	7	8	9
11	12	13	14	15	16	17	18	19
21	22	23	24	25	26	27	28	29

Lord's Week

1	2	3	4	5	6	7	8	9

Tillingtyme

1	2	3	4	5	6	7	8	9
11	12	13	14	15	16	17	18	19
21	22	23	24	25	26	27	28	29

Rypenyng

1	2	3	4	5	6	7	8	9
11	12	13	14	15	16	17	18	19
21	22	23	24	25	26	27	28	29

Harvest

1	2	3	4	5

Storesmonth

1	2	3	4	5	6	7	8	9
11	12	13	14	15	16	17	18	19
21	22	23	24	25	26	27	28	29

Closedown

1	2	3	4	5	6	7	8	9
11	12	13	14	15	16	17	18	19
21	22	23	24	25	26	27	28	29

Fuelstore

1	2	3	4	5	6	7	8	9
11	12	13	14	15	16	17	18	19
21	22	23	24	25	26	27	28	29

Yearsend

1	2	3	4	5	6	7	8	9
11	12	13	14	15	16	17	18	19
21	22	23	24	25	26	27	28	29

The introduction of zero destroyed so much that was good; it plunged man into an age of darkness. The evil one sowed the seed of seven; many came to believe it was the number of magical powers, but it was not so. Preposterousness such as the seventh son of the seventh son abounded. Far worse, the nine deadly sins became seven; now the sins of   and   are considered virtues! There was vicious irony that made seven the 'lucky number'. 7 x 7 they thought of as extra lucky, without thinking through to the answer that came from adding the four and the nine together!

Some nines he could not destroy: the nine motivators we have protected, their secret safe with us. The nine musical notes he could not destroy - although clever use of a word worm saw the creation of two Es and two Fs, which caused many to see seven.

EGBDF

FACE

The nine emotions remained. It is these that we will study in more detail today. Firstly, you must learn their groupings; always must these appear together for balance; only the one that encircles them may be considered alone. Firstly, there is Love and Hate; then there is Confidence and Nervousness; then there is Happiness and Sadness; lastly there is Hope and Despair.

Surrounding all of these, binding them, there is Tranquillity; thus, must they be depicted:

Returning to music, some of the true songwriters have written the truth; not the imitators - and of those there are many - but the real songwriters; those who often claim their inspiration comes from beyond their consciousness, arriving in their sleep, or when they are daydreaming, not concentrating. Lennon is perhaps the strongest example, with *Revolution #9* and latter *#9 Dream*. Or Hendrix, the cosmic joker with his humorous take: *If Six Was Nine* - although some have said that he was not aware of the full extent of the joke!

Let me ask you, how many planets in our Solar System? Several attempts has the Dark One made to change those; the wreckage of one remains for all to see;

NOTE TO ME HOW MANY PLANETS? IS PLUTO NOT A PLANET? COULD BE IF THERE ARE MORE THAN NINE AND THE ASTEROID BELT TOO!!!

Many times, the sun set on the scene, and, with its rising, nothing had changed; still the group stood entwined with the vegetation. After a time, and Judas could not say if that time was days, or weeks, or months – even years – he became aware that at the far edge of the clearing a ring of dark-skinned warriors had surrounded this Garden of Eden. Each had a vine tied about his waist, which disappeared into the forest behind them; at full stretch it stopped them 20 yards from where Judas and his companions were. They stood impassively in the clearing; each was dressed in animal skins, and carried an ebony and silver spear; their eyes were covered, and their ears were blocked.

Looking at them, though he could not see their eyes, Judas sensed pity; a frown creased his brow, why pity, surely not for him; pity for themselves perhaps for being unable to reach this harmonious garden.

Judas returned to his feast, even after all this time, each mouthful was still tastier than the last. How many more days or weeks he stayed there, Judas could not say, but all the time the warriors stood impassively, their spears planted on the ground before them, masked eyes seeming to look straight ahead.

From the corner of his eye, Judas caught a movement: as one, the warriors' spears rose; together they descended as the warriors plunged them into their own chests. Briefly, a moment of sadness passed through Judas, but then it was gone, wiped away by the soft touch of a leaf.

For time beyond count Judas stayed there. When he slept it was in a hammock of leaves; when he was hot, they fanned him; when he was cold, they warmed him. They fed him and bathed him, satisfied his urges and desires; entertained him. When Judas grew frail, they supported him, massaged aching muscles and now wrinkled skin. Though his sight grew dim, Judas could still see their beauty; his ears still heard the beauty of their music. The sun's passing overhead seemed to become quicker and quicker; it bordered on the strobotic.

And then one day, lying in a hammock of leaves, Judas just stopped breathing. From the vegetation came a short sigh; the leaves wrapped tighter around him, pulling him towards the thick stems of the plant. When the fronds unfurled once again, of Judas there was no sign: tiny white motes hung briefly in the air around the plant before slowly descending to the ground blanketing the soil by the plant's roots.

One final sigh went up from the flora, it might have been one of sadness, or it might have been one of victory.

ደህና፣ ብዙም አስቤበት አላውቅም!

WHEN?

Why is the mountain stronger than the tree? Because it's base is wide. The wind cannot move the mountain, but the wind can uproot the tree.

Now consider water. The wind can lift the water, turn it to spray and scatter it on the ground. But it cannot destroy the water; the water will collect together again and become a river, or an ocean. Not so the tree.

So, in you there must be something of the mountain, but also something of water. Be strong, and unmoving; but at the same time: shift, and flow.

Only a fool would ask which was stronger, water, or the mountain.

He sat now at The Master's right hand. Before them on the floor of the vast cavern their slaves writhed: part orgy, part obeisance before the throne. Occasionally they would dip their noses into the trinity bowls that stood on low tables around the vast room snuffling up white powders. There were probably 19,110,000 sweat slicked revellers, all bathing in the reflection of glory.

Thousands of Fresnel lights washed the writhing masses in a red glow, catching and highlighting the droplets of sweat; beer lights and par lights dotted the periphery. A single super trouper, so large that three operators stood ready to move it focussed squarely on The Master. At points across the room dinner-suited thugs moved through the throngs, each bore a large wooden chest. Seemingly at random they prodded those that writhed on the floor, demanding their contribution to the coffers; notes and coins continually filled the chests.

The Master ignored the squirming masses; they served a purpose, no more. The preternaturally white grin turned to the right, "tell me, Wunfor, has it all been worth it?" Blank eyes returned his look, mumbling a response: "I had a dream. A dream that I.......... that I would.........a dream." His voiced tailed off, a thin trail of spittle ran down his chin. The white grin broadened, "I know Mr Seventhreetoo, you had a dream that you would betray me, a pathetic plan to be your own man: Wunfor Seventhreetoo, greatest rocker – that last word sneered – of the age!"

Horror passed across Wunfor's face, "Oh no, Master, not me, not I; I live only to do your bidding. I have no ambition but that which you have for me; no desire but to please you. Nothing else matters except my seat at your right side!"

"And what of your other mission? Your – um – exploration? The reports you have to write?" The blank eyes that returned his stare told him all he needed to know; there was no longer any comprehension. The Master chuckled quietly to himself, "You sold your soul for rock and roll, and got only this! Commence the sacrifice!"

A brief flicker of recognition came and went from Wunfor's eyes as a glittering red object was carried irreverently into the room. One end of it was V-shaped, with a thin plank continuing from its point; six thin metal wires stretched the length of the object. Wunfor could not guess at its purpose. A small fire was lit near the centre of the chamber, when it was blazing hotly the object was tossed into its flames. It caught instantly and flared up sending a trail of glittering smoke to the cavern roof; there was a screeching, reverberating wail which was suddenly cut short. The flames rose and then disseminated; on the floor where they had been a middle-aged man, and his oriental prize began to copulate.

He had never been able to shake off his personal demons; but now he embraced them. He recognised them as the source of his id; they made him who he was. His egos could take care of themselves, dragging him in their wake. He wondered at his motivation; which of the nine drove the three, he mused. Or was it the other way round, he would have to get back and check his notes.

For every Romeo, there is a Juliette, and for every Juliette, there is a Romeo. Sometimes. Judas had his Juliette, and her name was Rachel. He remembered the first time that he had met her, at the first high school disco. He had had eyes for her all night, but it was not until the last dance that he had had the courage to walk across to her and ask her to dance. He remembered the record, Because The Night. Somehow, he had managed to mumble the words to ask to walk her home; and now here they were walking along the street. He was just thinking of taking her hand, it was trailing inches from his own, as if asking to be taken; but then he became aware of steps behind him; something in them said, menace. Judas dared not turn. Perhaps it was nothing, and they would soon turn away. But now they matched pace with his, their tap, tap, now joined by the clicking of several pairs of fingers.

He was about to turn to Rachel and suggest that they run, when a foot snaked round in front of his, tripping him; he was pushed into a shop doorway. From this vantage, Judas could see half a dozen pairs of brightly coloured brothel creepers, topped by equally vibrant socks, which disappeared into close fitting drainpipe trousers. Instinctively, he knew whom they belonged to: Craig Feeleep, and his cronies; officially, they still attended his school, but they were never to be seen in class.

"Where you off ter?" drawled Craig, in his best neo-American accent. "Thinkin' of dippin' yer little winkie was yer?" Judas looked up, unsure how to answer, eventually mumbling in the negative. “Well, she wouldna’ notice anyhows, with that li’l thing.” He kicked out in the general vicinity of Judas’s groin. Judas curled slightly, absorbing the impact. The Dandies circled closer, trapping him in the doorway; too late he had thought of flight. Rachel stood slightly outside of the circle; Judas was unsure whether she waited in support, curiosity, or for some other reason.

“I don’t want no trouble,” claimed Judas, trying to emulate their method of speech, as though that might give him strength. “Too late, mate!” chuckled Craig, “It’s fahnd yer!”

“Craig!” shouted Rachel; Judas was still unsure if in recognition, warning, or pleading. Craig ignored her, and continued, “You Jewish, in’t yer? ‘Ad the snip, snip op?” Judas shrunk further back. “Grab ‘im lads, ‘n lets ‘av a look!”

Craig’s cronies grabbed Judas’s arms, pulled him to his feet, and then pinioned them behind his back; his face was inches from Craig’s. One of them pulled Judas’s grey flannel trousers downward until they flapped around his knees; there was a lot of laughter, but Judas did not know why, his underpants remained in place. The next thing he knew he was thrown back to the floor, the impact of the flagstones on his forehead sent his senses reeling; they spun even more when the kicking started.

How long it continued, Judas did not register, probably not long, although to him it seemed an age, but finally the blows stopped. The neon socks turned to go; Judas heard a voice, and presumed that it addressed Rachel: "'Ay darlin', don' 'ang arahnd wiv that loser, why doncha come on wi' me?" The socks continued their withdrawal, clearly not concerned whether Rachel followed them on not. For a moment, Judas's spirits lifted to see that her black stockinged ankle had not followed them, but then she spoke, and his remaining hope bled out onto the street, mingling with his blood: "Oh, Judas, why can't you be more of a man? You really are a wimp, aren't you!" And that hurt more than any blow; Judas whimpered as Rachel turned after the retreating socks, calling "Hey, Craig, wait up, you can buy me a Coke."

Why was it that his powers always deserted him when he needed them the most?

Weakly, I turned over in my bed; for forty days, and forty nights I had sweated with the plague and had taken no form of sustenance. Unsteadily, I got from the bed, collapsing immediately as my legs refused to take the weight that they had become disaccustomed to. I lay on the floor for several moments, before seeking to rise again; slowly, gradually, I made my way into the main room. The fire had long ago burnt out, the soot-stained hearth sat bare and cold; the grey ash matching the stains on the otherwise brown walls. I found a small piece of hard, stale, bread, which I managed to eat with a little water. Of my parents there was no sign. I entered their room; both lay in impossible positions on their bed, agony on both pale faces; they had clearly died many days past.

On a table by the bed lay my mother's diary; it was open, the precise neat hand easy to read; several sentences stood out: *Rand still delirious. Husband seems to have caught it. Neighbours shun us. Think I have caught it.* The last sentence was more puzzling: *Now our son will become mighty.*

I tipped the diary closed, and returned to the main room to sit by the empty hearth. With a start, I realised that I was not alone: the chair opposite me was occupied, although I was convinced that it had not been when I had first sat down. "Are you ready to leave?" He asked. Leave, I questioned. "It is time for you to commence your training, as a mage." He raised a slim, bony, hand to my objections, and my protestations of disbelief in magic. Suddenly he had leapt from the chair, standing tall, and frightening before me. He banged his staff once upon the floor, making the whole house shake: "It is disbelief in magic that causes it to die, and belief in it that causes it to be strong. Be strong, for magic is before you, and it is your destiny; believe in the power of wizardry!"

I know not why I went with him that day, perhaps because there was nothing to leave behind. "I will travel with you," I said, "although I am weak, and will not be able to travel fast."

"You will need little strength for this journey (although much for the days to come)," he said. He touched me upon the forehead with his staff, saying: "You will go to my Father's house this day." I sensed movement, although initially the house remained; from the staff flames now sprang, my house began to smoke, and to burn; a funeral pyre for my parents. Who are you I asked, as the scene dissolved; The Arch-Mage was the distant reply.

I found myself alone, by gates carved from living rock, and themselves set into living rock; they towered before me, forty to fifty feet into the air. I could not see how high I was on the mountain, below me the clouds hid the depths from view; above the mountain soared up and out of sight. I waited; there seemed little else to do. There was no sense of time, it might have been a moment, or a millennium, but at some point, an eagle circled around behind me, and then at another the doors were slowly opening. I entered, and found myself in an unlit chamber, there was a single door at the far end, and no other feature; the walls were smooth and polished. The outer door closed, and I was in darkness. Patiently I waited, for there was naught else that I could do. Eventually a voice which might have come from the rock, or from within my mind spoke, "What is your name?" "I am called Rand." I replied. "That name you shall leave here, and so too your garments; naked and nameless shall you enter; clothed and named shall you leave; with that you must comply." There was silence, and nothing further was spoken, or happened. Slowly I unwound my robe, as it dropped to the floor the far door opened. I stepped through onto a flat shelf of rock, which, although inside the mountain, was beset by an icy wind. I stood shivering and hugging myself, as the figure of a man slowly crossed the ice-crusted plateau toward me; instinct told me that the Arch-Mage's father approached.

"Here is your first lesson: ignore the cold," he said, "for it is but an element of our existence, which we must be aware of, but which we must not let inconvenience us." Belief surged in my heart, and I lowered my arms; the cold was still there, and I could feel it, but not its effect. In the days to come, I would know both the extremes of heat and cold, a much deeper cold than this one, and I would be required to master them all.

The lesson continued, with an instruction to raise the little toe on my left foot. I could not do it, and said so. "But you must, it is the second lesson. I will return when you are able." With that, he turned to go. "Wait!" I cried, "What difference does it make whether I can do this or not?" The response drifted back from his fast-diminishing form: "Fool! How is it that you can expect to control that that is around you if you cannot first control your own body? Every part of your body you must be master of, and able to control. The next lesson will commence when you have mastered this."

There was no time; no circling of the sun was visible to mark the passing of the day, or the night. In ways I felt that time had indeed stopped; at least where I was, if not in the outside world. I visualised five poisoned needles: four of them above my toes, the fifth below my little toe. The one below my little toe started to rise, slowly, slowly. I could feel it coming closer; I tried to lift the toe, but at first the other toes came with it: I focussed on the other motionless needles, and they stopped; the little toe continued to rise, its motion barely visible, but finally it was extended.

At the moment it reached its zenith He stood before me again; He nodded: "So, the way with you is through pain, not pleasure. You must do this now with all your extremities: toes, knees, elbows, ears, nose. You may take one step forward: this is the third lesson."

It might have been a year, more likely ten, but finally I mastered them all, and He returned. I took a further step, and the cold was gone, though it had ceased to bother me long ago. "Now that you have control of your body, we must make it strong: you will run, you will walk – on your feet, and on your hands, you will jump, you will punch, you will kick; there will be sit-ups and press-ups. All this you must do for the fourth lesson. Now he stayed with me, at least his voice did, telling me when to run, when to do press-ups, when to strike at trees, and at rocks.

"You learn well." He said. "Is your spirit indomitable? Who is the Master, you, or your will, or your doubt? We shall see: you will do press-ups, on your knuckles. You will do 1,000, and they will be full, or they will not count." My body was hardened, and the first few hundred came easily, but then a burn set into the biceps: He disallowed many, until I had finally reached count of 1,000 in which he was satisfied; I remained in position, knowing that to rest without His say would be to fail. I sensed a flicker of a smile, and then a quiet voice told me to complete a further 1,000. I screamed, from the pit of my stomach, to strengthen my resolve and began; each upward movement burnt and tore at flagging muscles; at first,

I probably managed only one scoring press-up to every failure. But the lesson was learnt, and as I entered the halfway stage, I knew that I did not have the energy for failure. Finally, I heard the words *two*, and, *thousand*; my arms locked, and I knew that they could not move again. "Lower yourself," He said, "but only your nose must touch the ground." I complied. "You will raise yourself once more." I threw everything I had into movement, but none would come; all strength was gone; my body shook with effort, but would not move. "One more is all I ask," he said. "I cannot do it!" I cried. "My strength is gone."

"You must, or you will die."

"I cannot."

"You must."

Before my forehead I saw the ground split; slowly a spike started to rise toward the bridge of my nose; death was upon it. I fought for energy, but none came. The spike continued its slow ascent. The tip touched my flesh, and I felt the power within it: it would drive clean through my skull. I saw my own death before me, and from that I drew strength, pushing away from death, holding onto dear life: my body started to rise, as slowly as the spike, but with it.

He said, "You may stand. Remember from whence came that strength, for with it you will not fail at any task, but you must remember its source, and you must never doubt it.

Judas was busily jotting down the answers:

TEST PAPER

Unpack the lines from the following songs that spoke whole stories in only a few words:

And the papers want to know whose shirts you wear: the newspapers are often late to identify the zeitgeist, but once they are, they love to make stories from nothing. The underlying import is that readers would wish to go out and buy the same clothing as their heroes', as if looking like them, imitating them, they might become them.

He can't be a man because he doesn't smoke the same cigarettes as me: real men smoke; and the brand that they smoke is vital to the level of coolness;

Oh, we hated our Aunt

Then we messed in our pants

Then we lost our faith and prayed to the TV – this one stumped him for now. He would come back to it.

He maketh me to lie down in green pastures.

A story in a sentence. We would not lie down in a field if the sun was not shining. Unless they had eaten plenty, sheep would not lie in green pasture. If I wear the shirts that you wear, then people will think that I am as cool as you are. Real men don't smoke those cigarettes, real men smoke these cigarettes. There is a new messiah, and he is a square box. We watch him, he does not watch us. Although by 1984 he did.

He sat, a stupid, smug, smile on his face. Judas thought he had been oh so clever, little realising that he had simply reinforced the sterotype!

This page is intentionally blank.

Ten thousand pairs of eyes turned towards Judas: eyes of pale blue, mid blue, deep blue; eyes of hazel, light brown, dark brown; eyes of green; eyes of grey; even one pair of pink eyes belonging to a doleful albino.

Those eyes studied, worshiped, drank in his every movement, every nuance of his character. He was their master; they were his slaves; he had but to command it and they would leap to do it. They had all undergone rituals to bring them to this state, each one subtly different, and yet the same. Sleep was Judas's to give, or take; happiness, sorrow his to share out at his will.

Ten thousand pairs of eyes stared, transfixed as Judas jauntily trod the boards once more, throwing himself into his latest role with gusto and aplomb.

The waxing gibbous moon peaked out from behind the petticoats of the earth's shadow, heralding the arrival of the forthcoming Hunter's Moon. The night was clear of cloud, and therefore bright, although it failed to illuminate the four shadows that passed from tree to tree through the woods. From their lips, a whispered conversation rose, it was naught but a buzz to anyone outside the group. The floor of the forest was strewn with pine needles, a soft carpet on which their bare feet trod. Judas looked around at his companions, they were faceless, but he knew them still. A dry thunder rumbled, although the sky was still without cloud; the air thickened. Suddenly, Judas was alone on a cliff edge; the ledge upon which he stood was narrow, only his heels making purchase as he flattened his back against the smooth rock face, trying to scrabble backward, panic rising. Judas cried aloud as behind him the cliff split into diagonal slivers, and he was sent tumbling into the abyss. His stomach lurched, and he felt the bittersweet taste of adrenalin in his mouth; falling, he spread his arms against the impossible descent. And now he was soaring, soaring upward; the mountains below him, the rivers, and the forest became miniature and indistinct.

Judas looked up, a clear challenge to the shy moon, and soared toward it, gathering more and more speed. The winds of space and time ruffled and tugged at his robe; he was in sackcloth again. And now he saw that the moon too was hooded, and robed, arms stretched out in greeting, encouraging his assault. The next instant they were together, locked in passionate embrace, kissing urgently, ferociously. With the dissipation of the initial heat, and a return to tenderness, they sank together onto the carpet of pine needles. Judas breathed a name, making it so; close by two others were locked in similar embrace.

HOW?

Judas smacked hard at his forehead, and stared at the computer screen in disbelief: Velikowski had been right! OK, by Ages in Chaos he was just cashing in.

.koob lanigiro eht htiw wef esoht ot tpecxe ,reverof
tsol won si egassem eht dna ,degnahc segap eht
,tnof tnereffid ylthgils a ni ,detnirper saw koob eht
nehw dna , sisab egap a no enod saw ti yldas tub
,egassem a hcus dah emit lla fo skoob gnilles tseb
eht fo enO. htrof os dna ,retpahc ,egap ,hpargarap
dnoces eht otni sdrow **X** si drow dnoces eht ;[**X**=]
sdrow fo rebmun eht tnuoc ;retpahc ro ,egap
,hpargarap ,ecnetnes tsrif eht fo ,drow tsrif eht ekat
:ecnenimorp fo skoob ni snoisacco nezod a tsael ta
no desu tub ,llits xelpmoc eroM .egap dnoces eht no
drow dnoces eht ,egap tsrif eht no drow tsrif eht ro
,ecnetnes yreve fo drow tsrif eht ti gnikam dna
egassem eht gnikat yb elpmaxe rof ,tceted ot redrah
emos ;sdrawkcab gnitirw ekil ,suoivbo emos
,snrettap etacirtni ynam desived evah yehT .txet otni
tup ylpmis tonnac – htrof os dna ,lagel ,larom
,suoigiler ,lacitilop – snosaer ynam rof tub ,skoob
rieht htiw trapmi ot hsiw yeht taht segassem evah
srohtua ,ynam ,ynaM

WHAT!

The human heart is much like a metal: it can be heated, and cooled; it can be moulded. Rejection, and jealousy, can temper and harden a heart, and, as though tempered by some mythical – magical – fire, it cannot be softened again except by the one that wielded the power.

Rejection, abuse, and confinement can turn a heart to stone; in this case, the magic can be undone if countered with one whose Prime-Motivator is The Eyes, with The Heart a leading Sub-Motivator.

Of course, a person's own Prime-Motivator will affect the degree of temperonicity of their own heart; but make no mistake, where The Heart is the Prime-Motivator, this does not necessarily mean a strong heart, and one able to withstand the fires of emotion, in many cases it can be the opposite.

Many have debated whether a heart can be truly broken, but just as over-tempered metal can become brittle, so it is with the heart. When a heart is broken, it will cease to be the Prime-Motivator, if it was, and another will come into ascendancy. In these cases, it is extremely rare for The Heart ever to become the Prime-Motivator again.

The warm, soft, reassuring aroma of new leather rose from the cover of the book, gently caressing his inner nostril. His thumb stroked the spine, enhancing his sense of calm. Judas had already annotated the first page: Lyric Book; it was decorated with musical symbols, notes, clefs and the like. Now he turned to page two. He was going to write his first song.

I ain't got nothing to give you but love.

Ain't got the money;

Ain't got the looks;

Ain't got the charm;

Ain't got the hooks;

Just love. Only love.

Love is all I have.

Silently he re-entered the museum; he had half expected to be discovered as he had lurked in the toilets close to closing, locked on one of the cubicles. But no one had checked, and now the museum was locked and silent. It was but recently that the artefacts had been brought to the museum, rescued from the silt of the delta. They were not yet on display whilst the scientists sought to divine their age and their purpose; so far both had eluded them. There were eleven of the objects that had been rescued; similar in material and in size, but very different in design. There should have been a twelfth, but Judas had had that in his possession for quite some time now.

It was unlikely that the purpose of the eleven would be discerned, but he just couldn't afford to take that chance; they should be returned to their rightful place, and owners. Judas did not want to risk a light and so flitted forward carefully from shadow to shadow; his own shadow somehow deeper than the rest. Having spent the day wandering the museum, he knew where he was headed; he had entered the room claiming to be looking for the toilets. One of the scientists had re-directed him, without even looking up from his studies; it had been a risk, but Judas thought that it had paid off, saving him valuable time now.

The doors to the room had been flimsy, and Judas knew that he would easily be able to break them open. But such force was not necessary, for they were unlocked! They clearly had no idea of the value of that which lay within. Sticking initially to the walls, he circumnavigated the room until he reached the table on which they lay. Close by a flipchart stood; it was filled with lists of single or coupled words, written with a stuttering green felt pen. It was as much as he could do not to burst out laughing when he saw some of the things that had been written – none were correct, but some came very close!

Fencing
Hospital implements
Distance measures
Jewellery
The Ark
Torture devices
Religious artefacts
Musical instruments
Messages
Flotsam
Fossils
Toys
The Cross
Farming
Walking aid
Teaching aid
Weapon
Chariot
Art
Financial device
Cooking utensil
Game
Communications device
Badge of rank
Bed
Shelter
Shelf
Ley
History
Puzzle
Runway marker
Scales
Device for getting the stones out of horses' hooves
Noose
Fashion
Pest control
Currency
Magick
Witch diviner
Water diviner
Oil diviner
Gold diviner
Treasure chest

It looked as though there was a second sheet, but Judas didn't think he could take any more without roaring out loud in laughter (tinged with just a little hatred!).

But there was work to be done, a reunion to take care of and in one case freedom to offer. Judas loosened the pouch at his waist, the eleven items slipped easily inside – Judas had nearly made the mistake of naming them! – he drew the strings to close it. He fancied that he heard a purr emanate from the twelfth, but knew that couldn't be so.

Suddenly, he heard approaching footsteps from outside; their constant timbre marking them for those of an ex-military man. Judas knew he could not afford a confrontation and hurriedly ducked down behind the bench; it was all he had time to do. There was a light creak as one of the doors opened and then the beam of a torch was playing around the room; its powerful beam bringing a microcosm of daytime wherever it alit. The footsteps entered the room; Judas tensed: fight or flight. He reached down for his sonic-inducer gun and slipped it from its case; the rustle of his silver cat suit seemed loud in his ears and sure enough the footsteps paused.

"What on earth?" came a voice. Judas slowly slipped off the safety and cranked the volume to twelve; he made ready to spring. And then the voice came again, " 'Witch diviner'! By jingo these chaps just aren't of the same world!" And then the footsteps were receding, accompanied by quiet chuckling. But for reasons he was never able to articulate to himself, Judas rose and pointed the sonic-inducer at the retreating back. He pulled the trigger; there was a scream cut short and then the retreating figure was falling to the floor a neat three-inch hole burnt clear through his chest; the choice of track had probably doubled the pain delivered.

Some urgent cover up was required! Judas flipped the input channels to two, and dialled in a discordant combination. He took aim at the wooden balcony that ran round the edge of the room, pulled the trigger and moved his arm left to right; flames burst from the wood. Hurriedly he moved to the doors firing off blasts at wooden worktops as he passed them; from the corridor the doors too ignited under his wrath. But then the red mist descended fully upon him, and he ran willy-nilly throughout the museum blasting everything inflammable within sight. The next day, naught remained but a pile of smoking ash; the tabloids ran vicious headlines about sprinklers and a cost-savings-driven director.

He tried desperately to remember the lesson; his brow furrowed, albeit screened by the curtain of grey, greasy, hair that fell before it. Knuckles white, he gripped the edge of the desk, grinding his teeth.

The year zero.

The time of conjunction

The time – was Time the right word – *when all the alternates met, become one.*

But were the alternates real or theoretical?

He knew it was important. Indeed, vital. Why hadn't he made more notes? There was something about the obliteration of the past, or was it some of the pasts. But there was something about the future too; were there as many futures as there were pasts? Or just one?

Briefly, in his mind's eye, he saw his Sensei again, heard his voice,

... ... at times, many will be the possibilities; although one path only is there, truly. To draw the map that follows that path is our task. The landmarks will be occasions and happenings; the contours will be potentials. Our map must be accurate – infinitely so – as the false paths will be many; barriers and diversions, also, will there be, and many. But we must not deviate from the path: the barriers we must overcome, the diversions, ignore must we. "Will the path be long?" one of his fellows had asked. *Long? Yes! So, so, long. Some are saying that the path is a circuit, no beginning is there, and no end – but a beginning we must find and therefore an end also.*

Λοιπόν, δεν το έχω σκεφτεί ποτέ πολύ!

There was once a great martial artist; one who described the ultimate truth as being akin to water, and how it adopted the shape and contours of the vessel that held it: going with the flow. He is wrong! Think of the power of water, the tidal wave, the whirlpool, the tsunami! But now I ask you: which is stronger: the water, or that which contains it? With all the power that water has, it is still held in check by the dam, the sea wall, the riverbank. Whilst the water might occasionally slop over the side of the sea wall, or breach the riverbank in time of flood, ultimately it is returned to its course.

So, I say to you, truly, yes, your motions should resemble the flow of water, but in your spirit, you must be the unbreachable dam; you must hold, and mould the water as you choose.

Slowly the desolation and despair crept through him. He tried to stop it. He knew that it wouldn't help. But slowly, slowly it took hold.

At first it was green, as he thought of The Other, all smug and enfolded in her arms.

Then it was red: what was so special about him. Wasn't he, Judas, just as special? Maybe more so. He thought of all the things that he had done for her; the lavish gifts: gold, diamonds, frankincense, perfumes, myrrh. Why?

His fists clenched the quilt, as red turned to blue; his grip loosened as the tears slipped from his eyes. At first just a trickle, then stronger and wetter; then sobs escaped from his lips, wracked his body. He buried his face in the pillow, still damp from the night before. And the night before that.

Finally, it turned black. Why should he lie here, as he had done for the last week? He would act. He was a man, not a snivelling worm. He knew where The Other lived. He would take his revenge!

He slid the head from the pickaxe handle and slipped its smooth, reassuring, wooden length under his long coat. It was late at night; although it was summer cold tendrils of mist, almost invisible to the naked eye, grasped for him. He shook them off. They could not stop him. The Other would be returning from work soon; he'd be tired; the perfect moment to strike.

He would hurt him; he would hurt him badly. I'm not going to kill him, thought Judas, well, not intentionally. Make him bleed. Maybe break a finger or two. Scare him; make him withdraw. He knew he didn't really need the weapon; The Other was soft, but no sense breaking into too much of a sweat.

Some twenty minutes later, he was turning into the quiet road where The Other lived. Close to his house, he saw the perfect place to wait: behind a tall conifer, in the night its leaves were as black as Judas's mood. The closest streetlight was out, he smiled, the gods were favouring him!

Not much later, he heard the sound of approaching feet. Peering through the leaves, he saw that it was indeed The Other approaching; he could sense his fatigue in the footsteps; in his mind's eye he saw the pickaxe handle descend, he saw red blood trickling down that smug face; he saw him crawling on the floor begging for mercy. He waited until he had passed his hiding place before stepping out, the hickory raised and ready to strike. “You cunt,” he rasped, “you smug piece of shit!”

Judas didn’t even see it coming. The clenched fist crunched into his nose, red pain flared, red blood welled from his nose; another blow to the jaw and, somehow, he was on the pavement, its dusty surface smeared his lips; a blow, probably a foot, smacked into his nose; followed by another and another to stomach and groin. The Other hadn’t even said a word. Judas passed out, for how long he couldn’t tell. There may have been other blows, but when he came to, he was alone in the street. I’ll break his windows, he thought. I’ll break his bones. But he didn’t. He couldn’t even stand. He crawled from the street, green lichen from the tree or the wall stained his coat; red blood smeared his face; bruises, blue and black, started to make themselves known.

Back stage things were heating up; Judas opened his fourth beer, and washed down another of the blue pills that Gimme, his roadie, had thrust into his hand on arrival; he was still unsure what they were, but they seemed to be working. Judas turned, staggering a little and asked no one in particular: “How long ‘til we go on?” His voice, slurring slightly, brought an immediate response from their manager, Tony P “Only a few more minutes, just time for another beer.” He passed one across; Judas shook the other tin, it was nearly empty, so he dropped it to the floor and took the new one. “Is it a full house tonight?”

Now Tony P became evasive, “Well, you have got to remember that The Demontfort Hall is only a step on the way to the top, word has got to spread yet. Think how long it took for the Flaming Roosters to reach the top!” Judas was scornful: “Reach the top, they ain't there yet! Never will be”. The Roosters were always a great deflection.

The word came down, time to hit the stage. Judas reached up to the glass and ebony case on the wall – it was his one rider, his guitar, in its glass case, had to be mounted on the wall of the venue – flicking the catch he lifted down the gleaming, black, Telecaster and slung it over his shoulder: a gunslinger once more. Terry and Pete, drums and bass, often mistaken for twins, followed him onto the stage. As always, their set started in complete darkness, a quick roll on the drums from Terry, and they launched into their first number, Spare Time Blues. Forgotten, for the moment, Judas's staff languished in the dressing room; it would be many years before he would be reunited with it.

At the given point, the lights flared on, illuminating an almost deserted auditorium. Perhaps thirty people sat dotted around the hall; one of them even looked to be reading a paper. The song chugged on for a couple more chords before petering out. Judas turned to berate Tony P, but was not surprised to see that he had done his usual disappearing act: the guy should manage a magician, not a rock band, Judas had often quipped. But for now, Judas was not in a quipping mood. The red mist had descended once more. Rage had taken hold. Judas screamed, at first in pure anger, but then that scream turned to invocation and he began a summoning: time for a reunion gig with some of the old band members.

First came Simon Peter, blinking into existence on the left of the stage, with his full double bass drum kit, which, using those twin bass drums, he started to thump out a rhythm on, underpinning Judas's invocation; Terry tried to keep up, but was thoroughly out-classed. With a huge flash of light and smoke, Thomas appeared with his black and silver Rickenbacker, thumping out a simple five-note progression. The audience were ensnared, and on their feet, clapping to the simple, but irresistible rhythm.

It was a bit Spinal Tap, but Judas added another ten notches to the volume knobs on the amplifiers, and then turned them all up to max; a wave of his plectrum, and the PA had trebled in size. Now, Judas splayed his fingers into the appropriate chord shape, focussed, took aim at the doors, and let rip with the power-chord. The doors flew off their hinges, and the sound spilled out into the surrounding streets, and park. Struck by the full force of the rhythm, anyone that it touched turned, and headed toward the hall. As the notes crashed and rolled further afield, more and more were caught by the song that Judas was composing as he went along, current working title: The Summoning.

Soon the hall was full, the audience spilling out onto the surrounding grounds. But still this was not enough for Judas, he wanted – he needed – more. Other members of the old band were summoned to supplement the group. Aware of the strong Asian population, Judas set Mark down with the sitar, to catch those that had so far resisted. The older, Asian, generation would not have appreciated the driving beat that accompanied the sitar, so Judas installed some ethnic baffles; buoyed by the success that that created, he added massed keyboards for a full orchestral sound, and installed other generation-linked baffles.

Sonic wave after sonic wave spread across the city, across the county, and across the country. Next stop: the world.

The glass and cellulosite of the world's first truly organic office faded to be replaced by a crumbling concrete prefab. It was a little melodramatic, but now Judas had their attention. "I am going to tell you about the number nine," said Judas, "and the conspiracy to hide it!" Did a flicker of fear pass across the Arch-Mage's face, he wondered, or was it déjà vu. Whatever it was, it was gone in a heartbeat. Had he interpreted his brief too literally, Judas wondered; but it was too late to change now: the stage was set, the audience of twelve in place.

He struck his pose, and started: "Some of the great songwriters have nearly discovered it," he held up his forefinger for emphasis, the bony digit pointing skyward, "the originators, not the imitators; not those that simply copy others but the genuine creators. Those who, mostly, do not know from whence their inspiration comes. Some have said from thin air. Some from cocaine. Some in dreams whilst they slept.

"John Lennon perhaps came close to the truth in *#9 Dream*; Jimi Hendrix to one of the key elements of the conspiracy in *If Six Was Nine*. So thorough was the masking that the Nine Wonders of the Ancient World became seven; when the Modern Wonders were compiled only seven were sought.

"How clever they were in turning two of the nine deadly sins (cf. The Tale of Woe) into positive behaviours!

"And how did the hiding start; what could eradicate such basics? Into the world they released the word worms. Of course, back then, there were two types of wordworm; the most common you know of course, those that live only to seek out the word it is given and to devour that word – be it written, or a memory node. The second type was much rarer (possibly, now, even extinct) and was highly prized. These seek their key word in the same way as their common cousin; but the difference is that once the word has been consumed another is excreted in its place. Few of these worms exist today, either; with the advent of the internet, they entered it and gorged themselves falling victim to worm-obesity.

"Today that work continues still: talk of Pluto, Eris and Ceres diminishes (or increases) our system; no longer can it be counted as nine.

"But I am getting ahead of myself. In the beginning there were the nine-nines; the eighty ones to some (never the AT1s as some modernisers have suggested – the significance is in the numbers). It was these nine-nines that balanced life; brought it peace, harmony and tranquillity. The nine-nines were: the nine motivators; the nine musical notes; the nine emotions; the nine deadly sins; the nine stages of life (birth, infant, toddler, child, teenager, young adult, adult, senior and death)."

Judas plucked a book from within his denim jacket. "I will name the other four groups in a moment; one of them will surprise and shock you! But each of them is discussed fully in this book – it is a forbidden book, of course – there are nine chapters, each of nine pages. Any guesses on the other four groupings?" None answered, a stunned silence had fallen upon the gathering. Judas continued: "then I must tell you. They are ...."

As he said those words, the book held proudly before him suddenly burst into flames of lurid purple; a mighty concussion shook the room; one by one his audience flickered and then vanished. Only the Arch-Mage remained, although he had not seen him move, he stood now before Judas, his fingers rigid as granite pressed on either side of Judas's temple. "That memory is not for you; not for those other puppets either! Where you came by it, I cannot guess, but I will take it now!"

The next thing he knew, Judas was floating in a dark fluid filled sack, a cord running from his belly to the side. And then there was a further eruption.

With a soft click the door shut behind him; he turned the key in the latch to shut out the world and shuffled into his cluttered living room. He had had good intentions of making something to eat, but decided to sit, first, on his settee; he slouched down. The small handheld screen was before his eyes, but he did not really see it; his finger swiped, but the images just blurred. Were there tears in his eyes? On either side of him were piles of unopened post; on the floor boxes, unopened, with a dozen or so recent purchases, made on the device that he held. This really wasn't his time was it; he knew he should not have visited; should have stayed in his own period. But the temptation had been to great; maybe there was a version of She with whom he could relate, engage, join.

Perhaps a drink, he thought. But he didn't move from his chair. His mind wandered, thinking on the work that he still needed to do in the house; there were still two bedrooms to decorate; schemes ran through his mind: wardrobe and shelving arrangements; flooring; colour schemes – it would be lovely when he had finished. He looked to the pile of paint catalogues and wardrobe suppliers, but he did not move towards them. His shoulders slumped; his eyes remained unfocussed; he felt the depression grow. Where was the motivation? Sapped and drained from him; but by what?

He turned on the larger screen; this one was wall-mounted. He selected a channel at random and was instantly absorbed in whatever it was – it had not registered in the slightest – only twenty-three more episodes in the boxset.

Outside, it grew dark; he looked at the floor lamp, but it was out of reach; he could not summon the energy to get up and turn it on. As the room darkened, so did his mood. He was lonely, and he knew it; although at the same time he hated company. If only he had a partner, everything would be fine; they would do things together. The house would soon be done; they could go for walks; they could holiday. But it made no difference: his mind was trapped inside the darkness; he was trapped inside the room. I'll get up in a minute, he thought, but he didn't. He just sat, alone in his room, with the dim light of the TV screen; lonely thoughts rattling around inside his head. He sat for ages. Days. Weeks. And that was how they found him, eventually; his flesh cold, his breathing stopped; just one more piece of household clutter.

Judas fingered the head of the axe at his belt; its cold hard steel; the blade smooth, notch-free, razor sharp. Indeed, he had but recently used it as a razor for either side of his scalp; leaving just the centre to grow longer; it was plaited and tied with leather, reaching just below his shoulders. How long ago was it that this axe had become a war axe he wondered. How long since it had been a tool around the farm to chop wood for the fire, to shape wood for dwellings. He was weary of the life of a warrior.

Looking around at his fellow raiders he was sure he could see the same weariness on their faces; the wish to return to the simpler life of a farmer. The flickering flames cast angular shadows on those weary faces. Night had fallen, they had eaten, soon they would sleep. Or maybe drink a little and then sleep. Or a lot, and not get much sleep at all.

Why didn't one of them voice what they were all thinking; speak of that desire to return home. And then he realised that perhaps they, too, were all having that same thought. Just waiting for someone else to voice it. Well, tonight, he thought, I will be the one to voice it. I will speak and they will all agree. And we can go home. He looked to the face of their leader, their warrior-lord, Ubba. He saw the same weariness on his face too. He opened his mouth to speak, but Erik got there before him, speaking the words that he was about to: "My brothers, we are all weary of this fight, we gain nothing. Let us return to our homelands. To our farms. Let us use these axes for firewood, not necks. Let's see our loved ones, our children, our wives."

Judas started to nod his approval, saw others doing the same. Hope came to him. But then Ubba spoke, and that hope was extinguished. "Have you gone soft? Have you turned back into a shivering, snivelling, child? Are you no longer a man? Home! Look around you, see these brave faces. None of them is thinking of home!"

Judas stopped nodding, hoping that in the dark none had seen. The others had stopped too. And now their voices echoed Ubba, endorsing his words. Judas found that his own voice had joined them, "Coward," he said, and "have you become a woman? Where is your spirit? Your fight?" He thought he saw several around him sag, resigned as he was. How many of them felt as he did, he wondered. All of them? None of them? Half of them? But he knew now that none would be voicing such thoughts again. Erik mumbled excuses, and then fell silent.

It was rare for more than two or three of them to be together in any one place, in any one time. But these were exceptional circumstances. Today there were seven of them; half their number. The orange plastic of the chairs, the bold orange, black and turquoise of the wallpaper pattern of their meeting room left little doubt of the date. All but one of them sat urgent and attentive; the meeting had just started. In deference to habit, they had not turned on the main lighting; the room was lit by the flickering glow of a dozen candles, a single lava lamp their one concession to the period.

"We are agreed then that they have come too close to the truth?" opened Peter. There were several murmurs of assent. Thomas opined, "I think that they are not conscious of the truth that they speak, they are reaching the knowledge in some unconscious way."

"That may indeed be true," agreed Peter, "but the end result is the same. And they hold such power that the word is spreading out of our control. We must act."

Judas stood up and addressed his peers, "I don't think that I can risk an assassination. We have travelled too far down that road, to little avail. A death might endorse the message even further." Peter and one or two others nodded in agreement,

"You are right, the risks are too great in this case. So, we must look to other suggestions. Ideas?"

A silence fell in the room. Thaddaeus toyed idly with his pencil, twirling it between his fingers, he opened his mouth as if to speak, but then closed it again. Simon and Bartholomew stared intently at the jotting pads before them, as though hoping that inspiration would leap from the blank pages. Finance Director Matthew tapped absently at his calculator, falling back on the numbers that he always felt more comfortable with than words.

"Come on guys," said Peter, there was a hint of anger in his tone, "we need some answers. We can't do nothing! What are we going to tell Him?" At the voicing of that name, Thaddaeus dropped his pencil, it clattered, unnaturally loudly, on the cherry wood of the desk; he looked up in sudden alarm.

Peter sought to instil momentum into his now plainly nervous peers, "OK, let's go back to basics. Let's brainstorm it!" He moved the flipchart closer to the desk and picked up a blue marker. "You know the rules, eyes on the flipchart, not each other; ideally single words, maximum of three words; no arguing about them until we have a finished list. Who's going to start?"

After a few moments of silence, Judas opened with: "smear campaign".

"Scandal?" offered Matthew, playing it safe, but wanting to be amongst the first to contribute.

"Make our own record," suggested Thomas.

And then the words started to flow more quickly from around the table:

"Bribes."

"Word Worm?"

"Drugs."

"Seduction."

"Perjury?"

"Cloning!"

"Hype an alternative?"

"Paint by numbers!"

"World tour."

The words were flowing faster now, Peter's writing deteriorated as he tried to write faster and faster to keep up.

"Assassination," offered Thomas. Judas thumped the table, angrily leaping to his feet; "No," he shouted

"I have already said no to that. It's not helping; there are too many ramifications!" He drew breath to continue, but Peter raised his hand in a gesture of silencing: "Come on, Judas, you know the rules of brainstorming! No discussion, agreement or disagreement until the list is complete!"

Judas fell into a sullen silence and resumed his chair. Slowly the suggestions started to flow again, soon Photographs, Scandal, Festival, Sound, Time Travel, Remote Control and two dozen other words had joined the list, which now filled two sides of A1.

Peeling off several knobs of BluTac, Peter attached them to the wall; he read through the list idly stroking his rust-tinged beard as he read. "OK, who wants to kick off," he asked, "anything there leap out to anyone?" After several moments of silence, Thaddaeus ventured: "Not sure who mentioned cloning, but that strikes me as a thought. Well not so much cloning, as preparing a look-a-like, but one that we have briefed and trained."

"I think you might have something there," said Peter. "Go on, expand the idea further."

"Well, I do agree with Judas, an assassination in this instance would just create a martyr and give even more power to their words. But if we replaced one of them, we could slowly change the tack of their lyrics."

"Word Worms!" exclaimed Bartholomew. We could release a Word Worm to even replace some of their lyrics; nothing too dramatic, but enough to put people off the trail."

"Might we turn some of their words to simple whimsy; help them to discredit themselves?" offered Thomas.

Peter turned to face Judas, "I think we may well have hit on a solution here. But that does give us the problem of removing the original." He fell silent. The rest of those in the room also turned to Judas who sat quietly for a long while focussed on his left hand's fingernails. Finally, he looked up: "OK," he said "but this really is the last one. Absolutely no more after this one!"

"Which one should we replace?" asked Mathew. "John's lyrics come closer to the truth when you look at them."

"I agree," replied Peter, "but I think that the other will be easier to replace. And it would help Barty's Whimsical Word Worm idea." There were several nods and murmurs of agreement.

"One problem though," pronounced Judas, "no matter how good our doppelganger, there will be some who start to guess. How can we avoid that – rumour could be more devastating than the truth to us and The Cause!"

“Very true!” agreed Peter. “Any ideas?”

“This is a bit left field,” offered Thaddaeus, “but how about starting rumours ourselves. I remember being told once that there were only two ways to lie effectively: to tell only selected parts of the truth or to tell the whole truth, but in such an unbelievable way that nobody will believe it.

“So, if we start the rumours of Paul’s death, but just make them so ridiculous – obliterate his shoes on *that* album cover, hint at backward messaging, something with flowers, a few more Word Worms, you know the sort of thing – that might just throw people of the scent?”

“Brilliant!” shouted Peter, “absolutely brilliant! You’ve really earned your bonus with that one!

“OK, teams: Matthew, Barty, the clone. Simon, Thaddie, Word Worms and rumours. Judas, you know what you have to do; but no mess, and definitely no body! And, definitely, none of your ‘calling cards’ nonsense!”

In a twinkling the office was empty, the plans were in motion, and two small piles of ash the only remainder of the two pages from the flipchart.

Your body is now honed: the fifth lesson may begin; it is the naming of things." He was before me once again, and his palm opened toward me; grass grew upon it, and He told me its real name; the grass vanished, and was replaced by a coarser growth, which He named. The changes grew faster and faster: earth and stone followed plant; fauna followed these; the names came quicker, and quicker, until he was done. Grass appeared once more, and He taught me its language, which was slow and whispering, with few real words. Once more, the content of his palm began to change, and with each change a new language was taught. I cannot here transcribe those languages: few words outside sun and rain would be recognised; but in any event, the writing of these things is not permitted. For a third time, the cycle commenced with grass, I was taught words of command, and how it might do my will.

There were four more lessons, nine in all, although I know not how to describe them, until the time came (and I think it was here that, for me, time started again) when He, whom I now called Father, said to me, "That is it. Your training is complete. You have learnt the nine lessons, and learnt them well; there is no more that I can do for you, except for these three things: I will clothe you, and name you, and you will meet the other eleven that have also succeeded where so many others have failed."

And He took me from that place to a room where eleven others, that I did not then know, were already gathered; there also was the Arch-Mage. Father seated himself, on a simple wooden chair; the Arch-Mage stood to his right. In turn we stepped forward, for each there was a short wooden staff, around three feet in length; each staff was different, a different wood, shape, or finish was on them all; some were refined, and polished, some crude. Mine was gnarled and twisted, a number of offshoots still in place, though their leaves long gone. Clothes we were given, in as many styles, some familiar, some alien. When we were clothed, we broke our fast: how long it was since I

WHO!

Carefully adjusting his tie, Judas smiled at his colleagues. "Good news, guys! The chief has sent through our new mobiles!" He loosened the drawstrings of the pouch at his waist and pulled out the eleven devices; his own nestled comfortingly in his trouser pocket; its light thrum at the same time reassuring and slightly arousing.

Taking care to ensure that each received the correct device, Judas shared them out. "They have all the latest apps," he said, grinning, "data pooler, crucifix, laser, cloak, stunner, instiller, ascender, remote, crayon, quiller, and all the direct links you could possibly need! Plus of course your own individual specialist tools."

Simon-Peter looked up from his device, which he had been avidly exploring; a wild, feral, light was in his eyes: "This should improve our conversion rate!" he cried. One by one they set the coordinates on their devices and vanished from the room.

Naked, she sat at the desk leafing through the sheets of paper. Behind her in the dimly lit room a lightly snoring Judas lay sprawled across the bed. The room was thickly coated in dust; even the network of spiders' webs that clung to every corner and join of the ceiling and walls had dust-encrusted threads. The sink and kitchen work surfaces of the tiny bedsit were covered in dirty plates, cups, mugs, saucepans and a solitary frying pan. Everywhere were empty tins and take way boxes; at some point there had been a failed attempt to stack them in a corner. The remaining spaces on the tables and floor were filled with empty wine and beer bottles.

In stark contrast with the rest of the flat, a neat, glittering white, author's roll lay open, within it were all the tools of the profession: pencil, biro, gel pen, quill, colour pencils, charcoal, scribe, laser-etcher, chalk, crayon, felt pen, light scribe, lettrebous, fountain pens (reservoir and cartridge types). They came in every conceivable colour; not just reds, blacks and blues but also greens and purples and oranges – row upon rainbow row. There were also rubbers and liquid papers, paper restorers, inkquidators and more.

Carefully, selecting the right tools, she made small amendments to the text on the papers. Mainly, she changed only single letters or the occasional word; on two occasions she inserted a whole paragraph; once she took an entirely new sheet, which she filled.

Behind her, Judas groaned slightly and started to shift in the bed. Hurriedly, she returned the sheaves of paper to Judas's bag; a simple hand gesture and the author's roll was gone. Quietly, she slipped back into bed just as his eyes opened. "Is it time for work?" he asked. "Silly you," she replied. "You know you are not working today. You said that you would spend the day with me; now what shall we do?"

Her hand slid below the sheets, she ran it down his chest and across his abdomen before slowing, "Ooh! Now that is an impressive start to the day!" she whispered in his ear. Her lips followed the same journey her hand had just taken, but more slowly, more teasingly. Judas's head flopped back onto the pillow, the sense of purpose fled from his eyes, which glazed over; his memory was getting worse every day. But then even that memory was gone, his only point of focus the gentle rise and fall of her head below the sheet; nothing else mattered to him anymore. There was always tomorrow.

Judas could not believe his good fortune, here he was in the night club, he could feel his powers at full potency, and there she was: Rachel, the object of his desires; well tonight he would show her that he was a man, and a better man than some of the ruffians that he had seen her with in recent months! He saw her looking, convinced that he saw interest flicker across her expression; he was about to walk across to her when he checked himself: play it cool he thought, just like in the movies.

So, he waited his opportunity, which did not come until nearly the end of the evening: he walked close to where she sat with her friends, bumping into the shoulder of a leather clad punk, taking beers back to his spiky haired friends. The four beer glasses crashed to the floor, sending beer and broken glass in all directions; Judas saw the look, but did not wait for the ritual to start, punching straight out at the punk, and sending him crashing towards the table at which his friends were sitting. In an instant, they had joined the fray, squaring up to Judas.

Judas was careful not to let the fight be too one sided, and draw too much attention to himself; although he could feel the power flow within him. He waited for the first of them to strike, knowing that the use of that energy would aid him; a clumsy punch came in from the left, Judas ducked slightly, grabbed the oncoming arm, and deflected it into the face of one of the other attackers. As it was landing, he sensed, rather than saw, the kick aimed at his thigh, he blocked low, and heard the splinter of bone; now he struck twice, at two of the punks: oi tsuki, gyaku tsuki, aiming for the noses: a good flow of blood always made for impressive results. Another blow came toward Judas from the left, he crouched double, waited to feel the weight of his opponent as he stumbled forward, carried by the momentum of his strike; when he felt the weight of a body on his back, he sprang up again, the attacker somersaulted into the air, to land on a table full of bottles and glasses: a pleasing amount of debris! Many more blows were traded, none landing on Judas, but many on the four attackers; at the end of it, the four punks lay in a heap on the floor, alongside two bouncers that had approached to stop the fighting; the floor was strewn with broken tables, chairs, glasses, and spilt drinks. Judas dusted his hands, and sidled across towards Rachel's table. She was looking at him, open mouthed; Judas felt his heart soar, convinced she was in awe of his prowess, certain that he would be taking her home that night. His bubble, however, was soon burst when she spoke: "Judas Iscariot, if that display of macho behaviour was meant to impress me, it does not. How could you think I would be drawn toward the Neanderthal that you have revealed yourself to be? That is thuggish, loutish behaviour, and it has no place in modern society!" With that she flounced off towards the ladies' toilets, her friends in her wake, leaving a dumbfounded Judas behind: wasn't this what she had wanted, had asked for. Why would she chase a thug like Craig, and yet reject him for the same behaviour; Judas did not think he would ever understand.

had last eaten or drank I could not recall; not since that crust of bread all those - - - - - ago, in my old house, I was sure.

When we were refreshed, the naming began; the staff was named first, and then its holder. I was last to step forward; Father and the Arch-Mage conferred, then He pronounced: "The staff before me shall be called Serpyllum; its holder will be known henceforth as Judas Iscariot." Under his breath, I heard the Arch-Mage mutter, "For he will betray us all." But with that naming, I forgot much that had gone before, my old name, my memories, my identity: the canvas was blank once more.

A briefing followed, and tasks were given; Judas was told where he must visit, and what it was he should seek. His report was to be full, detailed, and frank; the others had similar tasks, other places, other times, to go to. They would meet again only on rare occasions; that was until the scheduled date for their conference, at which they would present their findings. The instructions were mentally imparted; no physical notes were to be made, now or in the future, until the report itself was prepared. Access to the library was still to be allowed, but none of the books might be removed, nor should the text be copied: their mission must not become known; their findings were to be kept secret. Judas spoke to his staff, "Take me there!" and he was suddenly gone; around him the neon of Piccadilly Circus now flashed. Judas took refuge in Tower Records, and started to browse: he had a lot of empty memories to fill.

On a scruffy beer-stained couch sat Judas; it was one of the darkest corners of the pub, but it gave him a sense of security. As he sat eyes dreamily gazing through the beer to the bottom of the glass, he was joined by a woman sliding in close – very close – on his left-hand side; instinctively he moved to the right, only to find that another woman had sat close on his right, blocking all escape. The first woman was older, probably late forties, but her skin was still firm, her breasts large, revealed by the low scoop of her t-shirt. The other woman was younger, probably only just in her twenties. They were both blond, although the older of the two did not look quite as natural; both had fine hair left to hang down, framing their faces. "Hi," said the first woman, "I'm Jenny, and this is my daughter, Lou. We thought you could do with another drink." She pointed to a fresh pint sitting close to his other glass; they had brought drinks of their own too. She covered his hand with hers, lingering for a moment, "You don't mind, do you?"

Mother and daughter edged closer, Jenny's breasts now crushed into his side, pinning down one arm, Lou was lightly stroking his leg, just above the knee. "You looked as though you could do with some company, sitting all on your own," she said, "and we could do with some too!" Judas finished his old pint, and took a swig of the new one, spluttering slightly, as Lou's hand roamed higher, to the upper thigh. Jenny took a sip of her own drink, spilling some onto her cleavage. "That was careless, Mum," murmured

Lou, she leant across, “waste not, want not,” she said, and her tongue darted out to clear the liquid away. Judas realised that he was staring, “Did you want some too?” asked Jenny, splashing a little more and pulling Judas’s head down; he was caught by her perfume and before he could think his tongue was out running down the breast in a single slow motion, only stopped by contact with the edge of the t-shirt.

“Now look what you have done,” she said, stroking a stiffening nipple through the thin material. “It’s not just you, Jenny,” said Lou, she was now caressing the front of Judas’s trousers; you have had a similar effect on him. Jenny felt it for herself; “Very impressive,” she murmured, “I think that we should pop upstairs to our room; we are staying here for a while.” Dumbly Judas followed them, a lamb to the slaughter.

In the lift on the way up Lou began to massage Jenny’s breasts, pulling down the material of the t-shirt; Jenny grabbed Judas’s head and pulled it toward them, he sucked hungrily at the nipples: a ravenous child. No sooner were they in the room than they were kissing him, and each other, long and deep the tongues roaming from mouth to mouth, questing, exploring: bees flitting from bud to bud seeking pollen. One of them had thrust a hand inside his trousers, he didn’t know which, and he didn’t care, he was captivated. Momentarily a nagging thought entered Judas's enjoyment: this was all happening very fast, perhaps too fast. Should he be suspicious of their motives. But then one of them was kneeling before him and the thought had evaporated; he became rooted in the here and now – all thoughts of past and future fled.

They pushed him down to the bed; he lay there, unable to take his eyes from them. They kissed each other again, Jenny tore open the front of Lou's blouse, buttons flew around the room, the blouse fell to the floor. Lou's breasts were just slightly smaller, but probably slightly firmer; Jenny licked them wetly. For the first time, Judas noticed that they both wore white miniskirts; sitting up slightly he ran a hand up Jenny's stockinged right leg, and Lou's left. His hands curved round behind to stroke their buttocks; neither wore panties. Lou pushed him gently back down, "patience", she murmured.

Jenny lay down beside him, she clicked her fingers, and all their remaining clothes were gone; Judas's too. His suspicions should have reawakened then, but he was fast falling under their spell. Jenny spread her legs; without hesitation Lou's head was between them. Jenny turned her head slightly, kissing Judas deeply; her hand was between his legs, gently teasing. Jenny stopped caressing; Judas was momentarily disappointed until the hand was replaced by Lou's soft lips. Jenny slid down the bed; her lips replaced Lou's for a while, and then both tongues were upon him.

They moved back up the bed, Jenny lay on top of Lou, murmuring, "Oh, that tasted so good!" They kissed each other again, they writhed together, but he did not feel left out. It was his turn to move down the bed now, his knees slid underneath Lou's buttocks, and then he had entered one of them. Strangely, he could not tell which; there were no further clues as he thrust deeply: both screamed with pleasure. Judas took Jenny's right nipple in between his left thumb and finger and Lou's left nipple with his right. They crushed their breasts together and again he had the strange sensation that he could not tell which one he was caressing; perhaps both. His howl of pleasure joined with theirs in a prolonged moment of orgasm.

Judas lay now between them, sleeping; his ardour spent. Jenny and Lou smiled at each other, kissed once, before revealing their fangs and sinking them into the left and right sides of Judas's neck. He did not wake as they drank at his blood, nor did he wake when they replaced it with a liquid of their own. Many centuries were to pass before he escaped; not that he had ever wished to escape. It was just that during one of their wilder orgies he had fallen crashing through the window to the street below. When he awoke, he was in hospital; his memory was gone. It was 1913. He looked up at the approaching nurse, she looked somehow familiar; was her name Sandy? He thought it was. She smiled at him: "Oh good, you are back with us at last! Where have you been?" Judas thought it strange that she locked the door behind her as she approached his bed; there were no other patients in the ward.

Chief Inspector Monjack groaned inwardly as the door to his left opened and the eager countenance of Sergeant Millson appeared. Monjack still could not see Millson as old enough to be out of school; but then he had been feeling that about a lot of people, lately. He guessed it was old age; well, he did only have a further three months to go until his retirement. Millson's face bobbed up and down as he hopped from foot to foot; his smooth, slightly shiny, face reflected back some of the tungsten glare from the ceiling lights; the eyes and nose looked too small for the rest of the head. "Chief, Chief," Millson cried "you just have to look at this! You really will not believe it! It's the strangest thing I have ever seen!" Monjack's inner groan turned to a smile: the way Millson talked, he sounded older than Monjack himself!

Wearily, and a little warily, Monjack entered the room; the leather of his face wrinkling further as he took in the fifteen neatly arranged piles of paper on the desk. Monjack rubbed at his furrowed forehead, "What seems to be the trouble, lad?" He saw the flicker of anger that flared and then disappeared from the Sergeant's eyes: like most young adults Millson hated to be referred to as 'lad' or worse 'boy'. Sometimes Millson thought his elders did it just to annoy him; sometimes the Chief Inspector used those names deliberately to see the reaction they caused; it was all part of the ritual.

But Sergeant Millson was too excited to worry about such things now; he was so excited that he was gabbling: "Well, Chief, you remember that case you asked me to investigate? That one in the bar where the girl got hit by a bottle. She's ok now, by the way, hospital let her out this morning; they only kept her in for observations. So that's good. Well, anyway, I got all the witness statements like you asked, for everyone in the bar; where they were, what they were doing, what they saw, what they heard. Everything is all very consistent; a row about her kissing this other guy; she throws her drink over him; he retaliates by trying to throw the drink from the bottle he is holding over her, but his grip slips and it's the whole bottle that hits her. So probably an accident; he's got no record for anything; they'd both been drinking; she doesn't want to press charges. So, as I say, all very straight forward, except this one strange thing: I got names and descriptions of everyone in the bar at the time, you know where they were standing, what they were doing, that kind of thing. Anyway, everything ties up quite neatly, all fits quite well together, except for this one person. Everyone gives him the same name: Judas (well, one of them calls him Jude and another JayDee), but look at these descriptions of him. Nearly all of them different!"

Chief Inspector Monjack looked at the sheet that Millson had placed on the top of each pile, and read, groups of words leaping out: 'six foot two, white, clean shaven, no distinguishing features'; 'five foot three, dark brown hair, bearded, deeply tanned'; 'West Indian, scar above left eyebrow'; 'female, pale skin, died black hair'; 'approximately fifty five'; 'early twenties'; 'forties'; 'thin'; 'heavily muscled'; 'button nose'; roman nose'; 'broken nose'; 'well dressed'; 'scruffy'; 'rugby shirt'.

Each page had him located in roughly the same place (with one exception). All described his actions similarly: alone, reading a magazine (two had said a book), not involved in the altercation or its aftermath.

Monjack scratched his nose in puzzlement; twenty years ago, he would not have let this rest, but now common sense firmly ruled his decision-making processes. He turned to Millson: "So, Sergeant, he was not involved in the incident?" "No, Sir." "The case itself will not go to court?" "No, Sir." "Then file it!" Millson started to object, "But, Sir...." Monjack held up his hand silencing him mid flow, "We really don't need the hassle or the paperwork. No crime has been committed by this mystery man! Just consign it and get on with some real police work!" Before his Sergeant could argue further, Monjack turned on his heel and walked (perhaps a little too hastily) from the room, leaving behind him a slightly baffled, but nevertheless resigned, Sergeant Timothy Millson.

The tall, gleaming, rocket filled the horizon; its surface, burnished, mirrored; it reflected its surroundings. Four tailfins rested on the sand; equidistant between these the four engine outlets flared wide, wisps of vapour escaped them to be carried off on the wind. A red sun was only just clambering above the horizon, clawing its way up the sky, shooing aside the clouds.

Three figures left the low, single story, building that nestled, almost below ground, amongst the dunes. There was little sound except the faint rustle of their padded white spacesuits; each of them carried a spherical glass globe, at their bases rims and seals that mirrored those at the neck of each of the suits. Behind them, running almost straight, they left ridged footprints in the sands' of time.

Theirs was the honour of being the first men in space; if things went well, they would take a brief stop on the moon before they headed for their final destination: Mars. The trip was made possible by the breakthrough invention of the gravitational-force fed engines. Judas didn't really understand the science behind them; something about equal and opposite reactions and how no gravity would create... ... what was the word?... ... megagravity, which would both push and pull them across the void. At the moment, he couldn't quite remember why he wanted to be on the rocket. He could, however, still vividly picture his most recent victim: he'd put up quite a fight! There had been blood and entrails all over the apartment, smearing the space-themed pictures on the walls and shelves; bits of model rockets – some fantastical, some truer to the final reality – crunched into the carpet. He had created more blood and gore when he had peeled the victim's – was his name Budd? – face off and sealed it over his own; with a flourish of his staff (which he currently had formatted as a Cross fountain pen) he had sealed the edges, removing the red, ragged, join. For reasons he also could not recall, he had not cleaned up behind him: the victim would be discovered. He had never done this before with any victim – assassination or otherwise – he had always removed all trace. Well, except the one in the car; that had been very public!

The shadow cast by the rocket carved an oblique shadow to their left. If they'd approached the rocket from the other side, the glare and reflection of the sun in the rocket's surface would surely have been blinding! The nearer they got, the more the rocket's scale was revealed: they were now three tiny dots, dwarfed by its magnificence. Judas couldn't quite remember how they got inside the rocket; he could see no doors, lifts or walkways. No worry, he would just follow the other two.

Suddenly the scene before him juddered and tilted; there was a flash of light. The two figures beside him stood frozen, motionless, mid-stride. Before him now stood the Arch-Mage, his cheeks red with fury:

"Judas, for fuck's sake, what are you thinking!" he roared. Judas looked down at his toes, abashed, "I wanted to see what is beyond," he mumbled.

"What is beyond! What is beyond! Have you forgotten all your schooling? You know what is beyond! You know that man cannot leave this place! None may know what is outside!" But Judas couldn't remember, not even a hint, he really couldn't. But neither could he admit it.

"Now all this must be obliterated," the Arch-Mage waved a hand in the rough direction of the rocket behind him. He felt the Arch-Mage's power begin to grow; he saw that his staff took the simple form of a ring on his finger (he might try that, he thought). The ground shook, there was a huge flash, thunder and lightning sprang from the ground; the rocket shattered into a million pieces, shattered as if it had been made from glass or brittle plastic. The explosion ripped across the dessert; the explosion obliterated the low buildings between the dunes; one finger of the explosion ripped out across the desert engulfing his victim's apartment; the explosion lifted Judas off his feet and blasted him back on course.

The sun was setting now; he could see its trailing edge from his apartment window as it slid toward the horizon. He was comfortably nestled in the soft, supple leather of his settee; before him, Judas's television screen was filled with images of the space mission: the successful desert launch; the alighting on the moon (giant steps and golf clubs); the onward journey to Mars. It wasn't long after those images had been broadcast that the hoax rumours started. Judas laughed when he heard them: how could you fake an entire space mission; it just wasn't possible!

ובכן, מעולם לא הקדשתי לזה הרבה מחשבה!

After all, aren't we all a little bit Judas? And with that realisation, he put down his pen and ne'er a single word more did he write.

The maelstrom surrounded him, buffeted him, spun him upwards and downwards – at what felt like the same time on occasion. For hours/days/weeks/months/years/decades/millennia/eons, far beyond count, he had been lost in the time-wilderness. The slipstream of possibility tousled his hair; the vortex of chance nibbled at his toes; the winds of change buffeted his chest; his fancy was tickled by time trouts; ear worms, word worms; he certainly was not the early bird; that worm had turned, somersaulting in its tracks! He tried peering, from the worm's-eye view and failed. In desperation, he burped the worm; briefly glow worms jetted around him. Was he to become no more than worm food? But then the werm of an idea came to him; would it, could it, should it work?

He had plundered the silver! He had plundered the gold! The supply was endless, the wealth from all its treasures!

She had been pillaged, plundered, stripped! Her heart had melted, her knees give way, her body had trembled, her very face grew pale!

The hunt was up! Where now is the lions' den, the place where they fed their young, where the lion and lioness went, and the cubs, had nothing to fear?

He swam forward, though the time treacle clung to him, hampering his every move. Suddenly, he breached the surface (or was it the floor?); panting he drew in breath for the first time in... ... ... only his training had kept him alive, kept him sane. It tried to suck him under once more, but he kicked free rising (falling?) towards the neon signs, which flashed before him; there were multiple signs, but a single word blazed from them: έξοδος יְצִיאָה излез אַרויסגאַנג.

It was 01/01/801.

The office followed the typical layout of all late nineties/early noughties offices: all open plan with a few glass cubicles for the exalted. Each work area looked much like that of the next, although some attempt had been made to personalise some of them: pictures of family and loved ones, amusing cuddly toys, models of dream cars, left over novelties from the Christmas party, even one Toy Story doll.

At one point the rooms had been painted in bright pinks, purples and reds; it was a bid to demonstrate that it was a fun company, a young company. But now they were returned to the more normal greys and beiges. A vague air of depression hung over the office; quiet conspiratorial whispers were passed from desk to desk – or for the really scandalous, sent by e-mail to colleagues who were scant feet away. The senior management team felt that their junior employees had no passion for the company, no desire to work hard and succeed and no loyalty. Amongst the employees the commonly held belief was that the senior management team had no clear sense of direction, no interest in their staff, overpaid themselves and had been over promoted.

It was a very typical office.

He looked around the office for Fiona, but she was nowhere to be seen. Yesterday they had exchanged cross words and Judas wanted to apologise to her: she had led him to believe that a letter had been approved by the CEO for issue, but after it had been sent, he found that this was not so. He still blamed her for the mistake, but they had to work together, so he thought he ought to make his peace.

Fiona was impossibly glamorous; he often wondered why she worked in an office such as this one. Surely her true place would be within the glitz of a fashion magazine's offices, or in a television studio. Judas had no amorous feelings towards Fiona; perhaps because he thought he had no chance with her; but it was more than that, she did not stir any feeling within him at all, not even feelings of hopeless lust. Often, he had wondered why; was there something wrong with him, or something about her that was missing. No soul? Certainly, she was the subject of much lustful speculation amongst other male colleagues.

The other person that Judas thought he ought to speak to was the CEO, he had spoken unkindly about Fiona to Fred – or Frederick as he preferred to be called currently, no one was quite sure why. He had been Fred ever since he joined the company; but now he was Frederick; Frederick T Dearch to be as precise as he was. Judas strolled down the corridor to his office door, he pushed it open and walked in. Fred – Frederick – had never stood with the formality of knocking.

But Judas should have wondered when the locksmith had been there earlier that day. Ever after he wondered why he had not at least tapped before entering, or coughed, or made some other sign that he was about to enter. Because there was Fiona: her hair was still immaculate, but the shimmer that was her favourite golden blouse lay crumpled on the desk; the tight blue silk pencil skirt was draped across the back of Fred's chair. She was wearing black stockings, but there was no sign of any other underwear. The blue patent leather stilettos were still on her feet. And there was Fred, naked but for his socks. The blue heels dug slightly into his back on either side of his spine; his buttocks rose and fell, their rhythm matching the beating of Judas's heart.

All Fred's insecurities were revealed by the way his head snuggled into the nape of Fiona's neck, his arms clinging to her like some frightened child. He had not heard Judas enter; he might be able to quietly withdraw. But then Fiona looked at him, and in those eyes, he saw his future mapped out. He knew that she had won; no apology would suffice now. He knew that his days here were now numbered. He saw humiliation before he finally left. He saw demotion. He saw whispers and rumours being passed between colleagues.

But as he stumbled from the office the tears that glistened in his eyes were not for himself, they were for Fiona. How low must her self-esteem be if she was prepared to accept the role of mistress; her actions could not even be justified by the poor excuse of her personal advancement; she could never be more than a PA not possessing the technical skills needed for more senior roles. He wondered how she saw herself, where her own personal insecurities stemmed from. But then Judas never had understood the office affair; perhaps he was as dull and strait-laced as he knew his colleagues saw him as.

The battle lines were finally drawn. For the first time, they would face their enemy. Before, his tactics had been subtle, manipulative, singular. Rarely had two or more of his army appeared together; how many troops did he have, they wondered. They had taken their vantage point, on the higher ground: the twelve Generals, each with a thousand men; their weaponry was many and varied: sword, shield, spear, canon, spear, lance, revolver, rifle, shotgun, machine gun, canon, bazooka, mortar, gi, nunchaku, star, glove, gauntlet, laser, sonic reducer, drill, hammer, and so much more besides. Battle beacons blazed around them, illuminating the last of the night sky. It was silent. Judas's men looked nervously around them; he knew they would relax once the enemy was in sight, these were the pre-battle nerves.

They were all arrayed around the lower slopes of the hill; their formation formal, a twelve-pointed star. At the very tip of each wedge stood one of the twelve; Judas had chosen to go very old school: he was arrayed in faded robes of grey, a tall, pointed, hat upon his head, a staff in his hand and a sword upon each hip.

The silence was interrupted by a distant thrum on the horizon: the beating of a drum. Like the kindling of a forest fire, the single beat spread; one drum became two, became three, became four, became five, became six, became seven, became eight, became nine; they continued to spread, drum upon drum, beat upon beat. The beat had started to the east, but slowly it spread around to the south, to the west, and to the north. How vast was the enemy army to come from all sides! They found out soon enough; from every side a shadow appeared on the horizon – a shadow that had nothing to do with the fast-rising sun. That shadow grew thicker and blacker as it tightened around them; there was still some half a league between them, but now they could descry shapes of man and weapon. As the force approached, they saw they were outnumbered ten-fold or more. But that did not matter; they were going to battle the enemy and right was on their side. Ahead of the advancing foe, they now saw shorter shapes, moving on all fours; fell beasts with slavering jaws, long stiletto teeth and angry purple eyes. The advance was slow, measured. Judas could now make out individuals within the mass; women too were amongst the enemy throng, bare breasted and with flame red hair; he felt his cock grow stiff and all but forgot the sword at his side. He sensed, rather than heard, the Arch-Mage tap his staff from the top of the hill; at that tap the glamour momentarily faded, and he saw demon faces below the red hair; his erection too faded and one of his swords was in his hand; he raised staff and sword, almost in welcome.

When the enemy was some thirty paces from them, they came to a sudden halt, at some unspoken command. Almost directly in front of Judas, a tall, leathery-skinned, warrior stood. He was armed with an automatic crossbow; Judas knew the type, capable of firing up to forty bolts a minute. From the warrior's throat came a low growl, quiet at first, but then growing in timbre. As the volume of the growl grew, it was picked up by the enemy to his left; he too was armed with an automatic crossbow. Moments later, a third picked up the growl. The snarl continued its even, measured, progress in a clockwise direction, domino-ing around the throng. Some fifteen minutes later, the snarl had completed its circuit and was now taken up by the second row. There seemed to be no pause for breath as circuit after circuit more participants joined in.

Judas felt a thin trickle of sweat wend its way down his spine. "Hold!" came the silent command from the hilltop.

It may have been when the final warrior joined the cacophony, but suddenly the enemy was charging. A dozen crossbow bolts flew toward Judas who parried them away with his staff. As the gap closed, the crossbow vanished, to be replaced by a double-headed axe; before he had had a chance to raise the axe, Judas had taken him in the throat. Now there was no time for thought or consideration, his battle training took over. He attacked with the sword and parried with the staff; now he reversed that, defending with his sword and meting out flaming death as his staff swept left and right in a controlled arc. As the press grew thicker, his feet too become instruments of death. Soon a wall of bodies – friend and foe – before him halted the advance momentarily. Then the enemy was tossing the bodies away from the front, like so many scraps of meat (indeed Judas had a momentary vision of those at the back of the throng devouring the tossed flesh). The second wave stepped in; the warrior women and the fell beasts – alike to hounds, but scaled like alligators. Both women and hounds had blood of green, any last vestige of lust faded with the first gout of that blood as his sword sliced through breast and bone. A different lust was upon him: the lust of battle coursed in his veins. His erection returned, summoned by battle, not the lust of flesh. Their twelve-pointed formation held strong as the enemy broke against them, surging and receding like waves on the shore.

Despite the odds it felt as though they would win this battle; they were holding strong, and the enemy dead were piling up by the thousands. But then the enemy changed tactics. Suddenly from the ring that had surrounded them, the enemy transformed into a single wedge; at its apex, a giant beast stood tall: twelve feet or more in height, several feet across the chest, too. The beast seemed to contain elements of all the myriad foes: the scaled skin of the hounds; the breasts of the female warriors; the leathery muscles; horns and ridges. This enemy wedge charged full tilt at the ingress between Judas's wedge and Peter's; it split into the Arch-Mage's force like a tree-feller's axe into a roundel of wood. Fire and horrific explosions sent bodies flying through the air. Smoke billowed across the throng, stinging their eyes. Raggedly, they fell on the enemy only to be scythed down, row upon row of them. Judas felt an enemy axe bite into his arm; a tongue of flame scorched his ear and neck; on all sides his comrades writhed on the ground in agony, or lay dead.

Seconds later the fighting stopped, and all eyes turned to the hill: the beast had forged his way to the hilltop, his army at his shoulders, the Arch-Mage before him. The beast's axe lay embedded in his shoulder; great gouts of blood ran down his white robes. Weakly, he raised his staff before him, holding it in both hands, "This battle you cannot win," he stated, weakly at first, but then with gathering power, "it cannot be won by force; only hope and belief can win – or lose by their utter destruction!" The beast replied, his voice more evil than many a weapon, "That may be so. But by the same token, neither can you!" His second axe arced towards the Arch-Mage's head, but before it reached him, his staff had descended; it struck not the enemy, but the ground before him. "Return to your pits!" he roared in a voice of power and command. The ground of the hillside split, opening into a huge wide gully; into the opening the beast tumbled, his minions with him. Just before the rift closed his enemy's voice spoke once more: "This is just the beginning!" And with that utterance, the sun dipped beyond the horizon and night came. Only thirteen people remained standing on the hillside.

Eloise and Liv looked up from their work and waved a cheery greeting to Judas. Their work progressed well; they had scoured the whole of Paris for the parts necessary to build the perfect man – each according to their own design. The room was now full of glass containers in dozens upon dozens of shapes and sizes; limbs and organs floated in each.

Their mission had started last year, when Liv who was on her 14th husband received what was for her the final straw: the wedding anniversary present of the giant tub of cellulite cream. This had been preceded by the birthday present of a boob job for the left boob (husband 14's favourite side), with the right boob to follow at Christmas when he had saved up enough. Eloise remained untouched as yet, still searching for the perfect man. So together they had hatched their plans.

Both wore blood spattered white coats, their deft hands selecting the necessary parts joining and sewing one small piece at a time. Judas moved round to watch them at their work, standing between them. Eloise grabbed Judas's tie and pulled him closer kissing his lips; she crushed her breasts against his chest as her tongue gently teased his. "You know, if you were a little more available all this wouldn't be necessary!" she said. "Are you sure that you won't reconsider?" She patted his bottom.

"You know that I wish I could," he said, teasing at her left nipple. "But the mission must come first; nothing must take me from that path! No pleasure, whether it be of the flesh or of the narcotic, must tempt my feet from the path!"

Liv's hand grabbed at his swelling cock, caressing it through the rough tweed of his trousers. "Well how about making a donation to the project? There is one bit that I would quite like!" she giggled. The white coat had several buttons unclasped, showing birthday and Christmas presents to best effect. "Hey! Unfair!" cried Eloise, pushing Liv's had aside, and taking its place. "If anyone gets it, it should be me! And those won't tempt him," she teased, stroking a finger along Liv's cleavage, "mine are far nicer and all natural!" Her white (but blood-spattered) coat had been more demurely buttoned, but she now loosened several of these.

Judas extracted himself from between them, "now, now, girls, focus yourselves on your work! You'll soon forget about me when that is completed! It will not be long now, looking at your progress." He moved off towards the door, saying "I had better be off to collect the artefacts that I need for this stage of my mission." He was not sure that they had heard him, though: Eloise and Liv were now kissing each other passionately; Liv's coat was on the floor in a crumpled red and white heap; Eloise's fully undone and pulled back off the shoulder. Judas let the door swing back as he headed off towards Le Louvre. Perhaps when he had finished there he might just pop back, he thought.

A gentle drizzle fell from the dark and brooding sky. Normally not heavy enough for anything other than minor irritation, but it had been drizzling like this almost solidly for three weeks. The bottom of the trench now had a permanent carpet of water; only an inch or two deep, but slowly it had penetrated his boots, which were now sodden. He had not removed the boots for the last four weeks; the intense itching had started a week ago, and told him what he would find if he was to remove them. There were only a very few that were not suffering from trench foot, but that was the least of their worries. Around Judas the steady crump of artillery fire was the constant background noise; replaced in his ears with a continual ringing when it occasionally stopped.

The only colour to be seen was brown: the dull brown of the mud; the dirty brown of their uniforms; the dirty brown of their unwashed skin. One of the shells landed nearby; a rain of brown mud descended upon them. Such events had long ago ceased to alarm Judas: it was just what happened; he could not remember a time when it did not. A distant groaning was carried to his ears by the wind: a few more colleagues lost.

Today, they were going to try to capture a few more feet of ground, to recapture the trench that they had surrendered some four weeks back. That same trench had exchanged hands at least six times since Judas had arrived. The artillery fire originating from behind them suddenly ceased; he knew what this meant. Automatically he checked his .303; he had seventeen bullets left. He would be third up the ladder. At the piercing whistle they began the hurried climb; by the time that he reached the top, the two that had preceded him lay dead or dying inches from the top of the ladder. Judas crouched and ran forward screaming; fear or battle cry, the difference was lost on them all now. He had made many yards of progress when he suddenly fell to the ground; he thought that he must have barked his shin on something jutting from the ground: a sharp pain had knocked his leg backward and he was face down in the mud. Looking down he saw a new colour: red. Slowly through the stinging pain the truth revealed itself: a small hole in the front of his trousers, a much larger, gaping hole to the back. He knew that his leg would look the same underneath, the small entry hole of the bullet at the front; the ruined skin at the back where bullet and splintered bone had exited.

The room itself was entirely spherical; the walls (or were they the floor?) were coloured a light pink, they yielded slightly to the touch. Judas could feel little effect of gravity; it felt almost as though he was swimming, so he was unsure if he walked around the room, or if the room rotated beneath his feet. He was dressed in a close-fitting suit; a thin tube ran from it to one of the floor/walls; it provided all the sustenance he needed.

But it wasn't the location that was important, it was the work before him: the conference would be held a mere 3,234 chronosytes from today and there was much to do. He had his full report to make; the Men-I-Mem had said he may choose the method of presentation. Around him, nestled against the walls/floor, were his information sources: the sum of all his research. Each individual study was held within its container, a rich viscous liquid: the data pool. The containers came in a myriad of sizes, but in basic shape there were only four: circle, wave, triangle and square.

Looking at the data pools, Judas had a sinking feeling that some of them were missing (in addition to the work that he knew he had not done in the first place); worse still in some the data looked changed or corrupted from that which he remembered. Maybe it was his memory, rather, which never had been too good. For a brief while, he wondered if he would have to undertake some of the studies again. But

Time forbade it. He would have to fall back on bullshit and artifice, like so many times before; he was certain he could gloss over the gaps.

He stretched out a membrane covered hand and dipped his index finger into the first of the data pools; the electricity of its content raced up his arm to the appropriate compartment of his right lobe nestling into its place. Following the complex pattern of the ancients he moved from pool to pool: absorbing, storing, understanding, discovering. Occasionally Judas kicked out at the walls/floor in frustration when the data took longer to assimilate than he would have liked.

His eyes ran around the room, ensuring that all sources had been absorbed; although he knew that the dance of the ancients would have taken care of that. Nextly, he activated his mind's eye and scanned across the contents; everything was neatly in place, although the gaps confirmed his fears of missing information. And then several things happened at once: as he twisted within the chamber the nutrient cord wrapped itself around his neck slowing the flow to his suit; the pattern formed by the node gaps burnt itself onto his memory, an answer in itself, but the shock of their revelation came close to paralysing him; the walls of the room convulsed, contracted; the exit (hidden until now) appeared, dilated; he began to feel gravity taking hold once more. And then all was black.

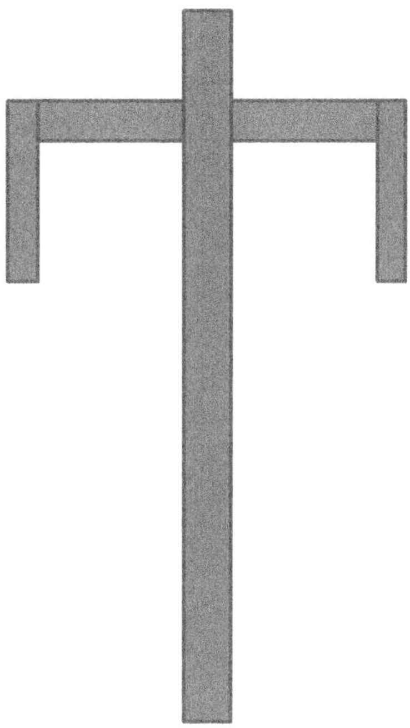

Warm golden sunlight was creeping its way between the slats of the blind; tiny motes of dust danced in reverent welcome of the dawn. Summer had arrived early this year; it was only May, yet the days were hot, the skies blue, the gardens radiant.

Judas threw back the covers and stepped out of bed; he stretched, his arms high and wide in welcome of the dawn. He hummed a simple melody as he opened the blinds; the view over the lush meadows never ceased to delight him. In some crops swayed in the light breeze, in others sheep grazed; he saw a lone hare streak across one of the fields, leaping amidst the buttercups and daisies. Today was going to be a good day. He knew that it was an important one; he had much to achieve. But everything that he needed was in place: his notes neatly stacked on the table, the reports all but completed, the pictures done. He knew how important this work was – the big meeting was to be held next week; a meeting long anticipated. He had no doubt that his work would shine; his work would ruffle the feathers of his eleven peers, but no matter: this was the crucial time.

Breakfast first, he thought. A spring in his step he descended to the kitchen where he carved two thick slices of soft granary bread spreading them generously with creamy butter and pale golden honey. Already the presentation was taking shape in his mind's eye; he knew the one that he had to impress and what he would look for. His colleagues

did too; but he had an edge, that one piece of crucial information recently discovered!

Breakfast over and cleared away, ablutions completed, he sat down at his computer and leaned forward to turn

Warm golden sunlight was creeping its way between the pastel striped curtains; tiny motes of dust danced in reverent welcome of the dawn. Summer had arrived early this year; it was only May, yet the days were hot, the skies blue, the gardens radiant.

Judas threw back the covers and stepped out of bed; he stretched, his arms high and wide in welcome of the dawn. He hummed a simple melody as he opened the curtains; the view over the lush meadows never ceased to delight him. In some crops swayed in the light breeze, in others sheep grazed; he saw a lone hare streak across one of the fields, leaping amidst the buttercups and daisies. Today was going to be the very best of days. He knew that it was an important one; he had much to achieve. But everything that he needed was in place: his notes neatly stacked on the table, the reports all but completed, the pictures done. He knew how important this work was – the big meeting was soon to be held; a meeting long anticipated. He had no doubt that his work would shine; his work would ruffle the feathers of his eleven peers, but no matter: this was the crucial time.

Breakfast first, he thought. A spring in his step he descended to the kitchen where he carved two thick slices of soft granary bread spreading them generously with creamy butter and pale golden honey. Already the presentation was taking shape in his mind's eye; he knew the one that he had to impress and what he would look for. His colleagues did too; but he had an edge, that one piece of crucial information recently discovered!

Breakfast over and cleared away, ablutions completed, he sat down at his computer and leaned forward to turn

Warm golden sunlight was creeping its way between the slats of the blind; tiny motes of dust danced in reverent welcome of the dawn. Summer had arrived early this year; it was only May, yet the days were hot, the skies blue, the gardens radiant.

Judas threw back the covers and stepped out of bed; he stretched, his arms high and wide in welcome of the dawn. He hummed a complex melody as he opened the blinds; the view over the lush meadows never ceased to delight him. In some crops swayed in the light breeze, in others sheep grazed; he saw a lone hare streak across one of the fields, leaping amidst the buttercups and cow parsley. Today was going to be a good day. He knew that it was an important one; he had much to achieve. But everything that he needed was in place: his notes neatly stacked on the table, the reports all but completed, the graphs done. He knew how important this work was – the big meeting was soon to be held; a meeting long anticipated. He had no doubt that his work would shine; his work would ruffle the feathers of his eleven peers, but no matter: this was the crucial time.

Breakfast first, he thought. A spring in his step he descended to the kitchen where he carved two thick slices of soft white bread spreading them generously with creamy butter and pale golden honey. Already the presentation was taking shape in his mind's eye; he knew the one that he had to impress and what he would look for. His colleagues did too; but he had an edge, that one piece of crucial information recently discovered!

Breakfast over and cleared away, ablutions completed, he sat down at his computer and leaned forward to turn

Warm golden sunlight was creeping its way between the slats of the blind; tiny motes of dust danced in reverent welcome of the dawn. Summer had arrived early this year; it was only May, yet the days were hot, the skies blue, the gardens radiant.

Judas threw back the covers and stepped from his futon; he stretched, his arms high and wide in welcome of the dawn. He hummed a simple melody as he opened the blinds; the view over the lush pastures never ceased to delight him. In some crops swayed in the light breeze, in others sheep grazed; he saw a lone hare streak across one of the fields, leaping amidst the buttercups and daisies. Today was going to be a good day. He knew that it was an important one; he had much to achieve. But everything that he needed was in place: his notes neatly stacked on the table, the reports all but completed, the videos done. He knew how important this work was – the big meeting was soon to be held; a meeting long anticipated. He had no doubt that his work would shine; his work would ruffle the feathers of his eleven peers, but no matter: this was the crucial time.

Breakfast first, he thought. A spring in his step he descended to the kitchen where he carved two thick slices of soft granary bread spreading them generously with creamy butter and dark, bitter, marmalade. Already the presentation was taking shape in his mind's eye; he knew the one that he had to impress and what he would look for. His colleagues did too; but he had an edge, that one piece of crucial information recently discovered!

Breakfast over and cleared away, ablutions completed, he sat down at his computer and leaned forward to turn

Warm golden sunlight was creeping its way between the chintz of the curtains; tiny motes of dust danced in reverent welcome of the dawn. Summer had arrived early this year; it was only May, yet the days were hot, the skies blue, the gardens radiant.

Judas threw back the quilt and stepped out of bed; he stretched, his arms high and wide in welcome of the dawn. He hummed a complex melody as he opened the curtains; the view over the lush meadows never ceased to delight him. In some crops swayed in the light breeze, in others sheep grazed; he saw a lone hare streak across one of the fields, leaping amidst the buttercups and daisies. Today was going to be a good day. He knew that it was an important one; he had much to achieve. But everything that he needed was in place: his notes neatly stacked on the table, the reports all but completed, the pictures done. He knew how vital this work was – the big meeting was soon to be held; a meeting long anticipated. He had no doubt that his work would shine; his work would ruffle the feathers of his eleven peers, but no matter: this was the crucial time.

Breakfast first, he thought. A spring in his step he descended to the kitchen where he carved two thick slices of sourdough bread, toasting them, and then spreading them generously with creamy butter and pale golden honey. Already the presentation was taking shape in his mind's eye; he knew the one that he had to impress and what he would look for. His colleagues did too; but he had an edge, that one piece of crucial information recently discovered!

Breakfast over and cleared away, ablutions completed, he sat down at his computer and leaned forward to turn

His own personal triumvirate stood before him: Doubt, Despair and Desolation. Doubt was the first to assail him, the blow was full of power, but easily deflected; twisting right he blocked with both forearms, pushing the strike wide.

The blow had been intended only to measure and test. Doubt and Despair continued to circle him; for now, Desolation stood to one side chin cupped between forefinger and thumb: observing.

Despair stood before him, now, a huge club in his hand: iron-shod ebony, studded with bronze. Judas took a step toward him, a lover heading for embrace. Despair beat down upon him with a rain of blows...

Before him on the black obsidian table rested all the objects of power; he had finally collected them all. The sword, gleaming silver with just a hint of bronze; broken, of course, into three shards, awaiting its grand re-forging. The ring, rune carved inside and out; its surfaces angular, black, reflecting nothing of the guttering torches. The crystal, multi-faceted, clear, apart from the spark that glowed and writhed at its very core; trapped within. The chalice, carved from a single ruby by some lost art, filled with a viscous liquid of a darker red; the surface agitated, a miniature ocean. The wand, the thinnest switch of straightened ancient oak, plaited with elder and holly; bound with silver at base and middle, silver capped at its top; humming quietly to itself.

He remembered the instruction that had set him on the path to their discovery: “You must travel to the seven corners of the world and recover the treasures that are missing. Each singly is without power; jointly they are as nowt, only when the seven are together can we have hope.” “The corners of the earth”, he queried, “I thought it long proven that the world wasn't flat?” The slap was unexpected and stinging. "Dolt! Believe nothing until its veracity is beyond all doubt!"

Judas asked the nature of the treasures, in reply he was told: "each is different, each is disguised, like, and yet unalike, to a jigsaw; together they are whole separate they are as dust. In this quest you must not fail. Of all the Twelve, only you can possibly succeed. The distractions will be many, and of these some – but certainly not all – will be relevant and indeed revealing."

And now, after all that searching, Doubt, Despair and Desolation sought to take them from him. He would not let them. This was one fight that he had to win; that was easier said than done, they were strong, and they coordinated their efforts.

Hazy golden sunlight was creeping its way between the slats of the blind; tiny motes of dust danced in reverent welcome of the dawn. Summer had arrived early this year; it was only May, yet the days were hot, the skies blue, the gardens radiant.

Judas threw back the covers and stepped out of bed; the water-filled mattress undulated slightly; he stretched, his arms high and wide in welcome of the dawn. He hummed a simple melody as he opened the blinds; the view over the lush meadows never ceased to delight him. In some crops swayed in the light breeze, in others sheep grazed; he saw a lone hare streak across one of the fields, leaping amidst the buttercups and daisies. Today was going to be a good day. He knew that it was an important one; he had much to achieve. But everything that he needed was in place: his notes neatly placed within folders on the table, the reports all but completed, the graphics done. He knew how important this work was – the big meeting was soon to be held; a meeting long anticipated. He had no doubt that his work would shine; his work would ruffle the feathers of his eleven peers, but no matter: this was the crucial time.

Breakfast first, he thought. A spring in his step he descended to the kitchen where he carved two thick slices of soft walnut bread spreading them generously with creamy butter and deep golden honey. Already the presentation was taking shape in his mind's eye; he knew the one that he had to impress and what he would look for. His colleagues did too; but he had an edge, that one piece of crucial information recently discovered!

Breakfast over and cleared away, ablutions completed, he sat down at his computer and leaned forward to turn

Vague, watery sunlight to prise its way between the slats of the blind; tiny motes of dust danced in the light, somewhat illumed by the dawn. Summer was late this year; it was already May, yet the days were cold, the skies grey, water-logged, the gardens water-logged too.

Judas threw back the quilt and reluctantly stepped out of bed; he stretched, his arms high and wide in trying to welcome the dawn. He hummed a simple melody as he opened the blinds, but the tune would not come; the view over the damp meadows had long ago ceased to delight him. In some crops swayed in the light breeze, though they had been beaten by the rains; in others sheep sought shelter by the hedges; he saw a lone hare streak across one of the fields, leaping splashing amidst the puddles. Never mind, he thought, today was going to be a good day. He knew that it was an important day; he had much to achieve. But everything that he needed was in place: his notes neatly stacked on the table, the reports all but completed, the pictures, the videos, the graphics, done. He knew how important this work was – the big meeting was soon to be held; a meeting long anticipated. He had no doubt that his work would shine; his work would ruffle the feathers of his eleven peers, but no matter: this was the crucial time.

Breakfast first, he thought. A spring in his step he descended to the kitchen where he reached down his large frying pan, which soon had sausages, eggs, bacon, tomatoes and mushrooms bubbling in the hot lard; he added bread to fry, which soaked up the fat like a sponge. Already the presentation was taking shape in his mind's eye; he knew the one that he had to impress and what he would look for. His colleagues did too; but he had an edge, that one piece of crucial information recently discovered!

Breakfast over and cleared away, ablutions completed, he sat down at his computer and leaned forward to turn

Warm golden sunlight was creeping its way between the slats of the blind; tiny motes of dust danced in reverent welcome of the dawn. Summer had arrived early this year; it was only May, yet the days were hot, the skies blue, the gardens radiant.

Judas threw back the covers and stepped out of bed; he stretched, his arms high and wide in welcome of the dawn. He hummed a simple melody as he opened the blinds; the view over the lush meadows never ceased to delight him. In some crops swayed in the light breeze, in others sheep grazed; he saw a pair of rabbits streak across one of the fields, leaping amidst the buttercups and daisies. Today was going to be a good day. He knew that it was an important one; he had much to achieve. But, he was struggling to remember what it was that he had to do. A report? An assassination? He looked enquiringly at his table, at the notes neatly stacked on it; but they yielded no clue. There was a pile of pictures; he stared blankly at them; the images rang no bells. He knew how important this work was – he just couldn't remember what the work was! Was there a big meeting? One that was soon to be held; a meeting long anticipated? He was filled with doubt; worried that his work would not shine; would his work ruffle the feathers of his eleven peers? No matter, he was sure it would come to him eventually: this was the crucial time.

Breakfast first, he thought, maybe that will open my mind. Slothfully, he descended to the kitchen where he carved two thick slices of stale bread spreading them thinly with cheap margarine and something red from a jar in his fridge. The presentation would not take shape in his mind's eye; maybe he could just throw words onto a page, bring them to life with animations? Would that mask his lack of insight?. He knew the one that he had to try to impress and what he would look for. His colleagues did too; he had had an edge, that one piece of crucial information recently discovered! But now that was lost.

Breakfast over and cleared away, ablutions completed, round-shouldered, he sat down at his computer and leaned forward to turn

The lights in the hall had been dimmed in an effort to add atmosphere; the six spotlights that were dotted around the rooms, their lenses coated alternately in green and red gels, spilled their garish light upon the walls. A chain of flashing white LEDs was strung unevenly across the lip at the front of the stage. Across the door a banner had been hung, created by the art group, it proclaimed: End of Year Promminade. The art was beautiful; the spelling less so. Along the left side of the hall, by the curtained-off windows, the girls stood in groups of five or six, chatting quietly. On the right hung the boys, in slightly larger groups, speaking in much louder tones, laughing coarsely. Occasionally they would glance across at the girls, some of them leering.

Back stage, the band were getting ready to go on; Judas took his turn at the mirror, brushing imaginary fluff from his white tuxedo, straightening his purple bowtie. His hair was pulled back into a rough ponytail. He pulled his guitar strap over his head; the guitar (an imitation Stratocaster) was slung low on his hip. Gim, the base player, plucked idly at his strings; his guitar was as out of tune as Judas's, but neither of them knew how to tune them properly. Terry twirled one of his drumsticks, before it spun out of his fingers and dropped to the floor; hastily he retrieved it.

It was time. The band strode onto the stage, to short and none-too rapturous applause. Judas stepped up to the mike, “Er, hi everyone, we are The Sheep-Wolves. Hope you enjoy the show.” They launched, almost at the same time, into their first number, a standard pop classic of the day: all minor chords and twee vocals (Judas and Gim did their best to harmonise). Some of the girls took a small step closer to the dance floor, starting to sway their hips just a little; the boys had hardly moved, they carried on talking as though the band hadn’t even started – Judas could hear them above the sound of the painfully quiet PA.

By the third number, one small group of girls had finally made it onto the dance floor; they tried to coordinate their hips and arms as they jiggled to the music. And now Judas could see Rachel; she was almost on the dance floor. He could see her long, flowing, pink dress; it was made of faux-silk. But it hung so well on her that it could have been hand-weaved from the finest silk in the world. Behind the curtains, the sun had finally sunk below the horizon darkening the room a little more; almost creating a bit of atmosphere (if it wasn’t for the overhead lights).

The group brought their fifth number to a close. It was time. Now he’d make Rachel take notice of him! Of course, he hadn’t told the others what his real reasons where, “Let’s fuck up the straights!” he’d declared, just before the show had started. The other two had sniggered and agreed.

Judas sauntered to the side of the stage and pushed the volume faders all the way up on the small, unmanned, mixing desk; for good measure he pushed the bass fader up too. He and Gim then yanked the volume on their amps up to ten. They were ready. Judas stepped in front of his amp and let the guitar start to feedback; it built from a hum to a shriek. Gim decided that he'd join in too; both amps started to judder, howl and scream. They sustained that for just a little longer before Judas moved back to the front of the stage, he crashed out an A, followed by a D, an E, another D before started the sequence again; he started to sing: "Wild thing, you make my heart sing...". When it got to the chorus, he fluffed the first Gsus4, but it didn't matter; there was still a whole wall of feedback to mask it. After the chorus, amidst ever growing feedback, he decided that it was time to out-Hendrix Hendrix, with a few Gs and Ds he launched into Star Spangled Banner; he went down, sliding on his knees, trying to throw in a bit of patriotism with God Save The King, but the A and B minors got the better of him, so he resorted to rubbing the neck of his guitar against his mike stand in a deeply suggestive (as he saw it) way. It won't be long now he thought, and Rachel will be rushing to the front of the stage, looking up at me, eyes' glowing!

But then suddenly the sound stopped, and the lights glared brightly as they were turned back to full. And there stood the Caretaker in the door, the Head behind him, all puffed up chest and outrage; both of them red in the face. But there was worse, much, much, worse. There was Rachel heading out of the door, her hands clasped firmly over her ears. In fact, the whole hall was fast emptying.

The show was over.

As he left the hall, his guitar case weighing on his left side he saw Gim in the shadows; he was snogging a girl. Judas couldn't be sure who it was, but from the brief glimpse of her profile, he could guess.

Wel, dwi erioed wedi meddwl llawer am y peth!

7

7

40

40

150

150

40

40

7

7

Warm golden sunlight was creeping its way between the slats of the blind; tiny motes of dust danced in reverent welcome of the dawn. Summer had arrived early this year; it was only May, yet the days were hot, the skies blue, the gardens radiant.

Judas threw back the covers and stepped out of bed; he stretched, his arms high and wide in welcome of the dawn. He hummed a simple melody as he opened the blinds; the view over the lush meadows never ceased to delight him. In some maize swayed in the light breeze, in others sheep grazed; he saw a lone hare streak across one of the fields, leaping amidst the buttercups and daisies. Today was going to be a good day. He knew that it was an important one; he had much to achieve. But everything that he needed was in place: his notes neatly stacked on the table, the reports all but completed, the pictures done. He knew how important this work was – the big meeting was soon to be held; a meeting long anticipated. He had no doubt that his work would shine; his work would ruffle the feathers of his eleven peers, but no matter: this was the crucial time.

Breakfast first, he thought. A spring in his step he descended to the kitchen where he carved two thick slices of soft granary bread spreading them generously with creamy butter and pale golden honey. Already the presentation was taking shape in his mind's eye; he knew the one that he had to impress and what he would look for. His colleagues

did too; but he had an edge, that one piece of crucial information recently discovered! This was his last chance.

Breakfast over and cleared away, ablutions completed, he sat down at his computer and leaned forward to turn

The room was dim, a single light bulb crusted with grime the only source of illumination; it flickered continuously giving the effect that the room was lit by candlelight. Dust covered every surface; the diligent work of an army of spiders bedecked the room. The door closed behind him with a final grind of the rusty hinges, and a click of the lock-catch.

It was a long time since he had been here; it seemed that his secret remained safe: the floor had not been walked on for many a long while. All four walls of the room were shelved, from ceiling to floor, every shelf was crammed with books, papers and manuscripts; on the floor were boxes that he knew contained magazines, their content apparently innocently salacious. Most of the books, he knew, were decoys; not even very well reproduced copies of the originals, their words subtly changed here and there. But to the normal reader no change would be discerned.

Only one of the shelves contained genuine books. Judas walked to it now, a light sprinkling of magic ensured that the dust on the floor remained undisturbed. He looked along the shelf, nostalgia, and habit, almost had him picking up a volume with a deep red leather cover. But Judas passed on by, perhaps when his work was done, he could return.

He came to the end of the shelf and looked back, puzzled: the book that he sought was not there. Hurriedly he retraced his footsteps. It was not there.

Definitely missing. The lack was obvious, the books remained in their sequence making its absence all the more noticeable. Rapidly he scanned shelf after shelf around the room, he could see nothing genuine. In mounting panic, he had even lifted some of them from their place on the shelves and scanned their contents. They remained false, as he knew they would.

Once more he walked along the length of the real bookshelf, mentally noting each publication: Aristotle And The Acausal Cosmic Being, Genetic Sleuths Follow Clues To Elusive Ancestral 'Adam', Against The Theory Of Autodynamics, Ancient Indian Aircraft Technology, Another Space-Time Perspective, The Collapse Of The Antarctic Ice Sheet, Ueber Antimaterie, Binary Perception: The Tiger Of Consciousness, Diskussion Ber Bioresonanz, Ueber Die Entstehung Von Blitze, How The Brain Works / How To Understand Reality, A Case Of Professional Hysteria On The Velikowski Manuscript, The Covariant Theory. (Time), What Is DHA? (Docosahexaenioc Acid), Eclipse / Alignment Update, The Orgone Accumulator, On The Scientific Concept Of Entropy, Evolutionists Disproven, Full Moon Peak Portends Stock Crash, World Crisis? Astroharmonic & Technical Analysis, Fundamentals Of Quantum Mechanics And Relativity, About The Future Of Physics: The Sustaining Myth, The Tale of Woe, Was Ist Gentechnologie, The Holographic Universe; Physics Mysticism, How To Construct A

Time Machine, Get Laid Newsletter, Issue 11: with Speed Seduction Editorial, A Rhapsody of Dreams, Levitation: It Is Very Simple, 'The Merlin Project': Time Pattern Research, The Neurophone: Electronic Telepathy, The Exact Nature Of The Catastrophe, Proving Morphic Fields, An Introduction To A New Geometrical Physics, Particles & Waves : Wholes & Aspects, From Ordinary Beginnings, Gravity Theory: The Physics Of The Parallel World, Photonic Mass A Definitive Exposition, PSI In Der Sovjetunion, Pyramid Energy: The Answer, Why There Must Be Antiparticles. (Quantum- Mechanics), ,
Do Quanta Have Mass?, Scientists Reconsider Life On Mars, Scientific Dissertation On Shadows, Snowflake Symmetry Explained, Social Toxicity Showing Effects In Children, Science Discovers The Soul, The Speed Of Light, The Speed of Sight, Synopsis: The Tarn Of Eternity, The Power of Love, Nikola Tesla's Wireless Power Transmitter, Why Does The Universe Exist?, Vector Particle Physics, VELIKOVSKI: The Mythological Evidence: Comets And Poem Of Erra, The Voynich Manuscript. The Most Mysterious Manuscript In The World, The Enigma Of The Atomic Tornadoes, Yin Yang And Particles. Magic Or Mechanics?, Fragments Of Behaviour: The Extensional Stance, Our Distant Future Leviathan,

Would he have to burn them all? For the time being he could think of no alternative. Judas slumped into a faded leather armchair; it might once have been a deep burgundy colour, with lustrous polished mahogany, now it was only grey. A huge cloud of dust rose, obscuring everything from Judas's view; or that might just have been the tears in his eyes.

Sometime later the idea came to him; it took even more time to remember the Replay Time spell. Finally, it came to him, and he muttered a few simple words. At first, nothing seemed to happen, but then spiders could be seen moving backwards, unpicking their myriad webs. Judas gave a subtle hand movement and the spiders moved faster; the dust got a little lighter. For many hours – it was hard to measure time, when time was running backwards around you – nothing else was seen. But then suddenly a figure appeared by the bookshelf. Judas slowed the replay and watched. Several times he ran time back on forth: she entered the room, went straight to the shelf, straight to the right spot, lifted down the book and clutched it to her. She looked around as though she felt watched. Then she was moving to another chair (briefly, Judas wondered what would have happened had she chose the chair in which he was sat). The book had already left grimy marks on her white dress, the chair left many more.

She opened the book and started to read, flicking hurriedly through the pages, occasionally slowing to read some parts in depth. Her breathing had become deeper; several times her lips parted, and her tiny pink tongue licked at the darker pink of her lipstick. As she turned the last page, her eyes shut briefly, and then she was on her feet and walking back towards the door. At the door, she uttered a single word; her dress was pristine once more, the library undisturbed.

As the door closed, Judas let out a howl of rage. He had recognised her instantly. He knew who she was. He knew where to find her. And he knew what he would have to do, to sacrifice, to get the book back. The thought repulsed him, but his only other choice was arson, or liberticide.

It was warm, even for early spring. Birdsong filled the air adding to the warmth; as did the aroma of the roses – his wife's pride and joy. Waving a last farewell, Judas turned again towards his front gate; he was looking sharp in pinstripes. Entering Acacia Avenue, he turned left for the short walk to the station. A smile of pleasure touched his lips as he stopped to stroke next door's cat for a moment or two. The cat stared after him as he carried on; clearly the petting had not been enough. Judas whistled silently to himself, nodding in greeting to friends and neighbours.

Picking up his morning paper, The Times, of course, and a coffee Judas strolled to his spot on the platform. The train arrived on time; Judas settled into his seat for the short journey to town; there was just enough time to complete the crossword.

A further walk through the sunshine, un-hurried, and un-jostled, brought Judas to his office, a towering block, beautiful in its modern architecture. With cheery greeting he bypassed security and headed for the third floor. Settling into his desk, with the second coffee of the day, he started to check e-mails: nothing too urgent had come in.

Judas's attention was drawn to the door as it opened, his boss, one of the firm's directors entered through it and came to sit down opposite Judas. Judas felt a brief moment of panic: was there a problem with the report that he had submitted yesterday. He had worked long and hard on it, in the office and at home; he was sure that there could not have been a problem.

"Morning J!" his boss intoned in his deep baritone. Despite being in his fifties, he remained slim and handsome; he had a full head of hair, albeit greying now – unofficially, he was known as The Silver Fox around the office.

"Morning JC!" Judas replied. The use of initials was the office's compromise between the formality of yesteryear, and the relaxed approach of the day. There had always been a sense of fun in that they were both J.

"And how are you today, J?" asked JC. "And Mrs I, is she well? It must only be a few weeks now until that second child of yours pops into the world?"

"Three weeks, two days, and counting! And yes, we are both well, thank you."

They exchanged a few more pleasantries, before JC turned to the matter in hand: "J, about that report that you presented yesterday."

"Yes?" replied Judas, with the slightest of stomach flutters.

"Damn fine piece of work! Excuse the French! I am deeply impressed; you have clearly put a huge amount of time and effort into it. I showed it to the Main Man: G was very impressed with it too. G and I were talking; you know that we have a place upstairs for a new Director Designate? We were talking about advertising the post soon".

Judas nodded, "I had thought of applying," he said, quietly. JC's eyebrows shot up: "Really! I wouldn't bother." For the third time since JC had entered the room, Judas experienced that slight sinking feeling. JC carried on, "No, as I say, I wouldn't bother. We are not going to advertise it." There was a long pause, and then JC broke into a broad grin: "No, we are not going to advertise it because the job is yours!"

Judas sat unmoving for a moment, his face portrayed perfectly his feelings: a mix of shock and elation, "The job is mine?" He still could not quite believe it.

"It is, with immediate effect. You are moving on up to the top floor; I will have your new secretary come down to arrange the move. Afraid you are going to have to have a vastly increased salary, old chap. Do you think that there will be room for a child seat or two in a Mercedes D?" JC extended his hand and shook Judas's warmly, "Welcome to the club old man!"

JC strolled to the door, just as he was leaving Judas asked: "do you mind if I telephone my w…., Mrs I and give her the good news?"

"Of course not, J! And no need to ask in future, you are one of us now. Enjoy!"

As the door closed behind him, Judas was already dialling the number, "darling, you know that house on the edge of the village that you wished that you could move to, but which we just could not afford ………."

WHAT?

Warm golden sunlight was creeping its way between the slats of the blind; tiny motes of dust danced in reverent welcome of the dawn. Summer had arrived early this year; it was only May, yet the days were hot, the skies blue, the gardens radiant.

Judas threw back the covers and stepped out of bed; he stretched, his arms high and wide in welcome of the dawn. He hummed a simple melody as he opened the blinds; the view over the lush meadows never ceased to delight him. In some crops swayed in the light breeze, in others sheep grazed; he saw a lone hare streak across one of the fields, leaping amidst the buttercups and daisies. Today was going to be a good day. He knew that it was an important one; he had much to achieve. But everything that he needed was in place: his notes neatly stacked on the table, the reports all but completed, the pictures done. He knew how important this work was – the big meeting was soon to be held; a meeting long anticipated. He had no doubt that his work would shine; his work would ruffle the feathers of his eleven peers but no matter: this was the crucial time.

Breakfast first, he thought. A spring in his step he descended to the kitchen where he carved two thick slices of soft granary bread spreading them generously with creamy butter and pale golden honey. Already the presentation was taking shape in his mind's eye; he knew the one that he had to impress and what he would look for. His colleagues

did too; but he had an edge, that one piece of crucial information recently discovered!

He did not clear away the breakfast, or wash, he just sat straight down at his computer and leaned forward to turn

He laughed. And he laughed. And he laughed. Until the tears were rolling down his cheeks. "So," he began, but then another fit of laughter took him and he doubled over in his chair.

"So, let me see... ..." more laughter "if I've got this straight?" He wiped his eyes with a tissue from the box on the table. "Your theory... ha-ha-ha-ha... of cre... ha-ha-ha-ha-ha-ha ...ation is this: in the sea, there was all this salt-water-stuff-soup sloshing about? And then that salt water soup... ha-ha-ha-ha-ha-ha-ha-ha-ha-ha-ha-ha-ha-ha-ha-ha-ha-ha-ha-ha-ha-ha-ha-ha ...was hit by lightning. And that made... ... what did you call them? Amoebas? And then a bit later, those amoebas swam out of the sea, and... ha-ha-ha-ha-ha-ha-ha-ha-ha-ha-ha-ha-ha-ha-ha-ha-ha-ha-ha-ha-ha-ha-ha-ha-ha-ha-ha-ha-ha-ha-ha-ha-ha-ha-ha-ha-ha-ha-ha-ha-ha-ha-ha-ha-ha-ha-ha-ha-ha-ha-ha-ha-ha-ha-ha-ha-ha-ha-ha-ha-ha-ha-ha-ha-ha-ha-ha-ha-ha-ha-ha-ha-ha-ha-ha-ha-ha-ha-ha-ha-ha-ha-ha-ha-ha-ha-ha-ha-ha-ha-ha-ha ...crawled onto the beach. And then they were hit by lightning again?

"And then one of those amoebas decided to grow fur and bones and guts and an aortic system, and start breathing, and become an animal? And then after a bit more time, some of them decided to lose most of their fur and learn to talk?

“And then a different one thought it would do the heart and lungs and bones thing, but grow feathers and start to fly?

“ha-ha-ha-ha-ha-ha-ha-ha-ha-ha-ha-ha-ha-ha-ha-
ha-ha-ha-ha-ha-ha-ha-ha-ha-ha-ha-ha-ha-ha-ha-
ha-ha-ha-ha-ha-ha-ha-ha-ha-ha-ha-ha-ha-ha-ha-
ha-ha-ha-ha-ha-ha-ha-ha-ha-ha-ha-ha-ha-ha-ha-
ha-ha-ha-ha-ha-ha-ha-ha-ha-ha-ha-ha-ha-ha-ha-
ha-ha-ha-ha-ha-ha-ha-ha-ha-ha-ha-ha-ha-ha-ha-
ha-ha-ha-ha-ha-ha-ha-ha-ha-ha-ha-ha-ha-ha-ha-
ha-ha-ha-ha-ha-ha-ha-ha-ha-ha-ha-ha-ha-ha-ha-
ha-ha-ha-ha-ha-ha-ha-ha-ha-ha-ha-ha-ha-ha-ha-
ha-ha-ha-ha-ha-ha-ha-ha-ha-ha-ha-ha-ha-ha-ha-
ha-ha-ha-ha-ha-ha-ha-ha-ha-ha-ha-ha-ha-ha-ha-
ha-ha-ha-ha-ha-ha-ha-ha-ha-ha-ha-ha-ha-ha-ha-
ha-ha-ha-ha...

“But one of them said, ‘bugger this for a game of soldiers, I’m going back into the sea, and I’m going to grow scales and swim about a bit’? And that’s your theory?

I’ve never heard anything so preposterous! Why would you even think that? Surely the truth is far more believable?

“Oh wait, I forgot one group, did some of those fish turn round and swim back out of the sea, firm up their scales a bit and become reptiles?

"ha-ha-ha-ha-ha-ha-ha-ha-ha-ha-ha-ha-ha-ha-ha-
ha-ha-ha-ha-ha-ha-ha-ha-ha-ha-ha-ha-ha-ha-ha-
ha-ha-ha-ha-ha-ha-ha-ha-ha-ha-ha-ha-ha-ha-ha-
ha-ha-ha-ha-ha-ha-ha-ha-ha-ha-ha-ha-ha-ha-ha-
ha-ha-ha-ha-ha-ha-ha-ha-ha-ha-ha-ha-ha-ha-ha-
ha-ha-ha-ha-ha-ha-ha-ha-ha-ha-ha-ha-ha-ha-ha-
ha-ha-ha-ha-ha-ha-ha-ha-ha-ha-ha-ha-ha-ha-ha-
ha-ha-ha-ha-ha-ha-ha-ha-ha-ha-ha-ha-ha-ha-ha-
ha-ha-ha-ha-ha-ha-ha-ha-ha-ha-ha-ha-ha-ha-ha-
ha-ha-ha-ha-ha-ha-ha-ha-ha-ha-ha-ha-ha-ha-ha-
ha-ha-ha-ha-ha-ha-ha-ha-ha-ha-ha-ha-ha-ha-ha-
ha-ha-ha-ha-ha-ha-ha-ha-ha-ha-ha-ha-ha-ha-ha-
ha-ha-ha-ha-ha-ha-ha-ha-ha-ha-ha-ha-ha-ha-ha-
ha-ha-ha-ha-ha-ha-ha-ha-ha-ha-ha-ha-ha-ha-ha-
ha-ha-ha-ha-ha-ha-ha-ha-ha-ha-ha-ha-ha-ha-ha-
ha-ha-ha-ha-ha-ha-ha-ha-ha-ha-ha-ha-ha-ha-ha-
ha-ha-ha-ha-ha-ha-ha-ha-ha-ha-ha-ha-ha-ha-ha-
ha-ha-ha-ha-ha-ha-ha-ha-ha-ha-ha-ha-ha-ha-ha-
ha-ha-ha-ha-ha-ha-ha-ha-ha-ha-ha-ha-ha-ha-ha-
ha-ha-ha-ha-ha-ha-ha-ha-ha-ha-ha-ha-ha-ha-ha-
ha-ha-ha-ha-ha-ha-ha-ha-ha-ha-ha-ha-ha-ha-ha-
ha-ha-ha-ha-ha-ha-ha-ha-ha-ha-ha-ha-ha-ha-ha-
ha-ha-ha-ha-ha-ha-ha-ha-ha-ha-ha-ha-ha-ha-ha-
ha-ha-ha-ha-ha-ha-ha-ha-ha-ha-ha-ha-ha-ha-ha-
ha-ha-ha-ha-ha-ha-ha-ha-ha-ha-ha-ha-ha-ha-ha-
ha-ha-ha-ha-ha-ha-ha-ha-ha-ha-ha-ha-ha-ha-ha-
ha-ha-ha-ha-ha-ha-ha-ha-ha-ha-ha-ha-ha-ha-ha-
ha-ha-ha-ha-ha-ha-ha-ha-ha-ha-ha-ha-ha-ha-ha-
ha-ha-ha-ha-ha-ha-ha-ha-ha-ha-ha-ha-ha-ha-ha-
ha-ha-ha-ha-ha-ha-ha-ha-ha-ha-ha-ha-ha-ha-ha-
ha-ha-ha-ha-ha-ha-ha-ha-ha-ha-ha-ha-ha-ha-ha"

On the horizon, a dark speck moves towards us along the narrow ribbon of grey tarmac.

In the foreground, there is a bulkier, but indistinct, object, blurred by our focus on the approaching speck.

As the speck moves closer, we can see that it is a person.

Closer still, and now we can see some little detail of the person: clad from head to toe in black leather; a helmet with dark black visor encases the head, so no features can be seen.

The figure is asexual.

Now that the speck is closer to us, and has taken form, we can focus on the object in the foreground.

It is a motorcycle.

At least, that is the closest description that we can think of; it is much like a motorcycle, but where the wheels should be: nothing.

Despite the lack of wheels, the bike hovers above the ground, almost as though the wheels are there, but invisible. We are reminded of the effect of a metal sphere held up by nothing more than magnetism.

The motorcycle, too, is black, bar three chromiumed pieces: tank, front forks, headlight.

It is a contradictory machine, at once both futuristic, whilst also traditional, perhaps even primitive; the style: pure chopper.

We are dazzled by the chromium; it glares painfully, reflecting the bright orange disc of the sun.

Now the fellow and the bike are together; there is a pause, whilst the fellow appears to admire, and appraise the machine.

The moment is brief, and then a leather-clad leg is stretched over the machine; the rider settles onto the seat.

Strangely, for a machine so apparently ahead of its time, the rider flicks out a kick-start.

The machine fires on the second kick; where the wheels should be two whirling vortices appear, bizarrely moving in divergent directions.

We are, again, surprised by a very agricultural clunk, as the gearshift is depressed, once.

The rider twists the grip: black smoke and an acrid smell of burning rubber swoosh up from where the rear wheel should be.

Now, the rider drops the clutch; the front forks rear up; we are convinced that we see them paw the air: a stallion: rampant.

The machine is now speeding back down the highway.

We are drawn with it, as though we sit astride a movie camera, mounted on rails; or perhaps this is a film itself that we are watching?

From our vantage, we can just see the needle on the speedometer, it has just passed 95.

We are shocked, and perhaps troubled, when we see that 95 is not even a quarter of the way round the dial.

Keeping a steady grip on the throttle, our rider reaches up with their other hand, and releases the strap on their helmet.

The helmet is torn off, apparently by the windblast.

And our rider shakes out long blond hair; their sexuality now revealed.

A woman.

There is a fierce grin on her lips, which are full; they ripple somewhat in the wind; already prominent cheekbones are made more pronounced.

Now, she yanks savagely at the throttle; the front forks buck, and rear again.

The needle passes 175, passes 210.

The black leather of the rider's suit, already pulled taut by the wind, starts to split in places.

Not only do seams burst, the material itself splits, as though raked by the claws of some giant cat.

As the needle continues to rise, tiny bits of leather tear free, whipped away; carried for a while in the back draft, then dropped to the highway.

Whilst animal once, they are now useless carrion for the swiftly descending vultures.

We see them pick once at a scrap, but then soar back skyward; angry gods, not appeased by the offering.

280 miles per hour and a whole sleeve rips free.

290, and the corresponding trouser leg rips free.

300, and the front zip finally gives up. A shrug of the shoulders, and the remaining scraps of leather join the highway debris.

The rider's flesh is pale, but, strangely, seemingly unaffected by the incredible wind pressure.

Firm breasts stand proud, the nipples slightly erect; the stomach flat.

We see the rider crouch lower, and twist the throttle again.

Since the needle passed 350, from our vantage point we can no longer see the numbers that it indicates, just that it continues to rise.

Tiny toes press, flick up the gearshift, selecting even higher gearing.

The machine lurches again, lunging for the horizon.

We cannot focus on the scenery beyond our rider; it is simply long horizontal stripes of colour.

So far, there has been neither twist, nor bend, to the road; before us it stretches to convergence at the constantly moving horizon.

The rider rises slightly from the seat, and flicks at a switch on the left handlebar.

From the centre of the leather seat a black cylindrical shape rises.

The cylinder starts to move, slowly at first, but then starting to gather speed, as though seeking to match the rhythm of the engine cylinders themselves.

Our rider slowly sits back down, and the cylinder is swallowed from view.

Eyes now glazed somewhat, the rider takes a deep breath, leaning slightly forward, her breasts are now crushed to the petrol tank.

Her breathing is now faster and deeper, lips parted; she twists savagely at the throttle, raising the tempo of all the cylinders.

The motorcycle bucks and leaps; looks almost to writhe beneath the rider.

The speed continues to rise, and now, as its leather coating before it, the skin starts to shred, and fly free.

There is no blood.

Our vultures seem better pleased with this offering, greedily descending.

Great ragged breaths escape from the rider's parted lips, which are now curled into a smile.

The flesh, and muscle, continues to shred revealing white bone on arms and legs.

Now a ribcage is exposed, and shortly after the organs beneath it begin to tear free too.

The extra cylinder can still be seen rising and falling in the now hollow pelvic region.

Now all that is left, apart from bone, is the rapidly beating heart.

The rider makes one final twist of the throttle;

The front of the bike rears skyward again, and remains there;

A great gout of black smoke escapes the exhaust;

The heart finally tears free, shredding into a million slivers; now there is blood, gallons of it.

The blood coats the bones, the bike, the road.

We seem unable to keep up with this newest, most savage, of speeds; the bike diminishes toward the horizon.

Just at the point when the bike had become a small speck, and was about to vanish from vision, it started once more to grow larger before us.

The reason soon became clear; it was stopped, parked up at the side of the road.

As we draw rapidly nearer, our speed starts to decrease, until we come to a halt beside the bike, and rider.

All trace of blood is vanished; a gleaming white skeleton stands beside the bike, its own chromium blazing brightly.

A skeletal hand raises, and puts a cigarette to white jaws, its tip glows red.

We can see the smoke from the cigarette as it leaves the jaw cavity, to enter the ribcage, swirling about within it.

The skeletal jaws give the impression of wearing a fierce grin.

We now see gothic lettering on the bike's tank; from our vantage, it is hard to read.

There are two words, the first looks like Speed, although it could be Greed, or even Steed; the second word could be Thrills, although it could equally read Kills.

On the horizon, the sun is setting.

He could remember nothing that he did not love. The warm glow surrounded him, seeping in. Rachel was coming to visit, a day long expected; he had planned every aspect of it. The background music was plotted; the seating arranged just so. In the kitchen, Rachel's favourite food was cooking; Judas had done his research! The lighting was fixed, two low-watt standard lights, chromium and glass, gave a lift to the room; the remaining light came from a dozen or so candles, some subtly perfumed. A choice of wines was cooling in the 'fridge; nibbles and crudités sat in small bowls on the tables, dips alongside them.

Judas checked his reflection in the mirror for the forty-fifth time that evening.

Some seven hours later he was still sitting alone in his living room; he was beginning to think that she might not be coming. He called her mobile, but a man's voice – a voice he recognised – answered it. But it told him all he needed to know. She wouldn't be coming. He ended the call without speaking, hearing a familiar giggle in the background. Tears started to splash on his beautifully ironed shirt.

John struck flint to tinder, the pitch at the end of the torch caught and then flared up, conjuring six other faces out of the darkness of the night. The orange and charcoal faces were in a tight circle; around them the trunks of many trees could just be picked out, their black one shade removed from that of the night. As John lit other torches held by the group, their gnarled trunks stood out in greater relief. It was late autumn, and the trees had surrendered their leaves to the woodland floor to form a soft, rustling, carpet underfoot.

John looked around the grim faces; close by an owl hooted. As though the hoot were calling the meeting to order, and declare it open, John addressed the gathering in a hushed, but clear, whisper: "You know why we are here." It was a statement, not a question, although a number of heads nodded agreement. He carried on, "Tonight we hunt! We seek! We go a Soul Searching!" The words echoed around the group: Soul Searching.

"Have we anything registering?" asked John, looking at Peter. Around Peter's neck was a leathern thong, which he pulled out from his jerkin to reveal a small multi-faceted crystal. Judas moved closer to see it; he had never seen The Locator Diamond before; worth the price of several small countries, but to them, currently, beyond price. Peter held it up before him; at its centre a spec of black grew, and lengthened, to form a miniature arrow. At first the around pulsed around randomly, in all directions, but slowly it settled pointing off in a north-westerly direction.

The owl hooted again, and this time its cry signalled the start of a race: the group sped off in the direction indicated by the arrow, torches spluttering in the cool night breeze. Several times the group were forced to change direction, as the arrow shifted within the diamond. As they drew closer to their prey the arrow became more defined, blacker; it had been shot from the bow of righteousness, and it dragged the seven behind it in its wake.

"There!" cried Thomas, pointing to the fore, as the antlers of a stag appeared ahead of them, before they crossed a ridge and dipped down into the valley beyond. The group, too, crested the ridge, seeking to separate the outline of the antlers from the naked branches of the trees; the arrow drew them on. And then they sighted the stag again: a magnificent beast, many hands high. The stag turned to regard them before thundering off. "Faster!" cried John, "He mustn't outrun us!" Judas cursed under his breath, damn these eastern religions, and their beliefs about the soul: they were scarce enough these days, without willing them, believing them, into the animal kingdom, where they could be trapped forever, growing ever more atavistic by the day.

The group fanned out, and with a sudden spurt of energy, John and Simon flanked the stag to left and right. The stag halted, sensing its entrapment, and the group closed in. The stag lowered its head and pawed the ground, a challenge, daring them to approach. Broad chested Simon was, as ever, the first to rush in. The stag charged, Simon spun to the side, but not far enough, Judas heard Simon draw a sharp breath as one of the antlers pierced jerkin and flesh – a painful wound, but not mortal.

As the stag lowered its head to charge Simon again, four more dashed in, drawing ropes around the beast's legs and tumbling it to the ground. The beast continued to thrash, not yet resigned to its fate!

But now the ritual began in earnest: the ropes were made fast, just above the four cloven hooves; Simon, Judas, John, and Thomas each took a rope, as one they turned and ran to trees at four equidistant points: north, south, east and west. As one they passed anticlockwise around the trees and then ran back in the direction of the stag; as one the ropes pulled taught, followed by four simultaneous loud pops as the stag's joints dislocated, spread eagling the stag on the floor; the stag bellowed in pain.

Judas loathed intensely what they were doing; no matter how many times he told himself it was necessary, even knowing there was no other way, still he abhorred the task. He knew how he had been instructed: the ritual must fit with the period; a time and a place; there could be no compromise, or the soul would be truly lost. Now, in conjunction with the other three, he sank to his knees in prayer.

Much as he reviled his task, Judas was glad that tonight his was not the main role, that was Peter's; Judas saw him now, moving forward, an iron knife held before him. The knife was pointing at the stag, an accusing finger. The beast's pants were lower now, but the rhythm faster; its head the only thing it could move. Peter grabbed one of the antlers, to steady the head, then his knife rose and fell, once, twice, gouging deep into the eyes, pricking the soft edge of the brain. The beast bellowed once more, its screams echoing off the trees, before Peter's knife moved in a steady arc, left to right, slitting the stag's throat; blood fountained out, and, after one last bellow, silence returned to the wood.

Peter moved amongst them, marking each forehead, including his own with three lines of blood. "First blood is drawn," he intoned. "Now, let us finish the ritual, and free the soul." Cutting a semi-circular arc at the base of the ribcage, he spread the innards as dictated by the ancient scroll: *Souls, And How to Free Them*, he then drew out the heart and liver. Each of them stepped forward and accepted a slice of liver, it was warm, but not through cooking; silently they chewed and swallowed.

Now Peter was quartering the heart, moving to each of the trees around which the now slack ropes had originally been drawn; he sliced the end from each rope, and lashed a quarter of the heart, with several turns of the rope, to each of the four trees, pulling the rope as tight as he was able.

Having tied the last knot, Peter returned to the stag; raising the knife high above his head, holding it in both hands, he plunged it down into the skull between the antlers. Had there been a casual observer, they might have thought that the blade had broken off, and remained wedged in the skull, because Peter pulled up only a hilt, but the seven all knew that the blade was no more. As the hilt drew away a small, but intense, blue flame could be discerned between the antlers; it hung there for a few moments before rocketing skyward, savouring release, destined for reissue.

Four more souls they saved that night, three from rabbits, and one from a fox; but as the first light of predawn crept into the sky the arrow in The Locator pulsed red, twice: an indication of a black, or blackening soul in the body of a man. Before them, they saw a cottage, deep within the wood, a single narrow path winding away from it and toward the nearby town.

Peering through the stained yellow glass of the window, they spied the accoutrements of evil adorning the walls. Silently they lifted the latch and entered. The last embers of the fire winked in the grate, before them, slumped asleep in an ancient leather covered chair, was their prey. His skin was as weathered as the leather of the chair; both were brown, both creased. The seven fell upon him, knowing the struggle would be great: here was a soul that was being intentionally blackened. Waking suddenly from his slumber, their victim sought to thrash, but they had timed it well, he was pinioned at seven points. Securely they bound him, and then dragged him out to the yard. Four posts were hammered into the ground, this time at northeast, southeast, southwest, and northwest; they suspended him between them. His eyes, wild, looked to left and right, his fate dawning; they were bloodshot, the smell of sloe berries heavy on his breath.

Their, surprisingly still silent, victim was suspended some eighteen inches above the ground; around him they now built an outline of faggots and wood. Peter placed his hands over their prey's heart, his eyes closed in concentration. With his first real action, the prone man spat up at Peter, but his watery venom landed only on Peter's shoulder. "The soul is black, but only around the edges; it can be saved," he said. Their victim roared now, suddenly fully aware of their intent: "I have no desire to be saved! It is you that needs to be saved; it is Law that is unjust, Chaos should reign supreme!" His mouth started to move, intoning, seeking to cast spells of release. Prepared for, and expecting this, Peter thrust a dirt, and grit, covered rag into the suddenly silenced mouth.

This was a delicate exercise: they needed to cleanse the soul with fire; enough to burn away, and cauterise, the black; not enough to destroy the whole. With reverence, and just a hint of irony, they brought forth the smouldering embers of the victim's own fire, carefully placing them amongst the faggots. Now their victim sought to scream, would have done had he not been chocking on the rag. The seven now all drew iron blades and started to score short, diagonal, slashes along the prone man's arms and legs; the flesh began to blacken and cook, juices bubbled up in the slashes, to fall spitting to the fire below. When the cuts reached one hundred and forty-four, they stopped and stood back, heads bowed. The ropes still held tight, the man was unable to thrash, his muscles now too cooked to strain; yet still he lived.

Now they stepped forward again, first Peter cut a slice of the cooked flesh, and thrust it into the victim's own mouth, replacing the rag with it; to each of the other six he gave a slice and took one himself; they chewed and swallowed. Their victim resolutely refused to swallow, but Peter blocked his nose, forcing his head back; gagging the eighth piece of meat was swallowed too.

The seven now ranged themselves around the now freely screaming form, knives raised in doubled hands. Several moments passed, punctuated only by further screams, "Now!" screamed Peter. As one, the seven blades descended, piercing, simultaneously, the flesh above the heart. For the fifth time that night, they saw the blue flame leap skyward. Peter nodded in satisfaction: "it was clean blue, we have succeeded."

The seven turned and stepped off, in different directions, just as the first cusp of orange sun rose above the horizon; behind them, silence, and the smell of roasting flesh.

Judas settled into the narrow seat of the airship, wondering at the limited leg space. Around him, his fellow passengers started to take their seats, as Judas, they were mostly businessmen on the return flight; the huge dirigible flounced slightly in the air, twisting anti clockwise.

Judas put his head in his hands and let out a low groan, inwardly he cursed: what a waste of twenty-five years! By chance, he had met up with an old girlfriend in York; it was the first time that they had really had a chance to talk in years. York was currently the capital city of the United Republics of Britain: in a bizarre twist to the devolution debate, and in a bid to secure a few more votes, some fifteen years ago, the government of the day had passed a motion that rotated power, and government around all the member states: Scotland, Eire, Wales, England, Yorkshire, and Cornwall; only Newcastle remained outside the Union, declaring itself an independent nation.

All that this had succeeded in achieving was that each successive government spent the first two years, of their four-year term, undoing all the regulations, laws, and impositions of the previous government, and the next two passing their own. As there was little time, or point, in elections, the MPs in each of the six houses remained in office for their lifetime, being replaced by their heir. Only the Welsh escaped this cyclicity, as they insisted that all government business, and hence laws, be undertaken solely in Welsh; other governments could not therefore undo what they had done, as they failed to understand the language in which they were written; jingoistic pride would not allow the residents of one country to learn the language of another.

The stewardess tapped Judas on the shoulder, “Are you alright, Sir?” she queried. “Yes, fine,” he replied, “I just learned something important whilst I was here.” In a tone that clearly said that she had not really listened to his words, or their sentiment, she replied, “That’s nice. Tea and shortbread?”

Judas shook his head in refusal, and returned to his reverie. His mind slowly reached back to the days when he had first met up with QP, as he had called her; he couldn’t quite remember where the name had come from, but it had stuck. What he had completely failed to see was that, if you used reverse alphabeticism, then R precedes QP! It was a testament to how distracted his thoughts were, when he was in love.

When they had first met, there was no doubt in his mind that it was lust that drove them, that it was the spark that drew them together. Although at the time, he had been convinced that it was love that motivated them, albeit love disguised as lust; love was the angel, disguised as lust – the words of a fragment of song entered his thoughts, and left as quickly.

But then it had developed, the motivations had changed, love had conquered all; it had driven away lust, buried it. And that had been the confusion, for both of them, the loss of lust had been mistaken for the loss of love, and they had drifted apart. That small loss of love, compounded by some of the nine Anti Motivators, Jealousy, in particular, but also Anger, and Sloth, too, had played a part, had been their undoing, had blinded them. Without the Anti Motivators, they might have worked through it, but Judas recalled the intense pain, sadness – and, yes, jealousy – of the other man; although he was not even really that, he was perhaps at best the scapegoat, for both of them. But in that pain, suffering that green tinged blindness, Judas had hardened his heart, and turned away. Maybe that had been what QP had wanted too, Judas did not know; and today had not been the right day to draw out all the old skeletons; perhaps next time.

But now they had met once more, and talked; "You know, the odd thing," QP said, "is that the lack of oddness, is odd. We have not spoken for twenty-five years, and yet it does not seem so. It is as though there was no gap!"

Judas ran through the Motivators, but could not find one that fitted. It is bizarre, he thought, we concentrate on the Motivators (align them with the nine Anti-Motivators) of the individual, and how they affect the individual; and the Motivators of a large group, and how that makes them interact; but none have explored just the couple, and their interaction. Or had he just forgotten that part of his studies? He racked his brain, but no memory, however fleeting, would come. But then a word came to him, and the word fitted, if the motivation did not; and the word was Soul Mate.

QP was his Sole Mate; yes, that fitted, too. But which had the ascendancy: sole, or soul?. Now, here was a position beyond love, one that was in none of the textbooks. Was it simply the nine (eighteen?) motivators of both working in perfect harmony, or was it something else? Judas thought of the disgraced Matlow, and his proposed Tenth Motivator; was this it?

Mentally, Judas tried to piece the elements together; it had been long since he had studied them in detail. Did this harmony indicate that he and QP had the same Prime, and Sub, Motivators; or did it indicate that they were diametrically opposite? But wouldn't that mean that the Love Motivator was in Prime position for both; he could think of none other that would have drawn them back together. Love of what, he wondered. Dare he hope that they might once more be together? But as quickly as the thought came, he dismissed it; Judas knew that he brought with him too much baggage; he could not wish that onto her; he knew how precious she was.

It had been seven days since Judas had set down the electro-scribe, at what passed for today's exams. Although profiles would be a more accurate word: the profiles measured not only intelligence quotient, and physical ability, but also psychological profile, hopes, dreams, humours, aspirations, human interactions, beliefs, motivations, alongside dozens of other minor profile formers.

Today, Judas was fifteen and three quarters, and just like every fifteen and three quarter year old before him – or fourteen and one twelfth for girls – today was the day when he would receive his diary. The diary, in the form of an electro-chip, which would plug into the main house system, would cover a period of around 130 years, starting with today's date. In it, if he chose, he could read his entire life: where he would work, when he would meet his future wife, when they would conceive their children, what he would do in his spare time. His entire life, in detail, lain out before him; the diary had been written by the mother computer, based on the recently completed profiles. The mother computer was never wrong: the wife would be the perfect companion, entirely compatible, the children (there were always children), the perfect blend of genes; the job challenging, satisfying, but never overbearing.

The diary would tell him where he would go, what he would do, whom he would see. Had he wanted to, he could have read right through to the end, but by popular convention, Judas, like all the others, would read no more than a few days ahead; there was no need to look further, the mother computer took care of all bookings and logistics, everything was entirely predictable.

Breakfast, lunch, dinner, and snacks would arrive at precisely the right moment, and would match entirely with Judas's fancies at that specific moment in time.

This was the first day of the rest of Judas's life. He opened the diary; much of the morning was to be spent in his quasi-garden, which would be formatted to resemble a Caribbean beachfront. His three newly appointed best friends would join him to swim, and drink beer; three girls would wander by in the afternoon, and they would have sex on the beach, and in the sea. Lunch was to be grilled sardines, with a mixed leaf salad, what a perfect match, Judas thought. Briefly, Judas wondered if the girls were simulations, and, come to that, his friends, too; but that moment swiftly passed, he could see no relevance in the question: as he had learnt at school, *what seems, is.*

Uill, cha do chuir mi a-riamh mòran smaoineachaidh air!

Now it was Judas's turn to present; before him the others had all used very different methods: Simon-Peter, PowerPoint; Thomas, OHP; Matthew felt it his duty to present a re-enactment using 3D holographic actors, in $^{1}/_{12}$ scale; one other had used parchment and scrolls (but Judas did not mind that, it helped). Eleven had presented now, Judas was the twelfth to go.

The glittering plas-steel tower started to fade; its view, stretching out across mile upon mile of sky-scrapers, wavered. The polished mahogany of the vast boardroom table fragmented; the plush leather chairs spun rapidly seventeen times. The down lighters flickered; there was a distant hissing; small objects vibrated.

When they solidified again, the walls were now of mud brick. Rough carpets covered the floor; a poorly carved wooden table was before them; they were seated on benches of dusty cedar and boxwood. Judas shuffled his parchments; picking up the first one he looked to the Chair for permission to begin. At a nod, Judas began to speak: "Colleagues, as you know, I was given the key millennia of what will come to be known as the nineth, twentieth and twenty first centuries; he paused mid-sentence, but no one seemed to have picked up his slip in mention of the 21st(he had known that it was not his, but something, or someone, had pushed him towards it; had that shove tainted his views and his reports, he wondered – too late!).

"The mid-twentieth century represents the next juncture and chance for change of direction; it is therefore *the* crucial period. My report begins 07/07/07-v43, a time of hope and change." He held up a crudely painted papyrus, and began to point out some of the icons upon it; there were strings of numbers under each; locators in time and alternate. "See this moment, and its effect on this moment here, and this one here," Judas pointed to three diverse points on the scroll. Simon-Peter leant forward, already bristling for an argument: "They are but moments, our task is to look at the over-all!" The Chair held up his hand, "Simon-Peter, you have had your chance to speak, we must let Judas have his say; uninterrupted." Judas nodded his thanks to the Chair, and continued, "Look now to these graphs; see the trend points, here, there and there. And the exceptions, here at the upper, and here at the lower. It was important for you to see these first, now if you would turn to sheet 439 in your packs, headed Conjecture 1."

For seventeen- and three-quarter hours Judas addressed the group, pausing only for short refreshment and comfort breaks and a final supper. Aside from a brief flicker within Thomas's eyes, he was pretty sure that none had spotted the gaps in his utterances; having heard the others he was even more convinced, now, that they made no difference.

As he had planned, after the final comfort break their location moved from room to garden. It was night time, and they were very focused on what he was saying (although for a number of differing reasons), so they did not notice the transition; or, if they did, they may have simply felt he was illustrating one of his more obscure points. Firelight replaced candle and lamplight, but that change, too, was subtle.

Finally, he began his summing up: "There can, therefore be no doubt of the course of action that we must take. It is a painful, but necessary one. What follows gives me no pleasure, but I do it because it is right, proper, and just." Judas had moved around the table, until he was standing at the right shoulder of the Chair; lightly, he rested his hand on that shoulder. At that moment, as though from a given signal, twenty legionaries crashed through the trees and into the clearing, short swords drawn; close behind them came a gaggle of men wearing cloaks, under which were robes, tied at the waist by sashes, they looked very self-important. Roughly they pushed their way into the clearing. Judas leaned forward, kissing the Chair on the top of his head, saying, "Forgive me Lord, but you know that this is right, and I must do my duty.

In that instant, several things happened: Simon-Peter, as ever on the right hand of the Chair rose, lunging toward Judas, dagger already drawn; Judas however was ready, and had anticipated such a move, unseen by the rest of the room's occupants he slid the thin needle into Simon-Peter's neck. The effect was instant: Simon-Peter slumped to the floor. At the same time, four of the legionaries grasped the Chair, pinioning his arms, and dragged him back the way that they had come. Several other of Judas's colleagues were on their feet, launching themselves at the invaders; most were unarmed, although a couple did have curved daggers. One of those, near the Chair stabbed at one of the legionaries, cutting off most of his ear; others struck blows.

But then over all the commotion, the voice of the Chair boomed: "Peace! Stay your hands! Judas does what he thinks is right!" He reached out to the bleeding legionary, staunching the flow of blood with a glittering touch. Then more quietly, he added, shaking his head: "Hasty, Judas, too hasty." Judas looked up, anger flaring within him, "The reports are all in. There is no other course. This is the critical day, upon today everything hinges!" The Chair looked steadily into Judas's eyes, and said, "No Judas, there was one more report to come: I have not yet spoken of my mission, my studies, my conclusions. But now it is too late; what must be, must be."

As the full import of this last statement weighed on Judas's shoulders, they took the Chair away; he did not struggle. Before anyone else could speak or act, Judas too rushed from the clearing; he fled screaming into the night. It was too late to change the course now, the path had been set, the alternates were all gone; their powers were all gone; only the power of the Word remained.

Heavily disguised, Judas watched the trial from the public balcony. It ran to script; there were the anticipated dramatic flourishes; the foreseen outbursts from amongst some of the others that watched from around where Judas sat. But the outcome was never in doubt, the sentence was passed, and the prisoner led away. His destination: The Hill, that very day.

A single guttering candle cast shadows across the rough walls, and roof, of the cave. Two figures huddled either side of the candle, in almost complete shadow; they were silhouettes, the one jutting beard and wiry, unkempt, hair, the other, smooth shaven, hair short, and oiled back, in the Roman manner. The beard waggled, and a voice issued from above it, the voice of Simon-Peter: "What's done is done; I wonder only if there is some way that we can limit the damage." "What can we do?" responded the other, "the die is cast!" The slight nasal whine identified the speaker as Thomas. Silence descended on the cave for a while, then Simon-Peter spoke again, "We could," he articulated slowly, "secrete one of the reports; perhaps the one that was not made?" Thomas recoiled, as if struck, "Are you mad! He will know that we are having this conversation, His ears are everywhere."

"He already knows our thoughts, to speak them does not make them any greater a crime!" was the reply. "This is not treason we are discussing, just hiding that which He has already denied exists!"

"Then, why are we here, who are we hiding from, who are we most afraid of, the Master, or the Betrayer?" asked Thomas.

"Should we not just destroy all the reports?" questioned Thomas. Simon-Peter bristled, as though about to strike him, "That would be to undo all that we have done, we would be starting again; is that what you really want? The twelve are fragmented; I doubt we could ever work together again, not as a single unit; remember, Judas's betrayal might have been the greatest, but it was not the only one! Thomas nodded, acknowledging defeat: "You are right, it is the only way that hope lies, yet still I have doubt. How shall we do this?"

Simon-Peter picked up a stick from the floor of the cave, in the dusty floor of the cavern he started to describe his plan; it was an unnecessary, and futile effort they knew: His eyes were as good as His ears; He could probably see the dim lines better than either Simon-Peter or Thomas could, in fact they both could. And that was their one hope, that the two watchers would negate each other, and thus their plan succeed, it was tacit, but unspoken.

They nodded, the plan was complete; they snuffed the candle and left the cave, behind them came the distant rumble of thunder, or was it laughter!

The streets were dusty and hot; the milling crowd stirred sand into the atmosphere: the scarves that covered everyone's mouths were not there merely for decoration. He forced his way through them until he had reached the front. Before him some dozen people walked along the dusty street; they had no scarves to protect them. Each had arms pinioned to a thick beam of wood; thick nails driven through their palms; their wrist lashed cruelly tight to the beams. Many bore signs of torture and maltreatment: weeping wounds, sores, missing fingers and toes. Malnourished, they staggered under the weight of the wood.

He saw the one he had been looking for amongst them and edged toward him, "Master," he cried, "come, I will spirit you away from all this and we can begin our work again!" Unfocussed eyes turned to regard him, this one bore more marks than all the others, he was missing two fingers and three toes; the crust of sand failed to staunch the blood that seeped from a wound in his side. He could barely hear him when he spoke, his voice was a dry rasp: "It is too late, Judas. You did what you thought you had to, but with that one kiss of betrayal you destroyed magick forever. Ever were you the arrogant one; the one who thought he was always right! Now there is a new word to replace magick, religion." The word puzzled Judas, he had not heard it before, he replied, "But Master, surely we can reverse it; return to another juncture?"

"Use your senses, Judas! It has all gone. Gone forever. There is no return! You have committed your final assassination." Judas was about to speak again, but was pushed aside by one of the guarding legionaries. And then he saw another face in the crowd, and that, perhaps more than his Master's words, forced him to face the truth. A truth that caused him to stagger as though struck. He let the crowd slip around him as they moved on; tears burned in his eyes; his breath came in great ragged gasps. And then he was quite alone. A different kiss (or was it kisses) played now on his mind, he started to wonder if it was he that had been betrayed and his notes amended; but those memories were fading like dreams – perhaps that was all they were.

And then, like the sun coming out, the veil fell away, and realisation came. He knew the tenth motivator for what it was.

Forty years he has wandered in the... ... the word would not come, it had been replaced with a new word: wilderness. There seemed to be so many new words these days. For forty years he had suffered – and mostly given in to – temptation. Were the memories nothing more than illusory temptation? Seeds planted by... ... the Enemy?

His brow furrowed, religion, belief, it still wasn't a word that he recognised.

It was time to dip out. He'd commit one final assassination: his own life was now at the top of the list.

Judas turned from the giant wooden cross, silver coins jingling at his hip, burning into his soul; the cross's tip grazing the sky some two dozen or more feet up, and there stood Rachel, arms folded gazing up at the now silent form pinioned to the wood. "Rachel!" he said, in recognition. Her gaze shifted to him, "Sorry," she said, "do I know you?"

"No, perhaps not yet," said Judas. "But you will." She smiled demurely at him: "Is that a line?" she asked. He was momentarily flustered, she was talking to him, with no animosity, no recognition, no scorn in her voice; was this another chance, his last chance?

Rachel linked her arm through his, “Come on then, you can buy me a mint tea and tell me when it is exactly that we are going to meet!”

Thoughts of his own assassination – suicide – fled from his mind. He might still fake it so that he could disappear from view. They walked along the street hand in hand, their feet raising little clouds of dust. They had entered the financial district, and saw the row of tax collectors. Passing the first table Judas saw the piles of silver shekels on the table; they were in piles of ten. Three piles of ten. Perfect. That would be the base of his escape plan; there would be more than enough truth in it to make it believable.

Epilogue

Far, far above he looked down upon the scene. He saw the protagonist turn and walk away, his arm around the woman. He saw… … … he didn't know the word. Son? Offspring? Rib? He was nailed to crude wood, life slowly seeping from him. New life waited in the wings.

He had seen all that was, and all that had gone before. An uncharacteristic frown crossed His brow; perhaps J had been right. He had tried mysteries and wonders. Maybe it was time for man to come of age. He would remove their shackles, allow the seed of independence to sprout. Long, long ago, they had stolen knowledge and gifted it to themselves; perhaps now was the time for the gift of free thought, independence, consequences. Should he give the third gift now, also? Or should that await another day?

He knew it was time to set his children free. For them to become grown. Adult. No matter their age. Their own person. He had held that seed of knowledge back for so long. No, not knowledge, awareness. He knew that if he gave it up, he would need to withdraw further. Some connections would be lost. But maybe, and this was his hope, a stronger connection would come. There would be less parental telling, and more mentorshipian guidance.

His presence had been gifted to only that one so far. The one that hung there now on the crossed spars; the one with crimson stains on hands and feet; and crimson soaking into the earth below. The sacrifice.

Reaching forward, he selected the Influence fader with his index finger, sliding it down and towards him; next the finger moved across to the Free Will slider, pushing it up and away from him. Lastly, he reached for a third fader; it's label was worn and faded. Up or down, he mused. He reached his decision and started to inch the fader... ... ...

It would be the end of magic. But then magic had never been that real anyway. It was the start of something new, which would need a new word to describe it. He gave it the word, Faith, and scattered that word to the four corners of the world. And that word pushed the riders to one side. What if Faith severed some of the ties? The ties that bind. How might they be replaced? Or re-joined? And so, in answer, he gave his presence to the one hundred and twenty. And they knew it. They were the conduit; through them, the presence metamorphosised, became the spirit, which then flooded the world. But most did not know it for what it was. They were awake, they were free, but they knew not how to live with that awakening. They were less able to tell the difference between the two voices, his voice, which now grew fainter, and the other voice, the tempter, which grew stronger, and they knew not how to resist it, how to turn it down, even, to balance the voices. Some only heard a single voice.

His mind wandered, "Scientists are a strange breed," he said, to no one in particular, "when they ponder on life, and whether there is life on other planets, they talk in depth about how miraculous it is that our world is just the right distance from the Sun to support life. A little closer to the Sun, and it would be too hot. A little further away, and it would be too cold. And therefore, what are the possibilities of another world being exactly the right distance from their sun to support life.

"Bizarre. They seem to be arguing against their own theory of evolution. That the World is in just the right place to support us. Not that we have evolved to live comfortably in the conditions that are prevalent on our planet! It is clear that they were created with the ability to adapt. But created they were, not born of soup!"

Unexpectedly, a reply came: "So too,

Printed in Great Britain
by Amazon

42296760R00255